D0765727

BUTTERFLY WINTER

BUTTERFLY WINTER

A NOVEL

W.P. Kinsella

Enfield & Wizenty
(an imprint of Great Plains Publications)
345-955 Portage Avenue
Winnipeg, MB R3G 0P9
www.greatplains.mb.ca

Great Plains Publications gratefully acknowledges the financial support provided for its publishing program by the Government of Canada through the Canada Book Fund; the Canada Council for the Arts; the Province of Manitoba through the Book Publishing Tax Credit and the Book Publisher Marketing Assistance Program; and the Manitoba Arts Council.

Design & Typography by Relish Design Studio Inc.
Printed in Canada by Friesens

Library and Archives Canada Cataloguing in Publication

Kinsella, W.P.
Butterfly winter / W.P. Kinsella.

ISBN 978-1-926531-16-8

I. Title.

PS8571.I57B88 2011 C813'.54 C2011-904143-X

MIX
Paper from responsible sources
FSC® C016245

ENVIRONMENTAL BENEFITS STATEMENT

Great Plains Publications saved the following resources by printing the pages of this book on chlorine free paper made with 100% post-consumer waste.

TREES	WATER	ENERGY	SOLID WASTE	GREENHOUSE GASES
25	11,373	10	721	2,522
FULLY GROWN	GALLONS	MILLION BTUs	POUNDS	POUNDS

Environmental impact estimates were made using the Environmental Paper Network Paper Calculator. For more information visit www.papercalculator.org.

ACKNOWLEDGEMENTS

Two chapters were published in somewhat different form as short stories: "Butterfly Winter," in *Red Wolf, Red Wolf*, HarperCollins, 1987; and "The Battery," in *The Thrill of the Grass*, Penguin, 1985.

For Barbara Lynn Turner Kinsella

SECTION ONE

THE WIZARD

"... anything that can be imagined exists."

—ROBERT KROETSCH, *WHAT THE CROW SAID*

"The word *chronological* is not in the Courteguayan language, neither is *sequence*. Things happen. That is all there is to it. In most other places, time is like a long highway with you standing in the middle of a straightaway while the highway dissolves in the distance in both directions, past and future. In Courteguay, if you picture the same scene, time occasionally runs crossways so that something that will happen in the future might already be behind you, slowly receding, while something from the past may not yet have happened."

—THE WIZARD

ONE
THE WIZARD

"You appear to be a man in your late 60s," the Gringo Journalist says.

"I have always been what I appear to be," replies the Wizard. "And," he adds, the words barely audible under his creaking breath, "I always tell people what they want to hear, whether it is truth or fiction."

"I am told that you move from place to place as if by magic," the Gringo Journalist continues.

"There is no magic, there are no gods," says the Wizard.

"You are currently referred to as a wizard, even by your enemies."

"It takes a wizard to know there are none," says the Wizard.

THE WIZARD LIES IN A HIGH, white hospital bed. The room is banked with flowers, bouquets made up of various combinations of the eleven national flowers of Courteguay. The Wizard stares up at the Gringo Journalist, who is lean and blond, holding a sleek black tape recorder toward the Wizard as if he were offering a bite from a sandwich.

The Wizard, who has discarded his hospital garb, is wearing a midnight-blue caftan covered in mysterious silver symbols that look like what a comic strip artist might use to intimate curse words, and insists on being paid for the interview, not in Courteguayan guilermos, but in American dollars. He forces a smile for the Gringo Journalist, his gimlet eyes twinkling.

"INTERVIEWS ARE SO TIRING. Even wizards die, did you know that?"

The morning air is cool and lustrous, rife with possibilities, silvered with deception, tasty as fresh lime.

"Here I am. Cool pillows, a clean room, a ceiling fan. And I still have a listener, something terribly important to one who is a storyteller. An excellent way to die. I close my eyes and my long life slides by like a newsreel, like a canoe floating on placid water. The room is liquid with memories. Me, planting baseballs like seed corn, waiting for the stadiums to grow and flourish.

"My enemies, and they are many, will deny it all. Without me there would have been no Julio or Esteban Pimental; their father was a gambler but I was a better one. It is not something I am exactly proud of. But it is all connected, as everything is. Knee bone connected to the thigh bone. Now hear the word...."

The Gringo Journalist asks another question, watches the Wizard's eyes, waiting. He wants to know how to find a place, a place important to his research.

"My friend, it is very difficult to give directions in Courteguay. Objects have minds of their own. In the night houses sometimes slip across a street, or change places with a house a few doors away. One might go to bed in a home on the south bank of a river and wake in that same house but on the north bank, and the basement not even damp.

"So, you want to know about Julio Pimental? Perhaps the greatest pitcher ever to play in the Major Leagues, certainly the greatest pitcher ever to come out of Courteguay. That is somewhat easier than giving directions. The rumors you have heard are true. Twin boys playing catch in the womb. An unusual event in many parts of the world, but not in Courteguay. Here the unusual is the norm. The sky once rained silken handkerchiefs. There was a woman with three breasts ... a man with a square penis.

"Well, you have come to the right person. The horse's mouth so to speak. Speaking of the horse's mouth did you know that there is a jungle spirit called a Loa that rides men like a horse? If you are unlucky enough to have a Loa land on your back it will run you until you collapse, if you are truly unlucky the Loa will ride you until you die.

"Of course Loas are Haitian. But spirits do not recognize arbitrary boundaries, Haiti, Dominican Republic, Courteguay, they are all the same to a Loa."

The Wizard takes a deep breath.

"I've seen it all. Not always through my own eyes, of course. I've spied on armies through the eyes of a predator, overheard the strategies of the Insurgents while lying comfortably in the undergrowth in the guise of a buzzard munching on a Government soldier. I can smell out conspiracy. Through the ears of an ivory-feathered cockatoo I have overheard young girls' secrets, eavesdropped on many a whispered plot, changed myself into a dewdrop and cooled a lovers back in the steamy dawn.

"You look skeptical. You question my veracity? An old fool on his death bed, you think, wizened to half his size. An old fool who has been President of the Republic of Courteguay, several times. I was there when that other El Presidente—it is a travesty that the words El Presidente should be uttered in the same breath as the name Dr. Lucius Noir, murderer of Quita Garza's father. Ah, I thought that would get your attention. But do not jump to rash conclusions. In Courteguay El Presidente is an all encompassing statement. You will, I'm sure want to hear about Quita Garza and Julio Pimental. But before we get too far into the interview, I must warn you that the boundaries here are different. Never forget that. Never be surprised."

The Gringo Journalist eyes the Wizard suspiciously, trying to find a suitable place to set the tape recorder, a recorder which he had to pay a bribe of three times its value just to bring into Courteguay. He gets no help from the Wizard. He finally swings the brown arborite arm that holds the food tray, into position, across the middle of the bed and places the tape recorder on it. The Wizard smiles again, the wrinkles around his eyes crinkling like crumpled newspaper. The old man coughs wetly.

"I crouched among the plumeria when the evil deed was done. Oh, yes, I've seen it all.

"It all began with the Wizard. If it wasn't for the Wizard there wouldn't be a story. You might say Courteguay began with the Wizard, with the coming of the Wizard, and the coming of baseball.

"Excuse me? Of course I am the Wizard, at least today. May I not speak of myself in the third person? Is there some new government regulation against speaking of oneself in the third person? My mind, the Wizard's mind, shifts constantly, my mind is like a record with a scratch, a tape with a flaw. Have you ever heard the name Jorge Blanco? Don't answer. Of course you have. All politicians have to reinvent themselves occasionally. Ah, for the simplicity of life when I was Jorge Blanco. Before the twins were born, before the dark shadow of Dr. Noir passed over Courteguay.

"But who's to say what is truth. People tell tales, and as the tales emerge they become as good as truth. In Courteguay, anything that can be imagined exists. The telling is the thing. Truth is spun like silk; truth is manufactured. Unlike you, a journalist, when I need facts I invent them. Here in Courteguay, the world is as it was meant to be, as it used to be everywhere before magic was hunted down, driven to the hinterlands, made extinct, like dazzling birds hunted for their beaks or feathers, or feet. People change, but shadows of their pasts remain behind, often have lives of their own.

"Yes. Yes. I do tend to ramble. But if you want the whole story, bear with me. You gringo newsmen are too impatient. You want the entire account presented in one minute flat, you want the tale in digest form suitable for *Courteguay Today*.

"It is? An imitator? I didn't know that. So long since I've been to America. Well, they say imitation is the sincerest form of flattery.

Besides, Courteguay has no copyright laws. I once published a book by this American fellow Hemingway, under my own name of course. It was very well received. I tried Shakespeare, a play called Othello, but though it has a wonderful plot it didn't sell at all. The language needed to be modernized. Too bad there are not more people in Courteguay who can read. I might not have had to go into politics.

"In Courteguay, whoever calls himself El Presidente is the law. A banana republic is how Courteguay is referred to in the international press. An irony. We do not grow bananas in Courteguay. Mangos, guava, passion fruit.... A passion fruit republic. You ever hear of such a thing?

"Yes. Yes. I do tend to ramble. Are you afraid I will die before you finish this interview? You pay your money. You take your chances. Didn't someone in baseball say that? Leo Durocher? Casey Stengel? Yogi Bear?

"Berra, of course. You will encounter this rumor eventually, if not already, so it is better you hear it from me. The reason the Wizard lives so long, people will tell you, my enemies, and there are many, possibly also my friends, is that he takes the future of others and appropriates it. He is there when a government soldier breathes his last—maybe that soldier had only four months to live, but the Wizard, his hand on the dying soldier's chest, adds four months on the end of his own life. The Wizard, some will say, is like an ambulance-chasing lawyer, always there within minutes of the crash, his wizened hands leaving a veronica on the chests of the dying. Wizards live forever some people believe. Not me. You should try being a wizard sometime. Perhaps I could persuade you. As you can tell by my demeanor, I am in the market for a successor.

"Has anyone told you of Dr. Noir's method of population control? No? Yes, I am getting ahead of myself, but bear with me. The contraceptive was much too slow for Dr. Noir.

"'There are more people than there are mangos,' he is reported to have said. 'We cannot increase the number of mangos, therefore we must decrease the number of people.' Consequently, Dr. Noir decreed that anyone with the first name Tomas, who lived within a forty-mile radius of San Barnabas, the capital, was to be executed.

"On the day Dr. Lucius Noir seized power in Courteguay for the first time, became El Presidente, he decreed that as long as he was dictator all the mirrors in Courteguay would reflect only his image.

"Children screamed. Women fainted. Mirrors were thrown into the streets.

"I'm sorry. Back to Milan Garza for a moment. Milan Garza, a baseball immortal, Quita Garza's father."

"But I was asking about Julio Pimental," says the Gringo Journalist.

"Pay closer attention, please! I was there, lurking in the ferns, like a lion in a Rousseau painting, when the deed was done. Milan Garza overestimated his own importance, felt that being named a Baseball Immortal actually made him immortal. Bad mistake.

"Later, camouflaged by a thousand funeral wreathes made from the eleven national flowers of Courteguay: bougainvillea, hibiscus, red and white plumeria, bird of paradise, orchids, poinsettias, anthurium, lehua, vanda orchids, and ginger—did you get them all down? I forgot that black biscuit absorbs my words like the earth does rainwater. I listened to the evil man who called himself El Presidente, as he eulogized Milan Garza, then had him interred in a crystal-domed coffin at the Hall of Baseball Immortals.

"But, again I am ahead of myself, it is the Wizard you want to hear about, amigo."

"I was asking about Julio Pimental."

"Time begins with the Wizard. I am speaking now as El Presidente. The President of Courteguay who began one of his lives as Jorge Blanco. With me you get three interviews for the price of one. Only in Courteguay.

"To know Julio Pimental, and his twin, Esteban, you must first know the Wizard. Courteguay began with the Wizard, the coming of the Wizard, the coming of baseball. I knew him well. There was nothing mysterious about him originally. His name was Sandor Boatly, the surname having been Anglicized on the spot by an immigration official when the threadbare Boatly family arrived in America from Europe, the spot being Ellis Island, the time being 1885. Sandor Boatly was nine years old, spoke only Hungarian, and the word *baseball* was not in his vocabulary, in any language."

W.P. Kinsella

TWO
THE WIZARD

Sandor Boatly saw his first baseball game in Providence, Rhode Island in 1887, when he was eleven, and his experience that day was more emotional, more magical, more prophetic, more of a grand call to service than that of other boys his age who claimed to have had religious experiences which inspired calls to the priesthood.

His father, Szabo Boatly, a glazer by trade, worked long hours in a crockery factory. Saturday afternoon was his only time off, except for Sunday, a day reserved for pious inactivity. On Sunday the Boatly children were not even allowed to play with their home-made toys.

On a spring afternoon in 1887, the father took Sandor and one of several sisters, Evita, for a walk. A few blocks from their home, outside the Eastern European ghetto, they were attracted by crowd noises, and the clear sharp thwack of bat on ball. The sounds reminded Sandor of his early childhood in Hungary. As he listened he recalled the crack of a woodsman's ax biting into a strong tree.

Sandor Boatly pleaded with his father to take the little family into the baseball park, and the father, being in a jolly mood, agreed. A man wearing a straw boater with a beautiful red sash, collected fifteen cents from the father; the children were admitted free. Once inside the park they made their way down the right field line to a spot where they could see most of what was happening on the field.

The elder Boatly was expecting a soccer game. He had played rather well in the old country, if his accounts could be believed.

"What is this?" he kept repeating in Hungarian.

By then Sandor knew the word *baseball*. He had been exposed to childish versions of the game played on the streets, playgrounds, and school yards of Providence. He had seen American boys trouping off after school, tossing a small, hard ball in the air, wooden staves perched on their shoulders like rifles. But he had never seen a professional contest, never dreamed that grown men engaged in the game, playing it with deadly seriousness.

Sandor Boatly had never guessed that, properly played, baseball consisted of mathematics, geometry, art, philosophy, ballet, and carnival, all intertwined like the mystical ribbons of color in a rainbow.

It was years before Sandor Boatly encountered a magician, but the thrill of seeing an orange turned into an endless string of bright silken scarves was nothing compared to what he experienced that afternoon.

There was a river to the left, the outfield sloped gently upward. There was no outfield fence. The game was unenclosed, the foul lines forever diverging.

"Bah!" said Sandor's father, settling on his haunches, chewing on a blade of grass. "A stick and a rock. What kind of game is this?"

But Sandor understood instantly. He intuited that baseball was somehow akin to the faded picture on the wall of the Boatly living room where two ballerinas twirled on toes as stiff as inverted fence pickets. It was only a semi-professional baseball game they were witnessing, two local athletic clubs, one sponsored by the Sons of Erin, the other by the Christopher Columbus Society.

Sandor, transfixed, studied the pitcher and catcher, connected inexplicably by the rope of leather they tossed back and forth. He watched the infielders scurrying after ground balls, leaping like cats to take a grounder on a high bounce and brace themselves in mid-motion to throw out the sprinting runner at first base.

Somehow, as if by divine revelation, Sandor Boatly was filled with baseball expertise; he understood the aesthetics of the game and explained each play to his father and sister, who after an inning or two had taken to cheering for the Sons of Erin, while, like the rest of the crowd, deriding the single umpire who wore a tall silk hat, and stood like an undertaker behind the pitcher, from where he made all decisions concerning the game.

In the space of a few moments, Sandor had not only become enchanted by the magic of baseball, but came to understand it instinctively. But, miracle of miracles, he was able to communicate his newfound love to his father and sister.

"Look! Look!" he kept saying. "The field is not enclosed. The possibilities are endless. There is no whistle to suspend play, there is no clock to signal an ending."

"Look! Look!" he must have repeated the words a thousand times that fateful afternoon. And when the game ended, the little family drifted dreamily away from the ballpark, the odor of fresh cut grass still in their nostrils, gauzy memories of plays that were and plays that might have been mingling in their minds.

It was Sandor's father who, as they walked toward home on the gritty streets of Providence, Rhode Island, articulated the essence of baseball.

"When," he asked his son, "may we return to this land of dreamy dreams?"

While his father remained a life long fan, Sandor Boatly dedicated his life to baseball. Instead of becoming a priest, as many of his boyhood friends did, Sandor Boatly became an evangelist of baseball, a Johnny Appleseed, who instead of flinging apple seeds in rainbow-like arcs as he walked the fields and backwoods of America, carried a strange and wondrous canvas sack across his shoulders so that at times he looked as though he was bearing a cross. The sack was filled with baseball bats, hand-carved from hickory, crafted with love to last forever, by men who knew and appreciated the feel of a smooth and sleek weapon, which like a gun, became an extension of the holder. The sack also contained baseballs, horsehide, hand-stitched with catgut, hand-wound by people who knew what they were building.

The day he turned fourteen, Sandor Boatly refused his father's offer (it was more of a command) to become an apprentice glazer and contribute to the family finances. Sandor set out on his mission, which was to introduce the magic of baseball to those who did not know of it, or if they did know about baseball, to teach them to regard it with the reverence it deserved.

On foot, Sandor moved across Pennsylvania, Ohio, Indiana, and Illinois, and eventually made his way to the plains of Iowa and Nebraska, where like a true evangelist he spread the word of baseball to the scattered multitudes.

Along the way he abandoned his name, for he found it took too much time to explain his ancestry, his recent history, his roots, for people were forever wondering if his family might have traveled to America with their family, plumbing the depths of their memories for common ground.

"Call me whatever you like," Sandor said to his multitudes, which, on the prairies, consisted often of a single farm family, dirt farmers living in soddies, some living in virtual caves built into the sides of hills. Sandor would thump at the gunnysack-reinforced door of a soddy. The pale face that answered would shade its eyes from the sudden glare of the prairie. He was often mistaken for a preacher, for he dressed in black broadcloth, wore a wide-brimmed hat, and, as soon as he was able, grew a bushy black beard.

After introducing himself, though not always his mission, for the tough pioneer women tended to frown on sport of any kind as frivolity, Sandor would find his way to where the men were working. He would pitch in and work side by side with the farmer and his sons, picking roots, or pulling stumps, perhaps carrying rocks to a homemade stoneboat, or walking behind an ox as it pulled a plow.

At the end of the day, by the fading rays of a low sun, or as the plains horizon flamed like prairie fire, Sandor would open his magical sack and toss a ball to a burly farm boy in work pants too short and clodhopper boots awkward as wood blocks. The three or four or five of them would lay out a rough diamond, perhaps using a barn wall as a backstop, if the homesteaders were fortunate enough to have built a barn. Sometimes there would be stumps for bases, with stringy trees in the outfield.

Often the only clear land would take in a slough, full of frog grass and cattails, where inches of water lay hidden under seemingly innocent greenery. But no matter the obstacles, Sandor's enthusiasm would shine through, and the big, lumbering boys would get word to their neighbors, and by the second evening of his visit there would be almost enough players for a side of baseball.

Then Sandor would spring the trap. He would mention the last area that he had visited, five, or ten, or fifteen miles away, and he would mention how *they* had taken to the game, and how they had formed a team and were waiting only for a challenge.

When he moved on he would leave behind a precious ball, after painstakingly demonstrating to his converts how to re-cover it. He might also leave behind a bat, or he might simply show them how to hew a bat from a sturdy piece of timber. On rare occasions he would actually see the competition through, choosing a site, scheduling the contest, acting as umpire.

He learned early on that the main objections to his mission would be on religious grounds. Sandor was quick to realize that pioneers, facing unbelievable hardships, often clinging to life and sanity by the thinnest of threads, needed not only to believe in the supernatural, but to believe the supernatural was on their side. Sandor realized too, that these primitive peoples lacked the sophistication to realize that there were many and various manifestations of the supernatural, Sandor Boatly himself being one.

Since he was often mistaken, on first contact, for a circuit rider, Sandor took to carrying a heavy, leather-Bound bible. He learned to quote the passages that urged the listeners to make a joyful noise and celebrate life. He never claimed to be a minister, but if his dress and demeanor intimated such, he found no reason to deny it.

If requested, he could conduct a brief nondenominational service of a Sunday morning, after which he would bring out his baseball equipment and retire to the nearest meadow with the men and boys. Even the most pinched and pious farm women could find no fault with a hard working pastor who regarded baseball as a sinless pastime for a sunny summer Sunday afternoon.

Occasionally, Sandor stumbled into a situation where a minister was clearly needed. He was known to pray with vigor over the terminally ill, preparing them for passage to the next world, easing that passage. When called upon he conducted funerals, baptisms, even an occasional marriage, though he loathed the intolerance of most Christians. "Christianity is the only army that shoots its own wounded," he said in one of his last letters to his sister, Evita.

As a boy he had heard or read that *it matters not what qualifications one possesses, but only that one look the part,* words that would have a profound effect on the many lives of Sandor Boatly. For instead of planting trees as a legacy, he planted the joy of baseball in several thousand hearts, and, as a seed grew into a sapling, then a tree, and eventually into a forest, so his own efforts multiplied over the years until baseball was everywhere in America, like the trees and the rain.

Sandor worked his way as far west as Wyoming, before heading south, touring Colorado, New Mexico, and Texas, crossing several Southern states before finding himself in Florida—Miami to be specific.

Though he had never lived in a truly warm climate he always sensed deep in his bones that the natural state of the universe was endless summer, though he had only heard rumors of its existence. He had heard of places where the grass was eternally green, where snow was spoken of with nostalgia by people who had not endured it for years. But Miami, and Florida, that tropical green finger with the angelic aura of white sand, was so perfect, so magical, the possibilities of baseball so endless, that its mere existence almost caused Sandor to acknowledge the possibility of a God.

What he discovered, something that disappointed him to no end, was that in Florida he was not a pioneer, for baseball was well known, played in every park, school yard, and vacant lot. Only in the furthest backwaters of the Everglades could he practice his calling, and then with only limited success, due to the lack of arable land.

THREE
THE WIZARD

His journey to the island of Hispaniola came about after he became acquainted with a group of Pentecostal missionaries on the Miami docks. They mistook him for a man of the cloth.

"We are off to spread the word of the Lord to the heathen," they confided in him.

"I share your dedication," he said obliquely.

Over his shoulder was slung a lumpy sack that might have been full of a many-armed invention. "Where might you be bound?" Sandor asked.

The Pentecostals explained that they were headed for Courteguay, on the island of Hispaniola, a tiny landlocked country nestled like a snail between Haiti and the Dominican Republic, bordered by both, the shape of the moon of a fingernail, and not much larger.

"We sent a team of missionaries to Courteguay a few years ago," one of the tall, pale men explained. "At first they sent back enthusiastic reports, then we didn't hear from them for a few months. Neither they, nor the follow-up team we sent have ever been heard from at all."

"Beyond there be dragons..." said Sandor, quoting from a medieval map he had seen in a museum. The phrase described the unknown, everything beyond the explored world.

"Haiti is full of dark visions and strange deaths," said a wiry-looking woman with bony, red-knuckled hands.

"And the Dominican Republic?" asked Sandor, willing to risk a good deal for baseball, but not anxious to be eaten by savages, or burned alive as a sacrifice to some primitive god.

"We are led to believe the Dominican is much more civilized than Haiti, though it is said to be heavily Catholic," a short, rotund man said.

"And Courteguay?"

"Unknown territory," said the leader of the Pentecostals, a red-cheeked man with a perpetual smile. "One of the newest and smallest countries in the world. Reportedly, a piece of useless mountain slope and swampy valley, given to a fierce old soldier, who so terrorized the governments of both Haiti and the Dominican Republic, so disrupted their attempts at civilization, that they gave him his own country just to be rid of him. His name—he was given the land some forty years ago and was an old man then, so he must certainly be dead—is said to be Octavio Court, though he was known to one and all as the Old Dictator."

"The trouble with an island is that it is the end of the world," said Sandor. "One cannot run and hide well on an island. People left with only themselves, with nowhere to hide, have to look inward, have to face the reality that they are trapped within their own skins forever. Sometimes they do not like what they see."

Sandor Boatly for some reason felt no fear at the idea of setting off for Courteguay. Perhaps they did not play baseball there, he thought, he hoped. He knew the Pentecostals would relish suffering, even death. They were fundamentalists so narrow they could look through a keyhole with both eyes. Martyrs have always been well regarded in religious circles.

"What do you think of baseball?" he asked the missionaries, tossing an ermine-white ball in the air and catching it in his large, calloused hands.

"A relatively sinless game," replied their leader, "as long as it is not played on Sunday."

"How little you know," whispered Sandor Boatly, smiling mysteriously, as he boarded the boat for the island of Hispaniola.

No one on the mainland ever heard from Sandor Boatly again.

He has become a legend, of course. You newsmen, journalists, writers, or whatever you call yourselves, must know all about that. By the time he departed America Sandor Boatly was already a folk hero, tales were told, songs were sung about his spreading the gospel of baseball across the continent. But because of his mysterious disappearance the legends grew, multiplied and prospered out of proportion to his actual deeds. Several books were written about him, the most famous, which I am told is still in print, titled *The Evangelist and the Ball.* In it is recounted how, when he stepped off the train in San Barnabas, the capital of Courteguay, he was met by two hyenas. They had been washed and perfumed and dressed in formal porter's uniforms. They walked upright and spoke enough Spanish to conduct their business.

"May we carry your bags, sir," the tallest hyena said, bowing slightly. Sandor Boatly, stared around. The station was bustling. No one seemed upset by the domesticated, talking hyenas.

"Certainly," he replied. One hyena carried his suitcases, the second managed a trunk and his mysterious bag full of bats, balls, and magic.

"You will have to help us with the station door," the tallest hyena said, "while we have evolved considerably we still have not mastered the doorknob."

As a famous missing person Sandor Boatly was a favorite subject for journalists. His followers organized expeditions to Hispaniola, though for some reason they concentrated on Haiti, where, one persistent rumor had it, he was buried under two baseball bats joined in the shape of a cross, while a dozen vanda orchids danced in a circle on his grave.

But as you must know, in Haiti they do not play baseball. They speak French in Haiti, a language not conducive to baseball. There they play soccer. I spit! Soccer is slower than watching stagnant water find its own level. A game for those totally devoid of imagination. Next to Ambrose Bierce and Amelia Earhart, Sandor Boatly is America's most popular and mysterious folk hero.

How do I know so much about him? I am Courteguayan. That is a sufficient answer.

LATER THAT DAY, more of the interview finished, if not satisfactorily (at least the Gringo Journalist had extracted enough information to continue to pique his curiosity and was alternately amazed, baffled, and annoyed with the elderly and capricious Wizard) something happened that made the Gringo Journalist a believer. After being given a drink from the hospital water glass with its crimped straw, the Wizard raised his head from the pillow and sniffed like an animal, a scavenger testing the air for carrion.

"I need your help," croaked the Wizard, reaching for the Gringo Journalist with a skeletal hand. "Help me out of bed." The Gringo Journalist aided the old man, who was light as a kite, from the bed, assisted him into a threadbare hospital robe and terrycloth slippers. The Wizard's talon hands fastened like intravenous needles to the young reporter's arm as he led the way down the hall of the hospital to the emergency ward.

There, even the reporter could smell blood, the coppery, electric odor of liquid death. Doctors were just turning away from, drawing a sheet over the face of an auto accident victim they had been unable to save. The Wizard detached himself from the young reporter, slipped both hands under the sheet and gripped the still warm chest of the deceased. The Wizard stood stock still in that position for several minutes. The reporter expected to be rousted by doctors or nurses or orderlies, but it was as if he and the Wizard were invisible.

Eventually, the Wizard produced his hands from under the sheet, and as he turned toward him the Gringo Journalist could see an amazing change had taken place. For one thing the Wizard had gained probably ten pounds, his hands that had been the claws of the very old, were younger, healthier looking, as was the Wizard in general. On the way back to his room he walked unaided, keeping up a steady one-sided conversation.

"A delightful twenty-two years," said the Wizard, smiling with both warmth and cunning, as he climbed, with a good deal of agility, back into his bed. "I expect I'll leave this hospital in a day or two. We'll continue this interview at my home."

FOUR
THE WIZARD

"You ask too many questions," says the Wizard to the Gringo Journalist. "Make up your mind. Do you want to hear about the old days politically, or the birth of the twins, or about Milan Garza, or the nefarious Dr. Noir?"

They are in an ice cream parlor in San Cristobel, the Wizard eating a concoction he has dictated to the wide-eyed boy in a white trough-like hat, who appears to be the only employee. It contains many kinds of ice cream and syrups, but also hibiscus blossoms.

"You're right, I have been asking too many questions at once," says the Gringo Journalist. "Tell me about the birth of the twins."

"El Presidente!" rasps the Wizard, "now there was a name that used to mean something in the old days."

"Did you hear my questions?..."

"The good times are all gone. The civil wars, the guerrillas, the government soldiers. The insurgents! I always liked being referred to as the Insurgent Leader. The tabloid newspapers manned by the only true journalists in the world, used to write about Courteguay's civil war. The tabloids have a feel for Courteguay; they understand the shifting time and space, and no matter how outrageous their claims, those claims never approach reality. For instance, they claimed that both sides in our ongoing civil war practiced cannibalism, and that both sides had pygmy warriors who fired poisoned darts from blowguns."

"Did you?"

"Which? What?"

"Were you cannibals? Were there pygmies?"

"Of course not." The Wizard pauses. "Did you know that roast soldier tastes a little like chicken? Or maybe frog. No, rabbit, I think rabbit."

"You just said..."

"Being government wasn't bad either. The poison from the pygmies' blow guns paralyzed their victims, turned them to granite. If you were to hack your way through the jungle today you would find statues. Some anthropologist uncovered one a few years ago. They claimed the statue was from some ancient civilization, and they shipped him off to Great Britain. The anthropologist's name was Mordechi Cruz and he grew up in San Cristobel, and he was no older than you are now.

"Revolution gets in the blood. General Bravura and I would trade places every few months."

"Excuse me," cries the Gringo Journalist. "None of this makes any sense. If what you say is true you are the Old Dictator, but from what I have researched you did not become El Presidente until after the passing of Dr. Noir. Which is it?"

"There is nothing like an unstable government to keep people on their toes," the Wizard goes on as if he didn't hear the question. "General Bravura was not without access to what some would call magic. I remember once, I was leading perhaps a thousand men and we were creeping up on General Bravura's camp at dawn. As we stood on a hill looking down on the small encampment, readying for the attack, at least twenty thousand soldiers rose from the banana grass like tulie-fog. We stared at them for a moment. General Bravura's army was supposed to be smaller than my own. There had to be some illusion involved. But what if there wasn't? If they were real and we attacked we faced certain defeat. In prudence we retreated quietly and waited for the sunrise.

"And a government, any government, must take good care of its own. In politics one rewards one's friends and punishes one's enemies. For instance, I know that a retired President of the United States receives a tidy pension, the Secret Service, CIA, FBI, and the Dallas Cowboy Cheerleaders guard him constantly. In his retirement, he becomes President of a college where he has his choice of concubines from each year's freshman class.

"Where did you ever hear such things?"

"The infallible tabloids of course. The fearless press who publish what the people want to hear."

"They also tend to exaggerate."

"There is no such thing as exaggeration."

"I might disagree with that."

"Today's El Presidente! I spit! Today's El Presidente has an image consultant. When he visits the United States he is brown. There are senators and congressmen with darker tans. When he speaks to the guava plantation workers here in Courteguay he is black as onyx, his skin glistens. His consultants spray his face with black dye. They have to burn his black-collared shirts after every appearance.

"The magic of leadership is gone. The public need to see coins pulled from ears, snakes curled from every orifice, they want to see beautiful girls disappear from before their very eyes. And can I help it if the beautiful girls always reappear in my bed?" The Wizard shrugs and smiles.

The Gringo Journalist throws up his hands.

"I'm not sure this is very valuable for the book I'm writing. I want to write a true history of Courteguay."

"Nothing is true. The concept is unknown in Courteguay." The Wizard frowns, take a bite of vanilla ice cream and hibiscus flowers. He chews thoughtfully.

FIVE
THE WIZARD

It was during the sixth month of his mother's pregnancy, that, inside her belly, Julio Pimental began to throw the sidearm curve, says the Wizard.

He glances surreptitiously at the Gringo Journalist to be certain he has his full attention.

"Yi! Yi!" screamed Fernandella Pimental, as Julio went into the stretch, hiding the ball carefully in his glove so the batter could not glimpse the way he gripped it.

"Yii!" shrilled Fernandella, as Julio's arm snaked like a whip in the direction of third base, while the ball, traveling the path of a question mark, jug-hooked its way to the plate, and smacked into the catcher's mitt held by Julio's twin brother, Esteban. The Wizard tips back on his cushioned rattan chair. The boy with the starched white hat brings them refills for their iced tea.

Many years later, on her deathbed, Fernandella Pimental, wizened and grey with age, attended by servants, small as a child in the queen-sized bed in the marble-pillared mansion her sons built for her, recalled the time of her pregnancy. She was residing on the outskirts of San Cristobel, which, though scarcely more than a village, was the second largest city in Courteguay. She and her husband lived in a cardboard hut with a precariously balanced slab of corrugated tin for a roof. The hovel was located on an arid hillside, surrounded by a few prickly vines, always in full view of the frying sun. Her husband, Hector, a sly young man with slicked-down hair, drooping eyelids, and a face thin as a ferret's, spent his life at the baseball grounds, winning or losing a few centavos on the outcome of each day's games.

Hector was proud of Fernandella's belly, which by only the fourth month was big as a washtub, forcing her to walk splay-legged as she trekked out each morning in search of fresh water and fresh fruit.

Fernandella had been the beauty of the San Cristobel, Queen of the annual festival at St. Ann, Mother of Mary Church, (though there was never such a church) fine-boned and light of foot, not at all like the peasant girls Hector Pimental was used to, who were heavy-thighed with faces like frying pans. Fernandella had courage as well as beauty; she could have done much better for herself. But the final evening of the festival she had walked the boisterous streets by herself, a yellow scarf twined in her long, straight hair. A summer storm hung on the horizon like a rumor; heat lightning peppered the distant sky.

As she walked she saw Hector leaning against the front of a booth that sold tortillas, and, as her clear, ironic eyes touched his, she trembled, as much from the night and the excitement of the festival as from the actual vision of the dark young man with hooded eyes who wore a black silk shirt open to the waist. She was enthralled as much by what he stood for as the man himself. For Hector Pimental had an aura of danger about him, a sexuality that widened Fernandella's nostrils as she breathed the tainted air.

They exchanged a few words. Hector feigned indifference, something Fernandella could not understand, or tolerate, for as the most beautiful young woman in San Cristobel, Queen of the Festival of St. Ann, she had all evening been rebuffing the advances of men more handsome, richer, more worthy of her. Her mother had whispered to her that Santiago the furniture maker, a widower, not yet thirty, with a fine home in the green hills above the village, painted the color of raspberries with a coral-slate roof of eye-dazzling white, had expressed an interest in her.

"I've seen you at the baseball grounds," Fernandella said, a delicate hand on her hip, one foot placed well in front of the other. When Hector did not reply she went on, "My father is a great fan of the San Cristobel Heartbreakers. We often come by in the evening to watch them play."

"I am a fan only of teams that win when I have money on them," said Hector, staring somewhere over Fernandella's head, not looking down the front of her dress as other young, and not so young men, had been doing all evening.

Thunder rumbled at a great distance; the colored neon of the ferris wheel cast yellow, green, and blue shadows across the faces of Hector and Fernandella, and Fernandella knew in her heart that she would marry Hector, whose last name she had yet to hear.

"Take me on the ferris wheel," she said suddenly; she had not until that second been aware of what she was about to say.

Hector counted the centavos in his shirt pocket. He grinned at her. "Girls are often afraid of great heights," he said.

"I am afraid of nothing," said Fernandella.

They boarded the ferris wheel amid the odors of grease, exhaust fumes, cedar shavings and the pounding of the motor that powered the rickety vehicle. The wheel worried its way up then lurched over the top, eliciting a scream from Fernandella who clutched Hector's arm in a gesture partly fear and partly an unendurable urge to touch this mysterious young man. The ferris wheel turned its requisite number of times, but when the attendant pulled the lever that would bring it to a stop, nothing happened. The wheel continued to turn, its green neon rolling across the sky like giant hoops. The speed of the wheel increased until it drew all the breath from the frightened passengers and the screaming died like bird calls on a breeze. The attendants worked frantically to stop the wheel. The motor was shut down, but a lessening of sound was all the shutdown precipitated. Eventually, the green neon, like parallel railroad tracks, disappeared into the distance of night like two illuminated green snakes.

Hector and Fernandella found themselves on a road outside of San Cristobel, the soft dust under their feet still warm from the day, the moon reflecting in a limpid pool, a stand of scarlet bougainvillea clutching at them as they kissed.

"When Hector Pimental takes his woman for a carnival ride, he takes her for a ride," the young man said, pretending not to be puzzled by what had happened.

Fernandella's knees were melting.

"You are magical," she said, "we will enjoy a magical life together."

Hector kissed her willing mouth, but all the while he was wondering about the outcome of his bets on that evening's baseball games.

SIX
THE WIZARD

Fernandella's family, who were stolid, hardworking, churchgoing people before the priests were relieved of their power, were horrified at her choice. Did I mention that the Old Dictator decreed that all priests were to leave Courteguay? Those who stayed were forced to live behind chain-link fences and quietly mold and disintegrate. Years later, Dr. Noir took credit for dispatching the priests from Courteguay and imprisoning those who stayed. Dr. Noir of course, was a liar, a thief, a cheat, a murderer and a scoundrel. And those were his good points.

When they weren't making love in some secret and forbidden place, Hector retained his indifference.

"I have no intention of changing my ways," he told her. "I will never work in the cane fields, or the guava plantations. I gamble. If you marry me my luck becomes yours."

Fernandella agreed. Within weeks they were married.

BUT BEFORE THEY COULD BE MARRIED there had to be a baseball game. The women of Courteguay played almost as much baseball as the men and some of them were exceptionally talented. Before a wedding could take place a team made up of the bride, her sisters and bridesmaids, and whoever else was necessary to a complete team, played against a team picked by the groom. The groom's team could be made up of anything from rank amateurs to semi-professionals. For the wedding to go forward the bride had to make an *adequate* showing as a baseball player. The word adequate could be interpreted in many ways. If the groom was reluctant, a bride who went only 1 for 4 and made an error in the field might be rejected by the triumvirate who made the decision, the groom and best man being two, the third often one of the moth-eaten priests who lived behind chain-link fencing. The priest never saw the game but would be told about it by the groom, and was the third leg of the triumvirate to give an appearance of fairness.

If the soon-to-be groom was madly in love, all the bride, if she was not an athlete, or many months pregnant, had to do was show up, stand helplessly in right field and swing weakly at the ball when she batted. But even if the bride was an excellent commercial league player, the groom might want an extra week to sow a few wild oats so would insist that she had not played well enough to be his bride, thus postponing the wedding for a week.

Fernandella was coached by a woman named Roberta Fernandez Diaz Ortega, who now lived in the United States with her lover, a woman who once won the Dinah Shore Golf Tournament, and happened to be visiting her family. Several years earlier in a Wedding Game like this Roberta had been seen by a scout for the Baltimore Orioles. In cut-off jeans, a loose shirt and with her boy's haircut, Roberta was mistaken for a boy, and the scout offered her a chance in A Ball in the USA. Roberta signed her name as Roberto and hopped in the back of the scout's Jeep after the game was over. As Roberto she moved quickly up the ladder and played two seasons for the Orioles, batting over .300 and coming second in All Star voting her second season. Her teammates did not suspect her. She was often seen in the company of women.

"Geez, Robbyo," said teammate Bubba, one evening before a game, "I seen you dancing last night. I thought that tennis player girl you was with was queer as a three-dollar bill."

Roberta stared him in the eye. "I am Courteguayan," she replied, "I am able to overcome any odds."

"Damn fine," said Bubba. "Maybe you could introduce me to one of them queer chicks, I've always felt that after one evening with Ol Bubba, they'd get over that foolishness."

"Maybe someday I will," said Roberta.

It wasn't until the last day of the season after Roberta had won the batting title in the American League and her teammates threw her into the shower that they discovered her secret.

Management quickly covered up by announcing first, magnificent player bonuses, then in December that a torn rotator cuff had ended Roberto's career. They paid out her contract, which made her a very wealthy woman.

SEVEN
THE WIZARD

Her mother was certain that an evil wizard had put a spell on Fernandella.

And, as if to confirm his mother-in-law's worst fears, on the day Fernandella first told Hector she was pregnant he took her to see a wizard who lived in a tent near the baseball grounds.

"If he is such a wizard why isn't he rich, or President of the Republic, or both?" Fernandella cried.

"A true wizard never uses his gifts for his own benefit."

"Who told you that? The wizard?"

Hector busied himself brushing dust off the cuffs of his pants.

The Wizard, who called himself Jorge Blanco, existed by predicting the outcome of baseball matches....

"You said Jorge Blanco was one of your names," said the Gringo Journalist.

"If I said that then it must be true," replied the Wizard, anxious to get on with his story.

In the mornings, a steady stream of gamblers made their way to the Wizard's tent, paying five centavos for each prophecy. The Wizard seldom gambled himself, and hedged his prognostications. Unless a game seemed a sure thing, he advised half the gamblers to bet one side, half to bet the other, swearing each side to secrecy.

The Wizard claimed that he had once been to America, had spent two whole days in Miami, where he had seen a hot air balloon. The moment he had seen it rise in the air, hissing like a million snakes, he knew the feel of magic, and realized his role in life was to be a wizard. It was the first time he had ever experienced wonder. His second exposure to wonder occurred the same afternoon when he stumbled on a Major League baseball team engaged in spring training, and by asking a few questions discovered that professional baseball players were well paid, well fed, and overly respected, considering that what they did for a living was play a child's game.

"THERE ARE INCONSISTENCIES HERE..." the Gringo Journalist began.

The Wizard glared at the Gringo Journalist.

"So, sue me," he said. "This is Courteguay. Sometimes two and two equal five."

"TWINS," THE WIZARD PROCLAIMED PROUDLY, pressing the newly-taut skin on Fernandella's belly. "Twin sons!"

The inside of the wizard's tent was stifling, and smelled of fruit rinds and stale clothing.

Hector beamed; Fernandella scowled at the wizard.

"How much is this going to cost?" she demanded.

Fernandella was not used to being so poor. Her own family had little, but their adobe home was whitewashed, had mats on the floor, and food had never been a concern. Since her marriage, Fernandella stole fruit from the tiny orchards of family friends. The hovel in which she and Hector lived had been abandoned by a family of ten, and their goats, when it became too filthy even for them, a group of people only one step removed from the animals with whom they shared everything.

Fernandella whirled about the hut like a Fury, making it livable. In a matter of weeks she was shrilling at her husband in a manner she had vowed she would never do, imploring, threatening, cursing, invoking saints that he might take a real job in the cane fields and provide for her properly. Still, in the night, when she slipped her hand inside the cool black shirt, when the sweetness of Hector's hair pomade was close at hand, she shivered with ecstasy and forgave him his indolence and lack of ambition, praying that the baseball teams he had bet on might win.

"The Wizard," scoffed Fernandella, "what does he call himself? Jorge Blanco? He is a scoundrel fallen on hard times who still wants to be the bride at every wedding, the corpse at every funeral. I've heard rumors that he was once known by the name Boatly, a Gypsy from Europe, an immigrant, a foreigner. I have heard that in another life he walked up out of the ocean like a fish learning to be a man. Some say he was deposited on earth full grown, that he arrived from outer space, emerged from a glowing, ball-shaped object that whined like an ominous wind and vanished the moment he stepped clear. He does nothing to dispel such rumors."

This was not the last time Fernandella railed about the ancestry and shiftlessness of the Wizard.

"He could not possibly be Boatly," said her studious son, Esteban, many years later. "Sandor Boatly brought baseball to Courteguay. Sandor Boatly, if he were alive, would be over a hundred years old."

"NEVER MARRY A HANDSOME MAN," Fernandella would tell her own daughters, when they became teenagers. But none paid the slightest attention, and all of them did marry handsome men, with varying degrees of success, except for her third daughter the dwarf, Agurrie, who joined a touring circus and fled to Europe, supposing rightly that her handicap would be more acceptable there. She sent postcards that often took years to arrive.

"TWIN SONS!" boomed the Wizard, "who will be great, no, not just great, but the two greatest baseball players ever to originate in the Republic of Courteguay."

The Wizard lived in poverty in a tent made of stolen canvas, saving the profits of his predictions in order to someday acquire a hot air balloon.

"I will fly like an angel over Courteguay," he proclaimed, "sizzling down out of the sky as a wizard ought to. My costume will be made of parrot-bright silks and will contrast favorably with the sleek brilliance of the balloon."

Removing his hand from Fernandella's belly, he said to her husband, "That will be fifteen centavos, please."

"Thief!" cried Fernandella, watching her husband digging in the pocket of his ragged trousers. It was at that moment she felt the first painful stirrings in her belly, though she could not comprehend the nature of the pain, and had no idea it was caused by a miniscule pitcher gouging out dirt in front of the pitcher's rubber, making a place for his forward foot to land comfortably.

"Eyyya," groaned Fernandella, grasping her belly with one hand.

"To be completely fair," said the Wizard to Fernandella's husband, "I will prophesy the outcome of three baseball games of your choice, for the same ridiculously low fee."

EIGHT
THE WIZARD

Excuse me, please. There *are* inconsistencies here. I am the wizard described in the preceding pages. I am at the moment staring over the shoulder of the author, a gringo journalist who is conducting interviews with me. He sits at a large oak table writing my story, the results of his interviews with me, on a pad of yellow lined paper. He was a guest in my own home. I allowed him to visit me when I was briefly confined to the General Omar Bravura wing of National Hospital of Courteguay, once known as the General Lucius Noir Hospital and Chiropractic Clinic.

The Gringo Journalist's handwriting is extremely bad, consequently I have to get so close I occasionally breathe on his neck and ear, dstracting him momentarily from his task. Even though I am indeed a wizard and as such can routinely be in more than one place at a time, I cannot influence what this author is putting down. However I can and will be certain to correct erroneous information, which I'm sure will keep me very busy.

This gringo is hardly qualified to write even a novel set in Courteguay. He once spent two weeks there as the guest of a famous baseball scout named Bill Clark who worked for the only Major League Baseball Club in the True South. The Gringo Journalist spent the entire two weeks whining about the humidity, the accommodation, the unpaved roads, the presence of the military at the baseball stadiums, and did not pick up his fair share of the bar tabs.

The one afternoon the famous baseball scout left him unattended he hired a taxi and attempted to cross the border into Haiti in order to investigate the origins of the infamous Dr. Lucius Noir, who was dictator and El Presidente of Courteguay during several of the years the gringo wishes to write about. The famous baseball scout, not wanting to be responsible for the permanent disappearance of the gringo, had stopped by Haitian Customs and told them that the gringo had once called Baby Doc Duvalier a pig, green pig to be exact, *un cochon vert*, and had said even worse things about his father Papa Doc Duvalier. Haitian Customs denied the Gringo Journalist permission to enter, and spat on the back bumper of the taxi as it turned around. The Gringo Journalist suffered from nausea and stomach cramps the final three days of his stay.

THE TWINS WERE MY FIRST PERSONAL TRIUMPH as a wizard. I think that, as an author, the Gringo Journalist could have spent a little more time on the gravity of that situation. If gravity is the right word. You see, one simply does not say "I am a wizard," and suddenly everyone treats you with the deference and skepticism that such a proclamation deserves and entails.

I remember once, not too long after my arrival in Courteguay, I had gotten myself into a rather precarious situation; it is a universal truth that gamblers who cannot meet their obligations are known to have their kneecaps broken, or worse. I was being approached by several sleek young men who had unexpectedly won a considerable number of guilermos from me because a no-account pitcher for a no-account baseball team had pitched a one-hitter against the San Barnabas Beasts, playing at home in the Jesus, Joseph and Mary Celestial Baseball Palace. I honestly did not have the guilermos necessary to pay my debts and was prepared for the worst when, as the young men, lean and vicious as coyotes, approached me, I flung open my shirt to display the gardenias growing from my chest hairs. The young men studied me, sniffed the air, glanced at each other with amber eyes. Without words their consensus was that a lucky flower would more than compensate for their financial loss. The only pain I suffered was from the flowers being ripped unceremoniously from my chest.

But what transpired was much more than being forgiven a debt, it established my credentials as a wizard. Word of a new wizard travels faster than pink eye, and within a day my reputation was known in both San Cristobel and the capital, San Barnabas. Though it took many more years before I could be a successful and nonchalant wizard, I, like that rookie pitcher who threw an unexpected one-hitter, had established my potential. No one would ever dismiss me at a glance again.

What transpired pertaining to the birth of the Pimental twins was secondary, for though it was perhaps my greatest triumph, my life was not endangered if the outcome was not magical or spectacular, or both. There is the story of the famous American golfer who, when asked if he didn't get very nervous when putting for hundreds of thousands of dollars, replied that nothing serious happened if he missed one of those putts; nervous, he said, was playing a wise guy who could have your knees broken, and putting for a hundred dollars with nothing but lint in his pockets.

NINE
THE GRINGO JOURNALIST

There is a certain heat in the city of San Cristobel. The daytime sky is always high and white, a carnivorous sun reflects blindingly off whitewashed adobe walls. Heat waves bounce from the walls and the red dust of the streets, until the air looks like it is filled with wavy spider webs.

The heat of San Cristobel saps the strength. Birds fall silent. Insects drone like overloaded aircraft. The heat of San Cristobel touches the mind. Eyes squinting against the fierce glare do not always see what is before them. The heat of San Cristobel is a magician pulling rabbits from hats, birds from concealed pockets, coins from ears. The temperament of the land is regulated by heat. Sudden and casual violence is a way of life, flaring like lightning, as quickly forgotten.

There are rumors in San Cristobel that Dr. Lucius Noir while he was El Presidente of Courteguay could command lightning to strike his enemies.

I've also been told of a woman who sold lightning, claimed she had learned the trick in Haiti. For a fee she would sell a lightning bolt from the storm that perpetually dumped torrents of rain on

San Cristobel every evening. Your personal lightning bolt would strike wherever the buyer desired. But, as with all magic, there were risks, if the mood of the people was bitter, sellers of lightning were sometimes stoned, other times tied to trees and burned alive.

It is said that nothing in San Cristobel has ever been exactly normal. At least not since baseball arrived, the accoutrements carried by a ragged, starved, fiery-eyed fanatic with a few chittering baseballs in a canvas bag, hanging from a bat. I have heard the Wizard's own story, but there is great confusion over whether a man named Sandor Boatly ever existed let alone brought baseball to Courteguay.

Easier to remember is the Wizard descending from the sky in a multicolored balloon, distributing baseballs like party favors. In this part of Courteguay, time is measured since the arrival of baseball. It was not all that long ago, and one or more of the versions of Courteguayan History begins just before the first baseball season. Those who remember the event, or claim to remember, sometimes refer to it as the Teaching Time. After-history being almost as interesting as history itself, the stories told by liars are often more entertaining, contain more truth than those told by people who actually witnessed events.

From the research of the Gringo Journalist:

A FIRSTHAND ACCOUNT OF BASEBALL COMING TO COURTEGUAY

The Teaching Time, perhaps a year, perhaps considerably longer, depending on whose story you believe. It is speculated that Time in Courteguay began on opening day of the Courteguayan National Baseball Association, at the moment when the Old Dictator, who may or may not have been Octavio Court, (I have so far been unable to determine if there ever was an Octavio Court, so ephemeral is his memory, so steeped in fog the short history of Courteguay) threw out the first pitch at Jesus, Joseph and Mary Celestial Baseball Palace, in San Barnabas, inaugurating the four team league encompassing two teams each from San Cristobel and the capital city, San Barnabas.

During the baseball season, a cloud in the early evening sky is an occasion. The temperament of the land is regulated by the heat. The season which is theoretically year round, is curtailed during the rainy months by hurricanes and torrential downpours, but not shut down. I am told that there was a law enacted against rain falling before nine in the evening, (but who enacted it?) a time when all but the longest extra-inning game was in the records and the fans and players had safely returned to their homes.

Sandor Boatly, the Wizard, as well as some historical sources, claim that Boatly demonstrated baseball by first teaching a would-be player to hit, first grounders, then flies. Boatly then played at every position on the field, showing how each player should conduct himself. He even visited the priests enclosed behind chain-link fencing and before long, though there were not enough for a single team, let alone two, they laid out a diamond and enjoyed a rousing game of scrub.

It is said that years later, Dr. Noir repeatedly mouthed the words, "There is no need for God in a warm climate," as he personally shot priest after priest where they were trapped inside their chain-link prisons.

As one must have in any odd or experimental project, Sandor Boatly had luck on his side. Just as the people in some societies have no resistance to alcohol, or religion, the people of Courteguay were seemingly born with no resistance to baseball, and it seems they were born with an innate knowledge of the game that only had to be scratched to bloom fully. Many of the young men were blessed with uncanny ability, the pitchers, with no training, able to throw 90 MPH fastballs, the hitters, equally untrained, able to club five hundred foot home runs, the infielders capable of performing contortions like gymnasts, able to retrieve sharply-hit baseballs from the short outfield grass and throw accurately to first base, always a hairsbreadth ahead of the fleet runner.

BUT HOW MUCH OF THIS IS TRUE? The Wizard is at best a charlatan. Could he, as many claim, actually be Sandor Boatly? It seems unlikely, but just as I feel I have a handle on him, he does something that makes me want to believe everything he tells me. For instance, no matter how many times I change it back, when I next open my manuscript my description of the Wizard in the second sentence has been changed to charming charlatan.

TEN
THE WIZARD

The birth of Julio and Esteban Pimental was my first triumph. I lurked in the dry weeds behind the shack while the births were taking place. My eyes glistened and my skin shone like polished teakwood.

Hector Pimental, who considered it unmanly to be anywhere in the vicinity of womens' work, still couldn't keep himself away from the birth. What if my prognosis was right? What if Fernandella were to produce from his seed the two finest baseball players ever to come out of Courteguay? Hector fancied himself selling his services as a stud, fathering an army of sons, graceful, powerful baseball players all. He fantasized the pleasure he would receive while doing his duty for Courteguay.

"The first one was born in the catcher's crouch," Hector cried, as he came upon me where I hunched in the brittle undergrowth eating a mango. "His little hands are already scarred. He has suffered several broken knuckles. He has a stolid face and full head of black hair. I will name him Esteban."

I stared at my reflection in the blue brook that had mysteriously appeared behind the tin shack that Hector and Fernandella called home. Handsome and lean as a coyote, I thought, rubbing my thin hands together and deciding that as a reward I would add a name, and henceforth be known as Alfredo Jorge Blanco.

An hour later Hector Pimental returned.

"The second one, the one we will christen Julio, was born wearing baseball cleats," he announced with wicked pride. He stared at me, dressed in my ink-blue robe covered with mysterious symbols. "The fingers on his pitching hand are like talons, the first two fingers splayed, the nails sharpened to fierce points."

"Did I not prophesy so?" I asked. I was now Geraldo Alfredo Jorge Blanco, having added yet another name as soon as I heard Hector crashing through the thicket toward me.

I continued to rub my hands together, maintaining a calm outward appearance as I tried to decide how to best exploit the situation. Hector Pimental's only motivation was greed; he would need much guidance.

"I am a wizard," I repeated several times under my breath, shaking my head as if to clear away confusion. I should not be surprised, I told myself. One has only to trail dreams obsessively in order to make them come true.

After the births, Carlotta, the midwife, swaddled Esteban and Julio in blankets made from freshly laundered sugar sacks. After she stretched Esteban out of his catcher's crouch, and attempted to force Julio to lie like a normal baby and stop the continual pitching motions, she propped the babies, one on each side of Fernandella, their tiny maple faces each resting against a swollen breast. It was then that the midwife discovered that, along with the twins, Fernandella's womb had expelled two miniature baseball gloves, one a catcher's mitt, three cumquat-sized baseballs and a pen-sized bat. If Julio was the pitcher and Esteban the catcher, who held the bat was never known.

ELEVEN
THE GRINGO JOURNALIST

The Wizard, after washing his most colorful costume in the clear stream that had appeared beside the home of Hector and Fernandella Pimental, set off for the capital of San Barnabas. He did not have bus fare so walked part way, then with the help of an acquaintance who was already on a bus, he was pulled through a window, suffering only minor sprains and a large rip at the rear of his caftan. He presented himself at the Presidential palace as an emissary of the miraculous, stupendous, fabulous, baseball-playing babies who had been born near San Cristobel. The Wizard lied outrageously, claiming that he had personally delivered the babies, and that he had a medical degree from Port-au-Prince Hospital in Haiti. The Wizard had heard that in Haiti, anyone with a sharp knife and more than one ounce of disinfectant could call himself a doctor, so he didn't exactly consider his story a lie.

The Wizard's message did eventually reach the Old Dictator, passing first through the head of the Secret Police, one Dr. Lucius Noir. The Old Dictator, who like the Wizard had a nose for a profitable situation, decided after leaving the Wizard waiting at the gate for 24 hours to give him an audience.

The Old Dictator donned his whitest uniform, one with flamingo-colored birds as epaulets, and stationed himself behind a huge marble-topped table, a bowl of peeled and sliced mango and a bowl of passion fruit the only decorations.

"I am humbled by your generosity," said the Wizard, shaking yellow dust from his caftan. "I have been a party to one of the more remarkable occurrences in a land of remarkable occurrences: babies that played catch in their mother's womb. Babies that even now, at the tender age of two weeks play catch in their crib."

The Wizard stopped and eyed the mouth-watering food.

The Old Dictator nodded for him to help himself.

The Wizard, rather than spoon out a dish for himself, pulled a full crystal bowl to the edge of the table and began to eat with the service spoon.

"Why exactly are you here? What do you hope to accomplish, other than a free breakfast?" the Old Dictator asked.

"Not a thing," said the Wizard between mouthfuls. "I have seen something miraculous, and as someone who has always supported you over General Bravura, I decided that you should be appraised of the situation. You are so much more astute than your enemy, I know you, in your infinite wisdom, will know what should be done to make the most of the situation."

"You are a toady of the first ilk," said the Old Dictator said with a smile.

"Thank you."

"What percentage do you want?"

"What is it we are planning to do?"

"That remains to be seen. First the business arrangements."

"A what is it they call it, a finder's fee, perhaps. Say, 40 percent."

"I would not even allow my banker 40 percent. You look like a charlatan, and a not very successful one. Five percent, take it or leave it."

"With all due respect, I will leave it. I am necessary because I have complete access to the remarkable and marketable twins. Their father is a close friend and confidant. Their mother is like a sister to me. Thirty percent, not a guilermo less."

"If I were not an honorable man I would send Dr. Noir and his secret police to pick up the twins and deliver them to me. I assure you that Dr. Noir, who is more of a toady than you will ever be, would be certain there would be no survivors, that the parents, and anyone associated with the family, I assume that would include you, would disappear forever. As a benevolent head of state I would personally adopt the orphaned twins. Now, I'm sure you wouldn't want that to happen. Fortunately, I am able to keep Dr. Noir's basest instincts under control. Ten percent."

They eventually settled on a fifteen percent share for the Wizard, of whatever might develop. After many hours of tossing ideas about it was agreed that the whole family would be moved to San Barnabas and set up in a fine home where tours would be held at least twice a day, possibly three, maybe even four times. The babies would be observed playing catch, and as their skills increased they would put on longer and longer displays. In return their family would be cut in for a percentage of the take, they would be fed, housed, and supplied with nurses and a personal physician.

Fernandella refused outright.

"I will raise my own children without the help of the state. How come a state that never helped me or even knew of my existence now wants to shower me with treasures all because my sons are unique?"

Hector Pimental lurked by the stream. A massive home in San Barnabas, good clothes, perhaps a car. His mouth watered at the prospect.

"We must work slowly," he told the Wizard. "We will make changes so gradually that Fernandella will hardly notice, and when she does, the changes will be so beneficial she will not reject them. My influence will cost you 10 guilermos per day."

The Wizard delivered the 10 guilermos which Hector immediately bet with him on losing baseball teams.

So as not to make Fernandella suspicious, Hector claimed to have been been wildly successful with his betting.

"With my winnings I am going to show my love of family by replacing the tin roof which attracts heat for a much cooler wooden one. Also the walls, and I will fill them with insulation to keep out the heat."

Though mistrustful, Fernandella allowed the remodeling.

"Next a nursery for the twins," proclaimed Hector, a few weeks later, flashing a wad of guilermos such as Fernandella had never seen.

The nursery was built, then a couple more rooms were added. Finally the grounds were landscaped, the brush and refuse cleared away, a low chain-link fence created a large front yard, with a sidewalk where passers-by could stare at the twins as they played by the miniature plate and pitcher's rubber that had been surreptitiously installed.

"The ticket booth will be at the foot of the hill where Fernandella will not even notice it," Hector told the Wizard who passed the information to the Old Dictator.

By the time Fernandella realized that people were paying for the privilege of watching her babies play catch, she was lulled by the comfort of her home, the fine clothes that had been provided, the abundance and variety of food, the new furniture.

"How are we being compensated?" she demanded of the Wizard, who now lived in a small home at the bottom of the hill, where from his window he could watch the tickets being sold and calculate his percentage of the take. He hired a housekeeper for himself, one who had formerly worked as a dancer at Miss Kitty's Bar and Pleasure Palace on the seamier side of San Cristobel.

"The profits are mainly being held in trust for the twins," replied the Wizard. "They will be very rich young men when they come of age. In the meantime your needs are being taken care of, are they not? You have to do nothing but put the twins on display three times per day. I myself receive a small fee for inaugurating the idea. The Old Dictator takes a percentage, for it is the Government of Courteguay that advertises the unique and stupendous Baseball Playing Babies, live and in color without commercial interruption. The Old Dictator also oversees the fees paid by foreign media for the privilege of photographing your beautiful sons."

Fernandella was suspicious but she was dealing with powers far beyond her.

JULIO WAS WALKING by seven months, however Esteban remained stable in the catcher's crouch until he was nearly three. Esteban stared straight ahead apparently concentrating on his pitching twin. He paid no attention to the throngs of people, many from the United States (the baseball playing twins increased tourism to Courteguay by nearly a thousand percent) who pushed against the fence, their cameras snapping photos constantly, clicking like cicadas. Julio often dazzled the tourists with a smile. The women immediately fell in love with him. He would stare arrogantly at the prettiest female in the audience, tug suggestively at his diaper, then unleash a wild pitch into the crowd, aimed, usually with great accuracy, at the stuffiest looking male present.

TWELVE
THE GRINGO JOURNALIST

I have more in common with the Wizard than I ever suspected. I often feel like the Wizard skulking in the underbrush witnessing events I was not meant to see. I am collecting material for my book on the history of Courteguay, incorporating my series of articles and features; to my knowledge no such compilation has ever been published. But I am coming to realize there is good reason for that because the history of Courteguay, such as it is, is so ephemeral as to crumble like pastry when put to any kind of test, to turn from a dew-studded spider web sparkling in the dawn to a useless daub of wet, black nothingness, only to reappear as a mysterious bright object visible only to certain birds....

AS HE GREW OLDER, Julio was able to remember the batters he had faced in the womb. He recalled them as being grey and spectral, faceless as fog.

When Julio began pitching in the Major Leagues, he treated all batters as if seen in the translucent memory of his mother's womb. When reporters inquired as to how he pitched to a certain batter, he replied that he did not know one hitter from another. When the press asked Esteban what pitches he called, he would shrug and say, "Julio knows the pitches he should throw." When pressed further, to mollify the questioners he would admit, "by reading Julio's mind, I always know what pitch is coming."

HECTOR PIMENTAL studied his children as his calculating heart expanded in the throes of love. The ultimate battery, he thought. The perfect pitcher, the immaculate catcher, not shaped by fathers and coaches and practice, but created by the universe. Hector Alvarez Pimental was poor enough to know that God was a rich man's device for theoretically keeping the poor happy, but always for keeping them subservient.

As a father, Hector allowed his imagination to fall in on itself, bringing him visions and memories of events in other men's lives, as well as his own, for which he would forever claim credit.

He saw hot air balloons, exotic as jungle birds, hissing like a dragon's breath, gliding across the sky like wondrous, garish melons. Hector Alvarez Pimental would wake in the night yowling, sweat-soaked, his mind like a box of photographs scattered callously on a floor.

He saw the Wizard dressed in harlequin-bright silks, in a flying basket, swishing over San Barnabas, the presidential machete held high in triumph. He was witness to his son, Julio standing like a general in front of a row of pregnant women, fresh as cherry blossoms. A contest of some kind? He was unsure.

He also dreamed that he saw Julio pitch the final delivery of a no-hit, no-run game, then be mobbed by players and fans alike. He saw Julio in a business suit, older than Hector Alvarez Pimental was now, the sleek black hair on each side of his head tinged with grey, being inducted into the American Baseball Hall of Fame.

But the visions were not all pleasant, for he saw his Fernandella in mourning. He saw her dressed in clingy black crepe like the elderly crones who creaked into what few priestless churches were left standing, on her knees clawing at an elaborate coffin. Hector Alvarez Pimental peered with trepidation over Fernandella's shoulder, his chest tight, afraid he was about to see himself in the coffin. What he saw, though not his own body, was equally shocking, for there lay his perfect son, Esteban, sturdy arms folded in death, called away at what appeared to be the prime of his life.

SOON AFTER THE BASEBALL-PLAYING TWINS were born, a clear brook, four inches wide, with water the cold blue of ice, began flowing down hill, passing only yards from the tin-roofed shack. The stream plashed softly and the cool waters held a plentiful supply of iridescent parrotfish, their larkspur-blue bodies darting like shadows. A guava tree in full fruition manifested itself among the bone-dry scrub on the hillside behind the shack where the Wizard had skulked. A dozen lemon-crested cockatoos appeared in a row on the tin roof and kept the area free of insects, while the yard filled with pheasants and game hens, tame and docile, anxious to lay down their lives to provide food for Fernandella and her family.

The babies slept at the opposite ends of their crib, each in their accustomed positions: Julio as if he had just delivered a sidearm curve, Esteban as if he had just caught one.

By six months of age the twins were playing catch with passion fruit. Julio was long and lean with an oval face and forehead, while Esteban was stocky and wide-faced with a low hairline and teacup ears.

"IF THEY ARE GOING TO BE FAMOUS, they will require some education," said Hector Alvarez Pimental.

"They must be able to do sums," nodded Fernandella, who sometimes was drawn in by the bombast of the Wizard, and the furtiveness of her husband. She changed her tone and immediately became jocular. "They will need adding and subtraction in order to count all the guilermos they will earn. You might give them practice carrying sugarcane so they will bear up well under the weight of their wealth."

The Wizard agreed to become tutor to the twins.

"In America," the Wizard pronounced, calling up distant memories, like a long arm reaching deep into a rain barrel, "in America baseball players are more powerful than Bishops, more popular than the slyest politician, more revered than the greatest inventors.

"Every October, the best player in the American League is carried to the President of the United States. There is a monstrous golden scale in the White House palace of the President. The player is seated on the scale, and his weight—he is allowed to eat a huge breakfast first—is matched in golden coins and priceless gems. When the player and his booty are equally balanced, the president takes off his diamond ring and tosses it in among the coins and gems, sending the delicate balance..." at that point the Wizard lost his train of thought and had to change marvels.

"At least so the tabloid press tells me. I am also told the water faucets in the hotels where the baseball players are accommodated, are made of gold," he went on.

The only faucet Hector and Fernandella had ever seen was the single water pipe in San Cristobel town square with its rough, hexagonal head that screwed up and down.

"Tell us about the food," said Hector Alvarez Pimental.

"Ah, the food. Everything tastes as you wish it to. It doesn't matter what you eat, it tastes exactly like what you crave at that moment."

"My cornmeal would taste like chocolate?" said Hector.

"Indeed," said the Wizard. "It is the American way."

THIRTEEN
THE WIZARD

At two years of age Julio struck out his father, using two curve balls and a sinking slider. Almost immediately after their birth, Salvador Geraldo Alfredo Jorge Blanco, as the Wizard now called himself, had a special pitcher's mound installed beside the stream where the blue fish darted like needles, the rubber stolen in the dead of night from Jesus, Joseph and Mary Celestial Baseball Palace.

Hector Alvarez Pimental saw to it that Fernandella became pregnant again as quickly as possible, in fact she produced four more children at ten-month intervals, two boys and two girls. The Wizard made no further predictions over Fernandella's belly, though her husband beseeched him to; the Wizard even declined to predict the sex of the unborn. To the great disappointment of Hector Alvarez Pimental all the children but one were born without abnormalities. The dwarf, Agurrie, might have had some magical appeal if she were male, but a female dwarf was merely bad luck in Courteguay, though even as a baby she had an ice-pick stare that was said to be able to spin the mobile that hung in the listless air above her crib. There was not a hint of magic about any of the others.

As the twins grew older Fernandella's vigilance slackened. Overwhelmed with newer babies and perpetual pregnancy she eventually became relieved to see the twins troop off with their father and the Wizard in the direction of the baseball fields. By the time they were five they were playing in a league for teenagers and winning regularly. Their father became almost prosperous by betting on them, until bookmakers, especially the Wizard, refused to accept any more bets on the battery of Julio and Esteban.

Years later, at the height of their career, shortly before his untimely murder, Esteban Pimental would look on his major league career with mild amusement. Esteban was the more passive of the brothers. Stocky and round faced, he was slow to anger, slower to smile, while Julio on the other hand, was taller, with his father's hooded eyes and sly smile, and a dangerous energy accompanied by a propensity to take chances.

Esteban even as a child in Courteguay was serious and studious, wanting to discuss with the Wizard questions of philosophical magnitude. Rather than discussing how to pick a runner off first base he was interested in questions of religious significance. Esteban often went to view the priests. Years earlier, the Old Dictator had, at great expense, imprisoned the priests by installing fourteen-foot chain-link fencing around every manse in Courteguay. When General Bravura overthrew the government and took power, he did nothing to remove the fences. Esteban would stand outside the frosty-bright metal fence, watching the old priests walk, hands behind backs, black cassocks sweeping the ground, their strides ungainly, lumbering like tall, mangy bears. The priests occasionally blessed a goat or a peasant who came too close to the fence. Esteban noted that the priest's eyes were rheumy and their teeth bad.

"Why doesn't God melt down the fence?" Esteban asked the Wizard.

"Why should he?" asked the Wizard.

"Because the priest is God's representative. He does God's work."

"What can the priests do on the outside that they cannot do inside the fence, except graveside services? If they wished to they could lead prayers, perform marriages, administer the Eucharist, hear confessions;

the sick could be brought to visit them. Because these priests choose to decay before your eyes, to choose as their only duties the blessing of goats and lottery tickets, is not the fault of God. If I were God I would turn the fence to stone so the priests might disintegrate in private."

"I have decided to be a priest," said Esteban. "And I will do the same work no matter which side of the fence I am on."

"You will go far," said the Wizard. "I will see that you are allowed to bless each new balloon that I add to my fleet." The Wizard, at the time, did not own even one balloon.

Word of the miraculous baseball-playing babies spread outward from Courteguay. In nearby Haiti, Papa Doc Duvalier, when he heard of the astonishing children, sent an emissary with golf ball-sized diamonds on his ebony fingers, who offered to buy the babies from their father in return for a twenty-pound bar of gold and six virgins.

"In Haiti, women who have had sex only with Papa Doc Duvalier or a member of his cabinet are still considered virgins. The gold bar has a leaden center and the virgins have the pox," said the Wizard, who had bigger plans for the battery. Hector Alvarez Pimental reluctantly turned down the offer. In America he knew, baseball players were rich and worshipped. They were idolized more than generals, bullfighters, plantation owners, rock stars or even Papa Doc Duvalier. Besides, what would Duvalier do with them, turn them into soccer players?

"They play soccer in Haiti," said the Wizard, "soccer is for rowdies who are not yet smart enough to tie their own shoes. When I become President of the Republic of Courteguay I will have a baseball installed on our flag." The Courteguayan flag was a solid green rectangle with a white cube at its center. The small square had no significance whatever, and the rumor was that the material for the first flag had had a flaw in its center that the flag-maker interpreted as a design.

FOURTEEN
THE GRINGO JOURNALIST

By the time the boys were seven years old they were playing in the best league in Courteguay, and were virtually unbeatable. General Bravura, who was now El Presidente, disagreed with the Wizard about possibly negotiating to send the boys to America. The Wizard went ahead and laboriously wrote a letter that he addressed to: El Presidente, American State of Miami, United States of America, The World. Or so the Wizard claims.

Since he mistrusted the Courteguayan Postal Service, a very small operation because sixty percent of Courteguayans were illiterate, the Wizard sent the letter to America by Dominican rumrunner, which would drop it off somewhere in the Florida Keys. He signed the letter Umberto Salvador Geraldo Alfredo Jorge Blanco, wizard, El Presidente of Courteguay in Waiting.

The letter, by a highly circuitous route, found its way to the Governor of Florida who, having ambitions to become at least a senator, if not President, forwarded it to the owner of the only Major League Baseball Club in the True South. If he was going to be a senator or President of the United States from the South he decided that the South should have a competitive baseball team in the National League. The only Major League Baseball Club in the True South had always had a reputation for mediocrity, even though the owner probably knew something about television stations, of which he owned hundreds, though he apparently knew little about Major League baseball.

The only Major League Baseball Club in the True South sent a scout to San Barnabas. The scout was a famous baseball star of the forties, who had had more losing battles with the bottle than Babe Ruth had home runs. After seeing the battery of Esteban and Julio in action he stayed sober for two full weeks, just to be certain that what he was witnessing was not alcohol induced.

"Julio Pimental is the best baseball pitcher I have ever seen," he wrote back to the only Major League Baseball Club in the True South, "but he is only eight years old. What do I do? Can I sign him? Can I sign his father? He has an agent of sorts, a man in blue silk dress that has silver stars, crescents, triangles and hammers all over it. How soon do you think we can introduce this boy to organized baseball? Aren't there child labor laws to contend with? Would something like this fall under the Coogan Law? By the way, Julio pitches to his twin brother, who is an average catcher but who couldn't hit water if he fell out of a boat. I understand they come as a pair, because the pitcher won't let anyone else catch him."

The owner of the only Major League Baseball Club in the True South was on intimate terms with the President of the United States. In fact, the President had once suggested to the Leader of the House, in a not altogether joking manner, that the leader of the House should introduce a bill to break up the New York Yankees. The President indicated that he would be happy to sign such a bill into law.

The President and the owner of the only Major League Baseball Club in the True South conferred deep into the night.

The alcoholic scout signed Hector Alvarez Pimental to a two-year contract as a scout. Though the father of the twins never realized it, he was paid more as a scout than the manager of the only Major League Baseball Club in the True South. Of course, the manager worked very cheaply.

The ball club also offered to rent the family a comfortable home in a pleasant district in San Barnabas. However, Fernandella refused to leave the cool stream full of flashing fish, the shady mango and guava trees, and the yard full of docile pheasants who did everything but pluck and eviscerate themselves so anxious were they to grace Fernandella's table. Reluctantly, and at great cost, for the Wizard somehow managed to become general contractor, the only Major League Baseball Club in the True South completely remodeled the home built on the side hill, adding a full basement holding an electric furnace. The plans for the house had been drawn up by a Minneapolis firm with a Federal Consulting Contract. When finished the renovated house looked like a cross between a Southern plantation house and a nouveau riche Albanian immigrant's idea of how a wealthy family should live. There were gold faucets, chrome lighting fixtures, garish carpets, and velvet paintings on the brightly-hued walls.

The only Major League Baseball Club in the True South, in consultation with the President of the United States, decided they would wait until Julio was ten years old before signing him. Deep in the bowels of the Capitol, the U.S. Government Printing office manufactured birth certificates for Esteban and Julio showing each to be sixteen years of age.

The bonus Julio's father demanded for signing was a hot-air balloon. The baseball club complied, for their negotiators were vaguely intimidated by the sinister demeanor of the Wizard, who always seemed present, his silks swishing malevolently in the background. They knew the hot-air balloon was for the Wizard and they hoped it would encourage him to travel extensively.

The Wizard, though he did not actually take part in the deal-making, was inclined to take the negotiators for a walk along the now yard-wide, crystal stream full of blue fish sparking like quicksilver; the Wizard made the negotiators aware that the stream began from nothing and diminished to nothing, and while he never claimed responsibility, he intimated strongly that he had something to do with its emergence.

FIFTEEN
THE GRINGO JOURNALIST

The twins, the day after their tenth birthday, armed with official birth certificates stating them to be sixteen, left San Cristobel bound for the mysterious United States, where, they had been told, baseball players were revered as idols.

They had first to be smuggled out of Courteguay, for there was no reliable airline in the country. The aging scout took it upon himself to do the job. Baseball management didn't understand the situation in these primitive countries.

"Be sure and get the proper visas," was their advice. They didn't know that if the boys applied for visas they and the scout might never be seen again. They also didn't know that Dr. Noir, the head of the Secret Police, was taking more and more responsibility for running the government of Courteguay, some of which the Old Dictator knew about, some of which he didn't.

The baseball scout bought a bicycle, an elderly, cumbersome thing with balloon tires, and a metal basket that weighed more than the vehicle itself. The three of them appeared at the border to the Dominican Republic, the scout squat, insect-bitten, with a three-day growth of beard. The boys were carrying the scout's equipment: the battery-powered speed gun, a sack of balls. The bats were in a canvas sack balanced across the black metal basket.

The scout explained in his halting Spanish that he was a baseball scout for a famous Major League team and that his car had broken down. He had hired the two boys to carry his equipment. He would pay them and put them on a bus back to Courteguay as soon he reached the Santo Domingo Airport.

"Beisbol," the immigration officer said, smiling vaguely.

The scout named a couple of famous Dominican players. "I am the scout who discovered their talents," he said, tapping his chest with a thick finger.

"Beisbol," the officer said again.

The scout opened the canvas sack that held the bats. He pulled one out and extended it to the officer. That morning, while the three were eating a breakfast of mangos and day-old tortillas, he had used a black marker to sign one of the bats with the name of a famous Dominican shortstop.

"Ramon Esquibel," he said, pointing to the black lettering.

The officer, clutching the champagne-colored bat, waved them through.

At the airport the scout used his team's American Express card to buy tickets for the boys. He made several phone calls to America, first asking, then demanding that a team executive meet the plane with proper documentation for the boys.

"Don't be fooled by appearances," he said. "They look very young. But they're sixteen. They are carrying their birth certificates, which were provided personally by the President of the United States, and El Presidente here in Courteguay."

"UNBELIEVABLE," said the field manager of the only Major League Baseball Club in the True South, as he first watched Julio hurl the ball toward Esteban's mitt. His name was Al Tiller, and *Sports Illustrated* would one day call him the dumbest manager in baseball.

"We'll start them in A-Ball," said the general manager.

"Double-A," said Al Tiller.

"Triple-A," said the owner, who had been sitting in a director's chair along the third base line. He was a slight, athletic-looking man with a soft, brown mustache, who was astronomically rich.

"I want them at spring training," said Al Tiller. "That pitcher, I've never seen such a curve ball, such movement on a fast ball. How old did you say he is?"

"Sixteen," said the owner. "The catcher's not good though, get rid of him."

"There's a problem," said the general manager. "They're twins, the pitcher will only throw to his brother."

"Offer the pitcher more money," said the owner. "Everyone has a price."

"Not these boys," said the general manager. When I asked them about a signing bonus, Julio said, "I would like a Meccano set, if you please."

"And a puppy," said Esteban, the catcher.

"Perhaps a bicycle with a banana seat," said Julio. "Candy-apple red would be nice."

"Are they really sixteen?" demanded the owner. "Have you checked their documentation?"

"Our scout says they're sixteen. That's good enough for me. Besides, we have their birth certificates."

"They're sixteen," the general manager assured Tiller. He produced birth certificates, 8½-by-11-inch parchments, bordered with blood-red bougainvillea, sporting the Courteguayan flag and the national emblem of Courteguay, the clinched fist holding aloft a glittering machete.

Tiller squinted at the certificates, counted on his fingers to substantiate that the twins were indeed sixteen.

"Joe Nuxall played his first game in the majors at fifteen, so I guess it's okay."

He did not notice the tiny blemish in the bottom right hand corner of each certificate where PRINTED IN USA had been removed by some terrible chemical known only to the CIA.

“They play cowboys and Indians in the locker room,” said Al Tiller.

“Learn to live with it,” said the owner, who amassed TV networks as a hobby, and was married to an aging movie star.

SIXTEEN
ESTEBAN PIMENTAL

Even my mother refers to me as Esteban the turnip, though she does it in a loving way, shaking her head at a son she cannot now, nor will ever understand. I am, indeed, a turnip. I stare dreamily into the distance, conveniently not hearing the racket of my brothers and sisters, of my contemporaries. Julio will come and tug at my ear when it is time to play baseball. I would just as soon not, but for Julio the game is everything. We appear to be extraordinarily talented, at least Julio is, and Julio cannot pitch unless I am his catcher. Many people do not understand this, and since I alone am only an average catcher and a dismal hitter, they try to substitute for me at every opportunity. A foolish ploy. If I am not catching him, Julio throws balls halfway up the backstop, or sometimes behind the batter, or he will deliver a sweet batting-practice pitch across the plate for the batter to wallop wherever he chooses.

We play in the highest ranked league in Courteguay. We are the battery for the San Cristobel Flamethrowers, and Julio is 13-0 with a 1.28 ERA. Scouts from the United States sit in the stands behind home plate, utilize their speed guns, scribble notes and marvel at the talent of Julio as a pitcher. In Courteguay no one cares that we are children playing with adults. However, for the benefit of the scouts, The Wizard has arranged false birth certificates for us, to show that we are sixteen years old, although in reality we are barely nine. The scouts have not yet come to realize that I am a part of the bargain.

On one of the happiest days of my life I remember watching as the wizard tossed blueberries into the stream behind our home. As each berry submerged it became a dazzling blue fish.

"How do you do that?" I asked the wizard.

"I will teach you," he said, handing me several fat blueberries.

I tossed one into the stream. It sank like a small rock as the water carried it downstream. I tried again with the same result. The Wizard tossed a berry and it changed immediately to a sparkling fish that leapt gaily in the water, turning its turquoise belly to the sun for a second before swimming away. He handed me a large handful of berries.

"It takes years of practice," he said. "But if anyone has the patience, you do."

MY WORD FOR TODAY is ullage: the amount of empty space in a closed container. Father Cornelius instructs me that the word is usually used to refer to the empty space in an opened bottle of wine. "With each drink poured from the wine bottle the ullage grew larger." That is the sentence I spoke for Father Cornelius to let him know I understood the meaning.

Father Cornelius, Father Joachin, and Father Bartholomew who has only one leg, live behind a chain-link fence that surrounds their residence. The house, of flaming white adobe, once sat next to a church, but the church was torn down by a previous administration, or perhaps by the present one, or simply by vandals, who knows?

An El Presidente once stated that "There is no need for God in a warm climate," and mandated that if the priests wished to remain in Courteguay they must forever remain behind the chain-link fences. They rely on the kindness of former parishioners for food and clothing. They are allowed to converse through the fence but are not allowed to perform religious rites, though I'm told they do, in fact I've seen them, in fact I have been a part of those forbidden rituals.

Father Cornelius teaches me one new English word a day. I was three years old when I decided that English would be the language in which I would think. I was leaning on the fence watching the priests eat some fried pheasant that my mother had me deliver to them. They spoke in Latin to each other, Father Cornelius spoke English and a smattering of Spanish, "Enough to be dangerous," he said. Father Joachin spoke Spanish Spanish, not the heavily accented, pidgin Spanish-French of Courteguay, and Father Bartholomew who has only one leg, originated in Warsaw and spoke only Polish, Latin and a few words of English. The one-legged Father Bartholomew used his few English words to say how good the fried pheasant was. Father Cornelius, who was tall and skeletal, his shiny bald head pointing like a beacon toward the sky, replied that the pheasant was indeed a gift from God, for which they would later give fervent thanks.

"Why don't you thank my mother?" I said in English, for I had understood every word they had said.

"How does such a tiny child as you come to know English?" replied Father Cornelius.

"I just know," I said. "It is a gift from God, perhaps?"

"You believe in God?"

"I don't know. Suppose you tell me what God is?"

That was the beginning of my spending most of my waking hours outside the chain-link visiting with the priests, discussing theology, philosophy, metaphysics. The priests lend me books. I read them, we all four discuss them, very heatedly sometimes.

I soon stopped discussing the situation with my parents and family. My father is a thinking non-believer, my mother is a non-thinking believer. Julio sometimes hurls a baseball into the chain-link at a high speed, the sound of the crash and the ensuing shudder of the fence causing all four of us to jump with fright. "I am my own God," Julio says. "I make things happen."

The Wizard is a charlatan (one of the first words Father Cornelius assigned me) of unprecedented proportions, though sometimes he is not. He has magic about him and is not afraid to use it. The church, although it believes in miracles, denounces the Wizard, which is apparently the same as denouncing El Presidente. This is a point I and the priests are not clear on. El Presidente in one of his incarnations turned on the church with a vengeance.

My fondest wish is to study for the priesthood, and perhaps serve in a country where the church and the power of the priesthood is understood and admired. Or, perhaps return to Courteguay and re-establish the church in this warm climate where the presence of a stable God would certainly enhance (to augment or intensify) the quality of life.

The priests, I'm sure even in the private of their tumbledown house, never refer to me as Esteban the turnip. They understand, though not completely, how a boy of nine can discuss religious history with them and have insights that sometimes engender (that was yesterday's word) hours of conversation and debate.

The problem that the church encountered in Courteguay was that they were, as always, completely behind the times. In a land of magical happenings they pretended to be blind.

My word for tomorrow is pylorus: the opening from the stomach into the small intestine. It was assigned because I was complaining of a bloated stomach. I have yet to construct a sentence using it correctly.

But, the Wizard. The Wizard, like God, can be in more than one place at a time. And, like God, he does not intercede where he is needed most, allowing the people who believe in him to suffer unjustly.

SEVENTEEN
THE GRINGO JOURNALIST

This was the first major league job ever for Al Tiller, manager of the only Major League Baseball Club in the True South. He had once been a promising minor league player but his hitting had been about as substantial as a politician's promise and he had withered in the minor leagues. Tiller had been a friend and teammate of the former manager, who when he was fired recommended Tiller for the job, not because of his ability but because he was the only one desperate enough and willing to accept the pitiful salary offered.

Tiller had not yet earned his reputation as the dumbest manager in baseball. Years later he would manage the Chicago Cubs to the last pennant before Armageddon.

Al Tiller had no idea what to do with the solemn, dark-eyed twins who appeared at spring training camp. They spoke virtually no English; Tiller spoke no Spanish. Not that Julio and Esteban actually spoke Spanish. Courteguayan was an amalgam of dialects, a bastardization of Spanish, French, English, twisted like toffee to fit the lilting tongues of the Courteguayans.

"How old are you?" was Tiller's first question.

The boys looked about ten, he thought. The slim one with the short hair, handsome as a child Valentino; the catcher, stocky with an almost Neanderthal air about him, was ugly as the famous Yankee catcher Yogi Berra.

The boys giggled nervously, play wrestled, stole each other's caps, and frolicked like children when they thought no one was watching them.

"I WATCHED THEM WORKOUT yesterday," said Tiller. "The pitcher is phenomenal. In three or four years he'll be the best in organized baseball. We're desperate enough for pitching that the boy can serve his apprenticeship in the majors. The catcher's all right defensively, but can't hit worth shit. He needs a few seasons in the minors."

"They can't be broken up," said the General Manager. "The pitcher will pitch to no one else."

"He should learn. I don't think keeping the catcher is a good idea."

"You're not paid enough to think," said the General Manager. "That's why we hired you."

"Who's gonna teach them English?" asked Tiller, who decided not to be offended. Major League managers, even if they weren't paid enough to think, still got their family medical bills paid. Besides, the only non-baseball job he had ever held was a summer on an assembly line, stacking cases of soft drinks as they came off a conveyor belt. He had been supervised by a 6'6" Jamaican who stared down on him with contempt and spoke only two words to him the whole summer, "Faster, asshole!"

"We'll find someone to teach them English," said the GM.

The next day a slim, dark woman with gimlet eyes appeared in the clubhouse. She had a hatchet face with lips thin as razor slits. She wore a white-belted raincoat with a cowl that made her look like a spy.

"Buenos dias," she said to the boys as they trooped in from practice, where Julio's sidearm curve had been dropping a full twelve inches, after gliding slowly toward the plate, fat as a full moon.

The boys, feeling as if they had been in solitary confinement since they left Courteguay, rushed to her and hugged her, babbling in Courteguayan, asking questions, making statements.

Al Tiller, never blessed with children of his own, took the boys under his wing. In the locker room he made a tent out of blankets and a bat. The three of them stayed long after everyone had left. They played cowboys and Indians. He took them to the zoo. He took them home where his wife cooked them burritos, and where he found they had an insatiable appetite for Popsicles. He would trade them half a Popsicle for proof that they had added a new English word to their vocabulary. He would reward Esteban with a lime Popsicle every time he got a hit. Esteban's average suddenly began to climb.

In Courteguay, Julio and Esteban had heard rumors of the radio though they had never heard one in person, had to believe the tales of their father and the Wizard concerning the talking box that told stories. They never even suspected television or the movies.

On their arrival in America they discovered the television set in their room. When it crackled like walking on sand and the multicolored picture emerged Julio was dumbstruck.

"I want to live in there," said Esteban. He watched the set deep into the night, understanding nothing, understanding everything.

"They never sleep," he said, when Julio woke deep in the night and found his brother still transfixed in front of the set.

JULIO WON SIXTEEN GAMES and lost four in his first season, and was named Rookie of the Year in the National League. Esteban batted .196 and was allowed to catch only when Julio pitched. The only Major League Baseball Club in the True South still finished last, the quality of the remainder of the team was so questionable that most of the players would have had trouble playing first-string in Triple-A baseball.

Esteban never learned the skill of giving an interesting interview. He was always indifferent to his accomplishments on the field, not that he was often interviewed about his own accomplishments; usually the press wanted to talk about Julio, and about their being twins. All too often Esteban would want to talk about religious or metaphysical matters. Reporters tended to duck away from him. Julio, on the other hand, never gave a bad interview.

Soon after he came to the Major Leagues a reporter asked, "As a pitcher what is your greatest asset?"

"Fast outfielders," replied Julio.

Back in San Barnabas, Hector Alvarez Pimental gambled with abandon. The Wizard, who now called himself Cayetano Umberto Salvador Juarez Geraldo Alfredo Jorge Blanco, ordered a second hot-air balloon, and began considering running for public office.

"The United States is not conducive to angels." The Wizard answered when asked why he did not accompany the twins to America.

"Treat your success with great respect," the Wizard told the twins. "Success is like a turtle climbing a mountain, failure is like water coursing down hill."

Julio nodded seriously.

"That is not original," said Esteban looking up from the book he was reading. I believe it is a Chinese proverb."

"There are no Chinese in Courteguay," replied the Wizard.

THE INTERVIEW WAS CONDUCTED in Spanish. It was difficult for her to tell how much English Julio understood. During English interviews, he answered questions in an arm-flailing combination of Spanish, English, and Courteguayan.

"How aware are you that you are considered a sex symbol by young women everywhere baseball is loved?" the interviewer, a dark-skinned woman of unusual beauty, asked.

"Everywhere I travel I appreciate the beauty of women," said Julio enigmatically.

"You must receive a great deal of attention from young, and not so young women. In the United States you were on the short list for the Sexiest Man Alive. Only the fact that you don't speak much English probably kept you from winning."

"I speak more English than many people might imagine," Julio said in Spanish.

"Millions of women would like to know about your first sexual experience. How old were you?"

Julio smiled his most charming smile, his dimples flashing, his teeth like polished marble.

"It was in the nursery at the hospital. Not as rumored, did I hop into another crib at the nursery, accepting the invitation of a beautiful girl baby, but it was a nurse who picked me up, held me to her bosom, then to other appropriate places on her body, hence my passion for older women."

"I know nothing of your passion for older women, plus, I am told on good authority that you were born at home."

"So, you have caught me in a lie," said Julio. "What is my punishment? What you do not know is that while my brother Esteban has had thousands of ladies, I have remained pure as rain water, saving myself for a beautiful and intelligent woman such as yourself." He smiled again, meeting her eyes as he did so.

EIGHTEEN
THE WIZARD

"Why in the world do you want to be a priest?" the Wizard asked Esteban, after it became apparent that the boy was serious about his choice of vocation.

"I wish to bring comfort and solace to those in need," said Esteban simply.

"By reinforcing their superstitions?" said the Wizard, for the boy was only five years of age. "Teach them instead about reality. Tell them that there is no comfort in praying to an empty sky. Point out that their saints are frauds. Point out that the Stigmata of San Barnabas, the bleeding heart of the Virgin, was caused by the bishop hiding behind the statue and squeezing pig's blood through the porous stone on high holidays."

"It is good for poor people to have something to believe in," said Esteban. "A little folk magic makes the nerves glow, gives people hope."

"The statue has not bled since the priests have been imprisoned."

"It is in mourning for the captive sons and daughters of the church."

"We'll talk another day," said the Wizard.

"YOU HAVE GREAT SKILL at baseball, that is close enough to religion," said the Wizard.

"Not for me."

"All right, what is a priest's first duty?"

"To God."

"I think not. Everyone's duty is to man. A priest's more than anyone's. God is an excuse for not being able to perform, whether it's bringing comfort to a troubled mind, or medicine to a sick body, or not keeping your glove on the ground when approaching a ground ball.

"If priests must be, their duty is to comfort their charges, but to comfort them with truth, not with lies about pie in the sky bye and bye.

"In America they have electric machines that blot out the unhappy part of the brain. Those machines are the true miracle workers. Priests need to provide forgetfulness. If I were a priest I would sell the stained glass from the windows and the pews from the floors. I would rent the church as a barn and use the money to acquire a wonderful electric machine that would deaden the part of the brain most full of grief or sorrow. Also, I would require my parishioners to attend baseball games on Sunday afternoons...."

"And you would require each one to bet ten centavos on the outcome of a game with you as the bookie."

"Forgetfulness is better than medicine or meditation, or false forgiveness. During a baseball game, for two or three hours whatever torment is raking the soul is put aside, forgotten. The spectator goes home refreshed; it is like he spent an afternoon beside a clear brook, birds singing, sun shining, flowers blooming. Baseball is redemption," said the Wizard.

Esteban occasionally sold peanuts in the parking lot of Jesus, Joseph and Mary Celestial Baseball Palace, hoping to earn enough to buy a Bible printed in Latin. The girl who approached him wore a half dozen leis of waxen orchids about her neck. She wore a red gown and was barefoot. She bought every bag of peanuts Esteban had with him. She piled them up in a little mound and led Esteban away. He followed her as if she was a pied piper; she led him to her home on the beach of Courteguay's only lake, a hut built of thick living vines and flowers; she fed him, undressed him, kept him for five days. She smelled of nutmeg, and live camellias grew along the headboard of her bed.

"Now you know," the woman said to him, though exactly what it was he knew, Esteban was not sure. "From now until forever, wherever you go, whatever you do, whoever you love, you will never be able to forget me. I will live within you like that pinpoint of green in the brown iris of your eye."

Esteban had never noticed the green dot the size of a pinprick in his right eye.

This happened during Dr. Noir's tenure as dictator, and Esteban had to journey outside the San Cristobel city limits—Dr. Noir's image now appeared in all the mirrors of Courteguay's two major cities—in order to view himself in a mirror. He took the green dot as a good luck sign, and he hit over .600 in the first twenty games of his next baseball season.

"Your chronology appears to be wrong," said the Gringo Journalist, suddenly paying closer attention to the wizard's ramblings.

"Have you forgotten you are in Courteguay?" replied the Wizard.

NINETEEN
THE WIZARD

"Forgive me Father for I have not sinned," said Esteban, as he entered the makeshift confessional, which consisted of a guava box wired to the outside of the chain-link fence. The bottom of the box had been removed and the open top was covered with black cloth. Those who wished to confess walked up to the fence, ducked down and poked their head into the cloth-covered guava box; the priest eventually noticing that there was a hooded body standing outside the fence, approached and listened.

"If you have not sinned, why are you here?" asked the flea-ridden priest, who knew full well who was in the confessional. Not only could he recognize the stocky body, but he knew the pious young Esteban's voice from having talked with him almost every day.

"I commit no sins, Father. I am an observer of human nature. It is no sin to observe."

"Perhaps not," said the priest, "but why come to confession if you are sinless?"

"I come to ask forgiveness for the sins of others, the sins I observe in my nightly meanderings and daily conversations and observations."

"What makes you think the sinners do not confess their own sins to me?"

"One of the things I know from observing is who comes to confessional and who does not."

"So what is it you wish to confess and for whom?"

"Li, the Korean greengrocer cheats his customers by pressing a thumb on the scale. He also cheats you, Father, for you have been behind this fence so long you've lost touch with prices. The mangos delivered to you here are twice as expensive as in his store."

"What else?" The priest sighed wearily.

"Reynoldo Javier beats his wife, flogging her with the wide leather belt he wears in the cane fields. He also whips his daughters, and does unspeakable things to them before, sometimes during, and after the whippings."

"Ah," muttered the priest.

"Mrs. Conchita Fernandez, your faithful housekeeper and treasurer of the bingo funds has been stealing 20 guilermos every bingo night for years, but she gives the stolen money only to the whores on Calle El Divisionado to keep them from degrading themselves for a few hours. The whores consider her gifts a bonus and continue plying their trade."

The priest sighed again.

"There is much more, Padre. Why my own father, Hector...."

"No. No. No." cried the priest. "I hear quite enough of the misery of this town from my own sinners. Sin needs no spies, Esteban."

The priest was immediately sorry that he had named the man in the confessional, but Esteban didn't seem to hear.

"My own brother, my twin, engages in immoral acts with young women."

"I don't want to hear," shouted the priest, covering his ears and turning away from the fence.

ESTEBAN LEARNED TO READ from a Bible supplied by one of the elderly priests who lived behind the chain-link fences at the edge of town. Esteban taught Julio to read.

"I am more interested in mathematics," said Julio. "I will need math in order to count the millions I will earn as a pitcher. Being Courteguayan, I will need math to count the women who will fall into my bed."

Esteban rolled his eyes toward heaven. He was reading Immanuel Kant. Each afternoon for an hour or so he would question the priests.

"I feel that the value of Kant's work, as an instrument of mental discipline, cannot easily be overrated," he said, quoting from *Critique of Pure Reason*. He had been reading a faded, falling-apart copy of the book that one of the priests had hidden away from Dr. Noir's book burners long after the churches had been closed. "I believe today I would like to ask a few questions concerning pure reason as the seat of transcendental illusory appearance."

"You are only eight years old," said the priest.

"Which means you are not able to answer my questions. How about a simple discussion of opinion, knowledge and belief? I will ask no questions, we will only speculate."

"At your age you should be playing baseball instead of worrying about such weighty matters."

"I am about finished with Kant. If you please I would next like the book of Descartes that you have buried beside the outhouse. I wish to meditate on this business of thinking in concepts."

The priest shrugged. "What do you think opinion, knowledge and belief have in common?"

Esteban gave a fifteen-minute answer that left the priest shaking his head in admiration. The priest dug up other hidden books: *Science and Moral Priority*, *The Basic Writings of St. Thomas Aquinas*. Esteban devoured them. He always read between innings at the baseball ground. Julio, on the other hand, watched the stands, the crowds. His followers consisted of little girls his age in communion dresses, teenagers shrieking at his every pitch, to groupies three times his age. The adult women frightened off the first two groups; there were sometimes hair-pulling matches, and occasionally a beribboned woman with a wasp's waist and overflowing breasts would pull a knife and send her opponent scuttling underneath the stands. The winner would wait, smiling redly, her arm extended to Julio as he appeared in his street clothes after a game.

"I HAVE A VERY RICH INNER LIFE," said Esteban. "I do not claim to be clever, but I am methodical and questioning. Always questioning. When, before we were born, Julio and I resided in that gauzy hinterland where I was eternally in the catcher's crouch, clothed in the tools of ignorance, the ethereal game of catch we played did not entirely hold my interest. I speculated about the world we inhabited, and the other world we would soon inhabit. If Julio had thrown the sidearm curve four times in a row, I would rouse myself from my reveries long enough to demand a fastball, then drift away again.

"Julio had no such spiritual inclinations. In that way we have always had of communicating, telepathy some would call it, we simply read each other's thoughts. I did not always understand Julio's thoughts, though I could read them clearly. He joked with me about sexual things that I would not comprehend for many years, and even then would not find them essential to my life.

"I must have been five the first time I wandered down the hill to the compound where two or three moth-eaten priests were caged like old bears in a dilapidated zoo.

"'What do you believe in?' I asked the priest who approached the fence, where I clung to the chain-link with my small, dirty fingers.

"'I believe in the salvation of the soul,' he answered, as if the question had come from a literate adult and not a peasant child with no religious experience.

"'Do you read?' the priest asked.

"'No one in my family has ever learned to read,' I replied honestly.

"'Come here, my child,' the priest said, himself moving closer to the fence, taking from under his ratty cassock a flat, floppy bible, worn with age, the edges of the pages curled with use.

"'I will teach you the two most important words in the mortal world. Hereafter you will always be able to say you are capable of reading.'"

"The words I learned that day were *Jesus wept.*

"Later on that same priest, Father Leopold, taught me to read, and I taught Julio, sometimes with the help of the Bible, but mostly by what I would call transplants of knowledge. I would think of the knowledge I had acquired and Julio would learn. Julio would do the same for me, pass telepathically to me the word and stories and rumors and gossip he picked up on the streets of San Barnabas. They were not always stories I wanted to hear. Nevertheless, they helped me understand and accept my brother.

"I remember the first time I held a book in my hands. I remember it the way someone else might recall the first breast they touched, their first kiss.

"Father Leopold had taken nothing in the way of personal effects with him when he was about to be interned in the compound. He was allowed only one bag, and he chose instead of clothing or food or religious accouterments, to carry a dozen books into exile.

"'Oh, dear, some of these books are in Latin,' Father Leopold said, glancing distractedly as them. 'Well, I will teach you Latin, after you master English, and Spanish.' Father Leopold was from a place called Poland, where he says the hills and forests are often covered in a kind of frozen rain he calls snow. I knew Father Leopold dealt in miracles, and I left myself open to such things, but waist high drifts of frozen water were too strange for me to comprehend.

"'You may take this one home,' the priest said to me, 'you must however keep it a secret from everyone, for we are not allowed such freedoms.' The book was small, inside plain blue hardcovers. I dug like a puppy with my hands, sending dirt flying back between my legs, until there was room for the priest to slip the book under the fence. I placed it against my heart, under my ragged shirt, it was cool and solid, and I felt I was holding a piece of the priest's heart. The book, of which I was unable to understand much, though I could read the words, was Aristotle's *Poetics*."

TWENTY
THE WIZARD

Julio and Esteban's great-grandmother, Fernandella's grandmother, had been stoned by duppies, the malevolent shadows of the Courteguayan cane fields and jungles. The dead, as everyone knew, went to live in the jungle as hunting spirits. Duppies, everyone also knew, were responsible for the rustling of leaves on a windless day. Duppies breathed on the back of your neck. And though never visible to the living eye, duppies, if angered by the actions of mortals, threw stones to let their displeasure be felt.

Fernandella's grandmother, a foolish girl of sixteen, with velveteen skin the color of a blue-black narcissus petal, deliberately picked an argument with her husband-to-be and stalked off swelling with feigned anger, wanting secretly for him to chase her and subdue her, in order to prove his love.

The man who would eventually be Fernandella's grandfather did not chase after the willful girl, for it was only an hour until the baseball match, and he was the star pitcher for the San Cristobel Heartbreakers.

While the girl sulked, her fiancé pitched badly, searching the crowd for her beautiful face rather than watching his catcher's signs and the stance of the opposing batter. San Cristobel was humiliated. It was a known fact that duppies often altered the outcome of baseball games. If an outfielder got a late start on a fly ball it was because a duppie held his belt, it was a duppie who kicked the ball from a second baseman's glove as he tagged a sliding base runner. And duppies who covered the eyes of umpires so that they had to guess at the outcome of easy plays, and, as everyone knows, when an umpire guesses, he always guesses wrong.

That evening as Fernandella's foolish grandmother walked barefoot through the quiet cane fields, the duppies unleashed a barrage of coin-sized stones at her. When she went to scream at the sting of the small rocks her mouth made no sound and as she tried to run away her legs suddenly felt as if they weighed two hundred pounds each. The stones seemed to come from all angles, and as the girl couldn't tell where the next stone was coming from, she curled on the ground like a snail and hoped that the duppies were not angry enough to kill her.

As it happened, other than bruises she received only one wound, an inch-long cut just above her left eyebrow.

"I hurt myself climbing to reach some ripe mangos," she lied, when her mother remarked on the congealed blood over her eye, and her generally disheveled appearance.

No more was said. But the girl vowed not to anger the duppies again. She married her fiancé and was a good wife, though her first girl-child, Fernandella's mother, was born with the same purplish worm of a scar above her eye. And, years later, Fernandella was born with the same duppie scar.

FERNANDELLA ACQUIRED A DOG, a two-pound, skeletal-looking, hairless Chihuahua, or rather the dog acquired Fernandella. It appeared at her door on a diamond-bright summer morning just as the last of the ground fog that hovered over the sloping acres of lawn which might have been made of the finest carpet, was evaporating.

The dog pawed at the heavily-timbered front door, yapping like a flock of starlings. The servant who opened the door stopped the dog as it attempted a mad dash into the foyer, and, not being fond of small, ugly, yapping dogs, was about to punt it to a spot near the edge of the property line when Fernandella appeared and rescued it.

The small, squirming mass licked Fernandella's face, while one scrawny paw massaged a nipple, moving in small counter clockwise motions.

Fernandella stilled the paw with one hand while holding the dog tightly against her body. The dog's coat was like worn carpet; his eyes were a muddy almost-blue. Like the Wizard's, thought Fernandella. The dog lapped at her cheeks with a raspberry tongue, he smelled of fog and fresh grass, and antiseptic, like a veterinary clinic.

Fernandella waved the servant away.

"I'll keep him," she said, for the dog was obviously a him, his tiny testicles, like unshelled peanuts, clearly visible. "Uhhh," said Fernandella, once again stilling the active paw. "I'll call him Juan," she said, "I once had a suitor who touched me in much the same way. He too, was called Juan."

The servant blushed and went about his business.

Hector and Juan hated each other on sight. When Hector returned from the baseball matches he found Fernandella curled on the chaise lounge in the green room, the dog cuddled to her breast.

Juan bared his tiny teeth and emitted a low, humming growl.

What Hector saw were needle fangs in an insane, badger-like face, a Tasmanian devil the size of a bloated hamster.

"What's that?" asked Hector.

"A little lost dog," replied Fernandella.

"A rat, you mean."

The dog's fur stiffened. It growled again.

"Get rid of it," said Hector Alvarez Pimental.

THE FIGHT WAS THE RESULT of Hector's gambling. And the fact that Fernandella seemed to keep the nasty little dog at her breast twenty-four hours a day. In spite of his monthly allowance from his sons of 100 guilermos (the annual income in Courteguay at the time was

78 guilermos), Hector Alvarez Pimental gambled away every centavo, betting on the baseball matches. The Wizard was his private bookie.

When his allowance ran out, Hector often appropriated Fernandella's household money. When that failed he would borrow from local merchants, who knew that Fernandella, or certainly her famous sons would honor his debt, out of embarrassment if not honor.

On a particularly bad day, Julio, who was 20-7, was pitching against the cellar-dwelling Cleveland Indians, against a pitcher with control problems that went far beyond finding the plate with his pitches and into the realm of alcohol and illegal drugs. The pitcher had a 6.49 ERA for the season. Hector bet 400 guilermos on Julio's team.

Julio pitched superbly, giving up only three hits and an unearned run in a complete game. But that evening the drunken pitcher had a curve ball that dipped like a ping-pong ball in a wind tunnel. He scattered seven hits and pitched a shutout.

Hector Alvarez Pimental smiled weakly when the televised game ended, and said, "I have left my wallet at home. How careless of me. I will gladly pay you tomorrow."

The Wizard replied, "You know I deal only in cash," then paused for a long time before adding, "and certain merchandise."

The word certain was spoken in underlined italics.

They struck a deal. The debt would be canceled in return for Leroy Nieman's portrait of Julio in full wind-up, his left foot a full eight inches above his head. It was when Fernandella discovered that the portrait, which belonged to Julio, was missing, that the terrible fight ensued. The fight when Hector beat his wife about the head and face with her evil little dog, doing neither of them any harm. It was many years before Fernandella entirely forgave Hector.

TWENTY-ONE
HECTOR PIMENTAL

It is a very frightening thing to be a poor man with a family. Sometimes I wish that the Old Dictator had not consigned the priests to the scrap yard, had not fenced them in behind chain-link where they pace like tigers, hands clasped behind their backs, eye burrowing into the ground. I liked the quiet of the church interiors, the smell of earth, varnish, incense. I liked being forgiven. In the years since the churches were outlawed, since they sit unattended, inching deeper into the earth, my heart grows heavier, my conscience dark and bulky within me, a metallic cancer without cure.

I remember the Old Dictator's speech. Fernandella and I, still courting in those days, walked into San Barnabas, stood barefoot on the rain-washed cobblestones in front of the presidential palace on a cool, sunny day, splashes of bougainvillea covering the adobe walls of the palace. The Old Dictator stood on the largest balcony, his white uniform emblazoned with many medals, his officers flanking him wore scarlet sashes, blue ribbons slashed diagonally across their chests like bandoleers.

"There is no need for God in a warm climate," the Old Dictator said. "We have been restrained by the church for centuries, could life be any worse without religious influence than it is now? It is time we found out." He went on to issue a proclamation that officially closed the churches, turning the buildings over to the people who were to put them to whatever use they saw fit. The military at that very moment were building compounds that would house the priests. All religious personnel were free to leave Courteguay at any time.

When we got back that night a compound was being built at the foot of the hill below the monastery, a fourteen-foot chain-link fence surrounding a vacant lot that was sometimes used as a baseball field. Canvas sheets, sticks and cooking utensils were supplied. There was a great outcry from the devout. The priests all vowed to remain prisoner as long as it took. The devout came to the compounds all over Courteguay, and the priests blessed them through the wire fence.

But time was on the Old Dictator's side. Time and the weather. The devout disliked kneeling on gravel and being blessed through a chain-link fence in a downpour. The priests found that living in makeshift tents and, though the Old Dictator provided them with adequate food, cooking over open fires, and having limited bathing and toilet facilities, and no replacements for worn out cassocks, was not to their liking. One by one they allowed as how a visit to their native land was not a bad idea. The few native born Courteguayan priests were allowed to choose a country of their liking, and all chose the United States, a country that while niggardly with humanitarian aid, is always a sucker for a religious refugee, fake or genuine.

TWENTY-TWO

THE GRINGO JOURNALIST

Courteguay from the air: centuries-old baseball diamonds visible.

The Wizard crammed them all into the gondola of the balloon, Julio and Esteban, Hector and Fernandella, the dwarf Aguirre home for a short visit, and a woman who claimed to be a psychic artist able to draw pictures of the future. The balloon, striped like a candy cane, hissed into the air over San Barnabas, the sky was turquoise blue, the wind soft as a rabbit's nose. What they saw below them as they swung out over Lake Verde and the jungle-like land in the direction of the Dominican Republic were baseball diamonds, not active ones where the Courteguayan boys of endless summer played ball from dawn to dusk, but baseball diamonds centuries old, appearing from the sky to be covered with layers and layers of gentle, verdant moss. They were unmistakable.

"Look!" cried the Wizard. "Look!" He pointed down at the mossy land where the ancient baseball diamonds were clearly visible.

"How do you explain it?" asked Fernandella. "You ... that is Sandor Boatly brought baseball to Courteguay. We all know that. Who played on those diamonds?"

"Baseball was not unique to Sandor Boatly. He discovered it in America. Perhaps it came originally from Courteguay to America and not vice versa. Perhaps baseball originally came from another galaxy. Thousands of years ago a space ship arrived here with bats and balls and laid out these diamonds where our ancestors enjoyed the game. How did it become extinct? I don't know. Like birds, animals, insects that have certain life spans then disappear into history, maybe that is what happened to baseball."

"Ever the charlatan," said Fernandella.

"You have a better explanation?"

"I do," said Esteban. "It is God's will. God allows us to fly above Courteguay to see it as few ever have. There need not be an explanation. God's will does not need explaining."

TWENTY-THREE
THE GRINGO JOURNALIST

The urchins of the green, that is how Julio, Esteban and their boyhood friends were referred to by parents and neighbors.

In Courteguay, where it was always summer, where the word snow was used only to describe a type of daisy, the boys played baseball from dawn to dusk, with teams forming, fragmenting, merging again, all in the space of a few hours. Some boys would leave to eat, run errands, or take a siesta, then reappear a few minutes or hours later, always welcome to fit into the loose structure of the game, like an extra bat on a bat-rack.

Only Julio and Esteban never left, their bolted breakfast of pheasant burritos lasting them all day. They never tired or rested or even answered nature's call. Only when the ball became invisible in the blueberry darkness of evening would they slog off home, with the slim Julio, tall and straight as a post, leading the way, and squat, muscular Esteban trailing him.

Even after it was dark the brothers would still toss the ball back and forth in the dim interior of their home. Julio liked to catch fireflies in a jar and watch the misty, dreamlike glow from behind the ice-colored glass. He would leave the jar beside his straw pallet, and as he went to sleep the baseball would slip from his grip and roll away a few inches until it nestled against the jar, the pinpricks of light reflecting softly on the scuffed baseball.

When they returned to Courteguay after their first season away it was the baseball fields that seemed to have changed the most. What they remembered as smooth, angora-like surfaces, were highly uneven and filled with hummocks, every step of the outfield an adventure. They had never realized that the grass was not shaved daily with mowers, in fact it never occurred to them to think of the grass at all.

On a cool, green evening some father or uncle, or neighbor, would be loitering on the sidelines, smoking, watching the game, when he would notice the grass was above ankle height. He'd smile slowly and produce, seemingly from nowhere, a scythe, and take one turn across the furthest arc of the outfield where if there had been a fence it would have stood. On the far side of the field he'd toss his cutting implement to another man, or one would be waiting with his own machete glittering in the orange spill of sunset.

And the fields were smaller than they remembered. Courteguay was smaller than they remembered; Julio recalled the first time he ever saw a map of the world and realized Courteguay was not only smaller than a postage stamp it was smaller than half a postage stamp, about the same size as the moon on his thumbnail, a crescent-shaped fragment cut from Haiti and the Dominican Republic.

Everything was small, even Fernandella was not the giant-sized mother they remembered. The boys were startled to find how small and almost frail she was, and their father was thin with bad teeth and a furtive air about him—which was about how they remembered him. And the Wizard ... only the Wizard remained larger than life, slicing down out of the sky, silent as a bird of prey, appearing out of nowhere in his spangled costume, part harlequin, part prophet, part priest.

But though the baseball fields were smaller, shabbier, their players less skilled than they remembered, the urchins of the green remained unchanged, as shadowy, as dreamy as always, and the languorous game went on from sunup to sunset, year after grassy-green year.

School for the urchins of the green had been a sometime thing, sometimes they attended on days when rain made baseball impossible. Uninspired teachers, some missionaries, some local people bewitched by the teachings of missionaries, held classes in humid church halls or basements, or in open air when the weather was fine. Students used the fine, ochre-colored dust as a slate, drawing letters, adding sums by scraping in the earth with a stick.

Then Eugenio Martindale arrived, a black man from Miami, heavy-bellied now, but formerly an athlete, a former outfielder who had made it as far as Double-A ball in the United States.

He chanced by one of the perpetual baseball games and his anthracite face glistened with sweat just watching the urchins of the green engage in their eternal baseball game. He became excited by what he saw in Julio and Esteban, coming forward to offer advice and coaching to the cinnamon-skinned Pimental brothers.

"How many of you know how to calculate your batting averages?" he asked the boys, hoping to induce them toward education by offering something they would desire.

"Courteguayan boys are born with that knowledge," assured Julio, "ERAS also. Esteban and I were a battery before we were born. My ERA in the womb was 2.04."

Eugenio discovered that in spite of Julio's statements only a fraction of the boys shared his and Esteban's knowledge, and that notwithstanding their ability to calculate statistics, neither could read more than a few words. Eugenio produced from a scarred leather briefcase a sheet of newsprint that held magic as an educational tool. He taught them all to read and write using Major League box scores first from the *Miami Herald*, and later local box scores from the commercial leagues. At his own expense he had score sheets printed, and refused to let a boy play unless he could write in his own name. Every boy learned to calculate his batting average, and he had also to be able to check his friends' averages, for once skill was acquired it was only a simple step further to cheat. The boy who had played the worst in the previous half hour was pulled out and forced to write a short summary of the game, naming stars, acknowledging great plays. He was force fed the five Ws of journalism: who, what, where, when, and why. He learned quickly in order to get back onto the baseball field.

SECTION TWO

BUTTERFLY WINTER

"Orderly things are wild on the inside."

—*THE SOURCE OF TROUBLE*, DEBRA MONROE

TWENTY-FOUR
ALI

Ah, yes, you have come to the right place. Welcome to my humble store. Booth, roadside stand would be more appropriate. Very far from famous American department stores, which I someday aim to emulate, is it not? I have seen Harrods in London, but it is Walmart that thrills my heart. That fine young man named Sam who began Walmart out of his back pocket so to speak, is my hero. He offered his friends a chance to invest $1,000 at the beginning, those who did so are multimillionaires today. I wish to make the same beginnings.

Your question? I have not forgotten your question. The Pimental brothers, Julio and Esteban. I have known them all their lives, indeed I have known their parents before them, the crafty Hector, the shrill Fernandella. Ah, how I came to be in this place is a long, sad story, of which I am sure you are not interested, though I'm sure you as an American recognize me as not being a Courteguayan. By the way, have I told you how much pleasure it is to converse with someone in English, you cannot imagine how little English is spoken here. Dr. Lucius Noir, the noble dictator of Courteguay speaks English, I know this for a fact, for he studied at a chiropractic college in your state of IdaHO. Ah, yes, IoWA, to be sure. Dr. Noir once graced my humble roadside stand with his presence, though that is another sad story, and the reason I limp, though I am certain you are not interested.

How old are the Pimental brothers? Well, yes, age is relative is it not? Some of us are very old when we are very young, some of us remain very young when we are very old in years.

I am not exactly evading the question. I have known the Pimental brothers all their lives. They have lived in a hut down that road to the left which is visible to the naked eye. I remember them coming to my humble stand with a centavo or two to spend. Different as night and day they are; Julio lean and wild-eyed, confident, like candy to the young women. Esteban, born with a scowl on his wide, dark forehead, stocky and lumbering, always eager to learn, the pleasure of the flesh secondary, or, how would you say less than secondary? It is so long since I have spoken English. You will notice that I speak English with an Oxford accent, for in my native country I was tutored by a fine young man who read history at Oxford, and could recite the details of every battle of the Peloponnesian Wars, a subject that I have to admit did not interest me a great deal, for I have always been an entrepreneur, though I tolerated his long digressions in order to learn English. Ah, I see you look askance at my meager supplies, at the warped lumber of the shelves, at the preponderance of flies on the fruit and meat. This is certainly not what I imagined when I agreed to come to this part of the world. I was offered a fine wife and acceptance into a prosperous business. In the Dominican Republic there are a number of families from India, all engaged in trade and commerce. One of these families had many daughters and few acceptable suitors so they advertised in India. I come from a family that had, with the early death of my father, a lawyer, fallen on hard times. I answered the ad and was presented with a photograph of a beautiful young woman, and a one-way ticket from Bombay to Santo Domingo.

Ah, yes, I can see your attention is wandering, you are curious about the Pimental boys. I do not know baseball, cricket is my game, but I recognize an excess of talent when I see it. Julio Pimental pitches the ball as if it were small as a grain of rice, it is not only speedy, but dips and glides away from the bat of his opponent. One can sometimes hear vertebrae cracking as batters miss the pitches thrown by Julio Pimental.

The brother? Esteban? He catches the balls thrown by Julio. He is an average catcher who always appears preoccupied, as if he would sooner be someplace else. He has a secret. He communes with one of the moth-eaten priests in the compound. I believe the priest has taught him to read. I feel sad for him, their religion has so many restrictions. In my country there are gods in every leaf or blade of grass and they are mostly benevolent except for Shiva and Kali, oh, they are most terrible, women of course.

I needed some benevolence when I arrived in Santo Domingo. Among the many people waiting to meet me at the airport was the beautiful young woman of the photograph, Bhartee by name. But when I walked toward her someone seized my arm. A trifling formality they assured me and I should not fall weeping in dismay onto the airport floor as I had already done. They did not have a photograph of the sister I was to marry, so they sent one of her youngest sister, Chandra. Bhartee was at home waiting with great expectation to meet me.

Oh, what an evil surprise awaited me. The family was very wealthy, very successful in trade and commerce. However, Bhartee, I do her no disgrace to say she looked like a warthog. In many instances I do disgrace to the warthog. I mistook her for a tent, but soon discovered it was all her. Her poor face looked as if she had participated in many boxing matches, all in a losing cause. Her voice was like a fork scraping on a plate. Her eyes were not connected to anything and rolled aimlessly in her head. They offered me wealth, and I greedy swine that I was, accepted. To my everlasting shame I married the woman Bhartee, was paid a fantastic dowry and welcomed into the family.

Ah, yes, your curiosity is not for my sad story it is for Julio and Esteban. An anecdote, that is what you journalists are seeking is it not? I will tell you one. As young boys they used to frequent my humble business; they would arrive a centavo clutched in a small hand seeking to buy a candy.

Sometimes, even when they had no money they would stare rapturously at the candies I kept in small boxes on the counter. Esteban was always somber, even at such a young age he had taken to walking with his hands clasped behind his back like the decrepit priests with whom he had become friends. Julio, on the other hand, was brash, outgoing, eyes full of the devil. The young girls in the neighborhood, if they were lucky enough to have a centavo or two, would buy candy and then share it with Julio without being asked, sometimes they would give all their candy to Julio in exchange for one of his smiles, a smile that would open a night-blooming flower.

One day Julio stole from me. I have developed eyes in the back of my head, yes. Almost everyone, except Esteban, is a potential thief if the occasion arises. Then I had occasion to relieve myself out among the dwarf palms and oleanders. As I returned I noted Julio slipping two centavo candies into his pocket. I said nothing. While I could not afford thieves, I could not afford to lose a long-term customer. A payback would be arranged.

A week later Julio came to my counter clutching two centavos and two candies. I looked sternly at him, seized both the money and the merchandise, and pulling my machete from beneath the counter, my defense against thieves and robbers, I brought it down harshly, cutting deeply into the countertop only inches from Julio's thieving fingers. "You know why I am doing this," I said. "I see everything, especially the work of thieves. I see even when I am out among the palms and oleander, or dozing in my chair behind the counter. I see everything."

Julio stared at me with incredulous eyes. Then he scuttled away like a whipped cur, not to return for many weeks, then with his hand thrust forward to show his centavo, and allowing me to pick and deposit the candy into his hand.

Had I only known. Had I only had some expertise in baseball. I would have fed him and his brother candies as if they were royalty. To think of the money he earns, the luxuries he can afford. Do you think my story is worth a small donation? I have an Indian passport, I need to first get out of Courteguay, make my way to Santo Domingo, where with any luck I will take the short flight to Miami where I will pretend to visit briefly but will disappear into the great American melting pot to seek my fortune.

But do not hasten away, you being a writer, a journalist, I'm certain my story would be of interest to you. A magazine article, a book perhaps? I would ask from you only as my share from the immense profits you would make from this entertaining story, a plane ticket to Miami, a few dollars on which to begin my new life.

It is a sad lesson to learn that wealth is not everything. Though, I suppose it was better to come early in my life than late. But I was a poor man in a rich family. In spite of being included in their wealth, I was an outsider, I was laughed at in private, whispered about behind my back. Here was someone, reluctantly accepted as an in-law, but ridiculed because I gave up my integrity for wealth. The woman Bhartee had no redeeming features, as you know sometimes someone without physically attractive features makes up for that loss by being brilliant in some other way, an artistic talent, business acumen, or displays an inner beauty that more than makes up for their physical unattractiveness. The woman Bhartee, while the size of three women, had the intellect of a child, the temperament of a hyena, the charity of a piranha, and the sexual appetite of three hundred mink in heat.

I lived with despair as my soulmate.

Then, one day in the hallway I passed the sister, Chandra, the beautiful one with whose photograph I was originally duped. A look passed between us, one of those about which there is no mistaking. Deep in the night, my feet in flannel slippers, I slid down the hall and, as I knew I would, found Chandra's door unlatched. Ah, the passion of my life, of several lives both before and after. Passion rules all, and though we knew our illicit love was self-defeating, and could only bring tragedy, agreed to carry on for as long as our luck held, which was only a few weeks. Chandra was engaged to a very wealthy and much older man who had agreed to a magnificent dowry, plus a million dollar investment to enlarge the family business. They were due to marry in a few months.

Oh, the hullabaloo when we were discovered. I will not go into the painful details. Chandra was shipped back to India, there to repent and regain her virginity, in order she might be married on schedule. Many meetings were held while the family tried to decide what to do with me. Ironically, the woman Bhartee voted to forgive and take me back. The betrayed family, however, had other ideas. I was taken from Santo Domingo to the nearest border with Courteguay, where I was unceremoniously pushed across that very same border into exile, accompanied by only the clothes on my back and a few hundred guilermos, not nearly enough to buy a ticket out of Courteguay, and threats of certain death should I ever return to the Dominican Republic.

I used my few guilermos to set up this pitiful confectionery and fruit stand where I have lived in abject poverty ever since, my one hope being that I might somehow earn enough profit to obtain a ticket to Miami.

Now, has my story perhaps touched you enough, my information about the Pimental twins been colorful enough that you might make a small contribution to my future? You could not imagine the joy that an American twenty-dollar bill would bring to my lusterless life.

I see. Journalists do not pay for information. How sad. Could I interest you in a lottery ticket or two?

Did I know Quita Garza? Of course. Beautiful in a nymph-like way, fawn-like, skittish. Very difficult to describe. She had sepia-colored skin and pale blue eyes that looked as if they had fought and triumphed over a century of genes demanding brown eyes. She radiated sexuality. Unconscious sexuality for she had eyes only for Julio. She had no idea the mayhem she caused in the blood of other men who looked at her. She was the Garza's only child. It is rumored she is the child of an American fan of Milan Garza. A groupie, yes, that might be the word. The Garzas accepted her as their own. Hence the blue eyes. This is important information, yes. Though you try to hide I can see the dollar signs in your eyes. That information will be worth many articles and many magazine stories. A small donation toward my future, toward America, toward ALIMART, the business I intend to open. Let me hint of what else I know, oh, I can tell you tales of Dr. Noir and Quita Garza that would curl your hair.

TWENTY-FIVE
FERNANDELLA PIMENTAL

"Marry in haste, repent in leisure," the Wizard has said to me a number of times when I complain about the way Hector treats me. It is not a Courteguayan expression. The Wizard has been around so long that everyone assumes he is Courteguayan, but I have my doubts. He is a charlatan, that is for certain. He used to cheat my poor, gullible Hector out of what few centavos he earned, by having him bet on baseball games in both America and Courteguay. I think the Wizard makes up the final scores. I suspect he falsifies the voice that comes out of the radio box down at the palm wine shop. Now that our babies are rich and successful the Wizard cheats Hector out of his allowance. The more things change, the more they stay the same. Another non-Courteguayan expression.

"DON'T YOU WANT to do something else," I asked, after watching the four-year-old battery fire the ball back and forth all morning.

"There is nothing else, Mama," Julio said, smiling slowly, staring at me with his heavy-lidded eyes. He looked as though he were a miniature of his father, the same cool, innocent-insolent stare, the sensual mouth.

"POOR ALI," says the Gringo Journalist, interrupting his interview with me, "I feel sorry for him. He's a bit of a whiner, but a charming whiner. I gave him ten American dollars toward his plane fare out of here."

I laughed. "I'm sure the coconut wine vendor did a brisk business until the money was exhausted. What kind of a sob story can I tell you that you will give me many American dollars."

"He's not trying to get back to India?"

"His family have lived in San Barnabas for several generations. They are merchants. Ali is a sorry swine. He has a weakness for coconut wine and theft."

"He was not brought here as a groom for a wealthy family's ugly daughter?"

I laughed again. "No woman would have him. He has never been off the island. His only skill is the ability to lie."

"I'm not usually so easily conned," said the Gringo Journalist.

"You've been indulging the lies of the Wizard. What he has is catching."

"Who can I trust?"

"Certainly not me," I said. "I am Courteguayan."

TWENTY-SIX
THE WIZARD

"They will believe anything these gringo journalists," the Wizard said to Julio. "Who started this rumor, anyway?"

"What rumor?" said Julio.

"That part of my duties as a wizard is to perform psychic surgery."

"You started that rumor," said Julio.

"I start so many," replied the Wizard. "I thought I might have. Well, what do I do?"

"I'm only a baseball player," said Julio. "But the operating room has been reserved at San Barnabas General Hospital, complete with a gallery for all the foreign journalists to observe your skill as a psychic surgeon."

"Ah, yes, I remember making those arrangements. Very good for tourism though. Dying people everywhere, if you will forgive the play on words, are dying to believe in psychic surgery. Why should charlatans in South East Asia reap all the rewards? I am as much a charlatan as they are."

"Indeed you are," said Julio.

The Wizard wore his trademark midnight-blue caftan covered in mysterious silver symbols into the operating room. The patient, a middle-aged Caucasian, had been prepared. The Wizard turned toward the gallery where two dozen foreign journalists sat on the benches eating a lunch provided by the hospital cafeteria.

"After your lunch I will personally provide whatever medical treatment may be necessary." There were a few dry laughs from the gallery. One journalist choked on his turkey hash.

"I use no scalpels," said the Wizard. "My magical hands are my scalpels." The Wizard moved to the far side of the patient. He waved his hands above the unconscious patient as though he were playing an invisible piano.

Suddenly, the Wizard appeared to thrust his hands into the abdomen of the patient. The gesture elicited a few cries of surprise from the gallery, and even one from an attending nurse. The Wizard dug around as if he were searching for an egg in a pillow. "Ah, I have found the trouble, at least part of the trouble." He pulled a bloody hand out of the patient, gore dripped from a large slimy object in his hand.

Whispers of *tumor* passed through the gallery.

The journalist with the weakest stomach ran for the door.

The Wizard held the object higher.

"It's a baseball," said Julio, his wonder shining like an aura.

"Indeed."

The psychic surgery complete, the Wizard bows to the applauding gallery. He turns and walks not to the door but to a completely blank wall where with his bloody fingers he draws the outline of a door. He draws a doorknob. He seizes the doorknob, pulls the door open and exits, closing the door behind him. What remains is the totally blank wall of a moment before. But the Wizard has vanished.

"That good old boy gets my vote for tour operator of the year," says a member of the gallery.

TWENTY-SEVEN
THE GRINGO JOURNALIST

The twins told Fernandella they wanted to buy her a villa on Lake Verde, in the richest section of San Barnabas. Unfortunately in their rookie years they made so little that they couldn't afford the materials for such a house, most of which had to be imported from America. They could have afforded something less grand, but decided to wait for the right moment.

Hector Alvarez Pimental wanted to take up the offer immediately. He was already mentally constructing exotic villas along the turquoise lake; he was counting the rooms, estimating how many he could rent, and to how many people and for how many guilermos. One of his fantasies was to acquire a telephone which he could see sitting, black as a rat, on an end table in his living room. But whom would he call? His cronies were all too poor to even use pay telephones, of which there were rumored to be three in San Barnabas, though none in San Cristobel.

The Wizard on the other hand, who had absorbed, or somehow been blessed with the best of political sensibilities, decided to wait and see what would be most profitable for him.

"I will never leave this place," huffed Fernandella, over a full-term belly, her cheeks blotched, her loose maternity smock sweat-stained. "The bounties of the hillside: fresh, cool water; tasty fish and succulent fowl, meet all my needs. What if we move to an expensive villa, and my boys disappear into the bowels of America, never to return? What if you die?" she said to her husband. "With my bounties, what do I need you for? To satisfy my lusts," she went on, answering her own question. "As I grow older my lusts grow less frequent while my appetite for fish, fowl, and clear water become more voracious."

Fernandella refused to leave her stream of plenty; she still killed pheasants for each family meal. It was the endless supply of fish and the pheasants that all but leapt into her frying pan, that saved the day for the only Major League Baseball Club in the True South.

AFTER WINNING THE CY YOUNG AWARD and being named Most Valuable Player, Julio, and Esteban because he was his twin brother, were invited to the White House to meet the President. After viewing the White House, Julio and Esteban decided that they wanted their mother to live there, in fact they made it a condition of their playing another season for the only Major League Baseball Club in the True South. It did not concern them when the owner waved signed contracts under their noses, and threatened to suspend them and let them rot in San Cristobal, and never play another Major League game. The twins pointed out through their interpreter, a cousin of the Wizard, though Esteban often had to correct the interpreter, whose English seldom surpassed a McDonald's menu, that the baseball stadium was full for every home game, though the team continued to finish dead last. They pointed out that the previous year Julio had won twenty-seven of the team's sixty-two victories.

The President of the United States agreed that Fernandella Pimental and her children, who now numbered eight, five of the final six unexceptional, except for Aguirre the dwarf, could visit the White House, even stay for a few days, two weeks at maximum, as guests of the State Department. The Pimental brothers found a Spanish-speaking travel agent and booked first class seats to San Barnabas. "We already have enough money to live comfortably forever in Courteguay," they told the only Major League Baseball Club in the True South.

Julio and Esteban were exceptionally generous with their father. They bestowed on him a large allowance which he gambled away. The Wizard was now the biggest bookmaker in all Courteguay. The only client he dealt with personally was the father of the twins. For one hundred and one consecutive days Julio and Esteban's father bet on losing teams. The Wizard, who never asked directly for anything from the twins, became a very wealthy man. He became interested in overthrowing the government. He acquired a fleet of hot-air balloons.

TWENTY-EIGHT
THE GRINGO JOURNALIST

The first time the battery returned home they paraded their money like military medals. They bought their mother silk dresses of iridescent greens and silvers; they bought her scarves and jewelry. On that first visit the brothers discovered that many of their neighbors, at the instigation of the Wizard, were worshipping the furnace in the basement of Fernandella's renovated house. It was the only furnace in all of Courteguay. The local priest refused to bless it, even from a distance, claiming it was an instrument of the devil; the Wizard conversed with it. Fernandella's children, and Fernandella herself, felt comforted by the way it hummed like a sleeping pet in the black hours before dawn.

Fernandella refused to even visit the United States.

"If the President wants to see me so badly, let him come here," said Fernandella. As for seeing her sons play professional baseball, she said sternly, "Watching my sons play baseball brings back painful memories."

"Look," the Wizard said, "the annual income in Courteguay is 200 guilermos or roughly $60 US. In Courteguay, a house, even a mansion, is very inexpensive to construct. The White House can be built in replica for less than its original cost, and, if properly handled, written off as foreign aid, charity, a gesture of international goodwill."

The twins hired an architect who reconstructed the White House on the barren, sun-scorched hillside on the outskirts of San Cristobel. The replica was built in such a way that the magic stream splashed through the rose garden.

FOR EACH OF THE NEXT THREE SEASONS Julio won thirty or more games. Each year the team finished above .500, and by developing a young and talented infield, were in a position to win a pennant. But in February, just before he was due to report for spring training in Florida, Julio was kidnapped by a rebel faction of the Courteguayan guerrillas, not the ones who at one time had been the government, and would be again, led by General Bravura. The government of El Presidente would then become the guerrillas, and the cycle would repeat itself. These were guerrillas within guerrillas. Their leader was a flat-nosed fellow with wild hair that blossomed from beneath a Fidel Castro cap. Because of his nose, his enemies called him El Puerko, the pig, though his name was said to be Colonel Castillo.

El Puerko first demanded, in return for Julio's safe return, money and arms from the government of El Presidente.

"Why should we care about the safety of a mere baseball player, who is fast becoming a gringo?" replied the Government. "Do with him as you will." Though in private, El Presidente, who had played baseball as a young man and claimed, since he had a reputation for being as honest as a politician was likely to be, that he had shaken the hand of Octavio Court after whom the country was named. El Presidente followed the career of the fabulous Pimental twins, and was exceedingly worried lest something happen to Julio. Still, he knew that there could be no negotiation with terrorists, which El Puerko and his band of idiots certainly were. Now if the kidnapping had only been carried out by General Bravura, an honorable man who had on occasion been President of the Republic, the problem would have been solved in a moment. He would have sent for General Bravura and he would have entered San Barnabas under a flag of truce. They would have had a leisurely dinner at the Presidential palace, and a variety of favors would have been handed to General Bravura, ranging from ammunition for his machine guns, to a case of brandy to keep him comfortable during the upcoming monsoon season. Julio would have been released. El Presidente would claim the credit, have Julio and Esteban put on a personal display of pitching and catching and he would warn Julio to be more vigilant in the future, and since Julio was very rich, perhaps ask for a financial hand in covering the expense of his ransom.

"You do not understand," the guerrilla-guerrilla leader replied. "In the United States baseball players of quality are revered as saints. If the United States deems your government responsible for the death of Julio Pimental, it could result in diminished foreign aid, which, as we all know, makes up most of Courteguay's gross national product. And since it is known that you use all agricultural and social service foreign aid money for military equipment, then where would you be?"

"We will take our chances," El Presidente replied, but with more bravado that he actually felt.

The kidnapping made the front pages of the *Atlanta Constitution* and the *St. Louis Sporting News*.

"I volunteer to seek out the offending parties and act as intermediary," the Wizard, Cayetano Umberto Salvador Alfredo Jorge Blanco, as he now called himself, said to El Presidente. He was reluctantly allowed to do so, though El Presidente warned him that he was allowed diplomacy only, that no money or goods would be paid.

The Wizard sent a message by short wave radio. The guerrillas replied that they would shoot down the Wizard's balloon on sight.

The Wizard promised to make himself invisible.

The only Major League Baseball Club in the True South offered the guerrillas five hundred dollars, no questions asked, for the return of Julio Pimental.

The guerrillas set an execution date.

"I will pay you one-quarter of my salary and all the residuals from my Mexican Bean Dip commercials," Julio told the guerrillas, some of whom were his childhood friends. When they rejected the offer he promised to buy all the guns in the largest pawn shop in Miami and ship them to the guerrillas by rumrunner.

Preceded only by an eerie hissing of calamitous magnitude, the Wizard appeared suddenly in the middle of the guerrilla fortress. He was freshly shaved and manicured, dressed in velvet breeches and knee-high boots.

"I will buy uniforms for all the guerrilla officers," he said. With his long, pale fingers he withdrew colored pens from the ears of the officers present, and a scarlet one from the nose of El Puerko, and sketched uniforms of turquoise fabric, spangled with gold braid and flamingo-colored epaulets, which quickened the hearts of the kidnappers.

"Picture yourselves dressed thusly, marching in triumph into San Barnabas," whispered the Wizard who knew the secret desires of every man with whom he came in contact.

"Perhaps you would care to join in our fight for freedom," said the guerrilla leader, who knew the Wizard's secret desire to be President of the Republic.

The guerrillas postponed the execution for two weeks. Cayetano Umberto Salvador Alfredo Jorge Blanco disappeared into the jungle as mysteriously as he had been breathed from it.

The only Major League Baseball Club in the True South upped the offer to one thousand dollars and a baseball autographed by the whole team. The American State Department hinted darkly that the kidnapping was communist inspired. The CIA airlifted twenty-three tanks to the government forces in San Barnabas with which to fight for Julio's freedom. The Government Department of Industry and Tourism sold half the tanks to Papa Doc Duvalier and declared a Festival day.

The deadline for the execution passed and the Wizard did not appear with the uniforms. In America the baseball season was due to open in a few days. The only Major League Baseball Club in the True South was frantically trying to trade Julio Pimental to a club willing to pay a larger ransom. The owners hinted broadly that the New York Yankees were probably behind the kidnapping, after the Yankees offered two of their superstars and a player to be named later in return for Julio.

The only Major League Baseball Club in the True South, in the meantime, refused to sign Esteban to a new contract.

"What do we want with a catcher who can't hit? Let's wait and see if we get Julio back alive."

In return for his release Julio offered to buy enough medical supplies for the whole guerrilla army; when that offer was refused he offered to buy guns and ship them to Courteguay as medical supplies.

"Shoot him!" said the guerrilla leader.

But he could not assemble a volunteer firing squad. Julio Pimental, in spite of playing his baseball in America, was a hero with the rank and file guerrillas. Since he had been held captive in the guerrilla camp, a makeshift baseball diamond had emerged from the jungle. Dense rain forest melted away, and the foul lines and base paths were illuminated by rows of tropical flowers, some white as wedding gowns, others indigo and orchid. The pitcher's rubber was a bar of golden poppies. Since they had no bats, the guerrilla soldiers used their rifles, holding them by the barrels, swinging with verve as Julio twirled the one battered baseball that had emerged from some irregular's duffel bag. A sandbag served as catcher, since none of the soldiers would even attempt to catch Julio's sidearm curve, or his seething fastball. There were a number of rather serious accidents involving batters who forgot to unload the bullets from their bats.

The guerrilla leader appointed a firing squad from the ranks of the non-baseball players. He stood Julio Pimental, the world's greatest living baseball pitcher, against an adobe wall, and gave the order for the squad to raise their rifles.

"If you please," said Julio in a strong voice, "I request to be shot while standing on the pitcher's mound."

A chorus of affirmative sounds emanated from the assembled guerrilla army.

"Very well," said El Puerko.

Julio Pimental stood on the bar of golden poppies, which were soft as velvet beneath his feet, and stared resolutely at the firing squad, which was assembled at home plate. The sky was low and leaden; the trees dripped sullenly. Julio refused a blindfold.

The leader raised his hand. The firing squad raised their rifles. Suddenly the air was filled with a sibilation, as if a million swords were slicing the sky.

The guerrilla leader lowered his hand slowly, so slowly that the firing squad was not certain if he was giving the signal to fire, or if he was just lowering his hand. Three discharged their guns. Three didn't. From the barrels of the three fired weapons there dropped three blood-red hibiscus, which lay in front of home plate quivering like fresh-caught fish.

As Julio and the army watched, the Wizard descended through the clouds in a blue teardrop of a balloon, of such color that those who remembered the sky, recalled it as being less perfect than the blue of the balloon.

Two more balloons followed, one red as the trembling hibiscus, the other orange as the sun. Beneath each balloon, the wicker gondola was piled high with exotic uniforms, while in the lead balloon the Wizard was arrayed in the most magnificent uniform of all, a uniform that caused the guerrillas to develop magnificent erections.

TWENTY-NINE
THE GRINGO JOURNALIST

"Here he is," said the Wizard, "the player to be named later."

"Hmmmph," said General Bravura, his medals glinting like gun barrels in the sunshine. "He looks to me as if he has a club foot."

"Nonsense," cried the Wizard. "He is a fine second baseman, agile as a panther, with the speed of gazelle on the bases."

The player stood in front of General Bravura's massive desk, eyes downcast, a hangdog expression about him. He was slumped forward, his shoulder blades prominent beneath his khaki shirt. He needed a haircut.

"He is thin and starved-looking. Have you just taken him out of solitary confinement at some military stockade in order to bring him to me?"

"By keeping his weight down he is able to sprint faster after ground balls," said the Wizard. "He is a veritable vacuum cleaner when it comes to sucking up ground balls."

The repartee continued for several minutes, until General Bravura had exhausted his stock of insults, and the Wizard was running low on praise.

"Very well," said General Bravura. "I think Edisto Montanez is a name that sounds like a second baseman."

"Ummmm," said the Wizard. "I would prefer something more, ah, distinctive, but it is your choice. However, he will require a nickname. May I suggest, *El Gato*? It offers a sense of quickness, does it not?"

"El Gato Montanez," stated General Bravura, frowning. Yes, I think that has possibilities. Distinctive and quick."

"If I might be bold once again," said the Wizard, smiling, "something American either before or after the nickname. Whether we like it or not American Baseball is very big and influential in Courteguay."

"American?" said General Bravura. In one of his previous terms as El Presidente of Courteguay, General Bravura had banned the importation of the *St. Louis Sporting News*. There had followed a series of terroristic bombings of public latrines and the uprooting in the dead of night of the statues of famous generals. At the scene of each bombing or uprooting was left a small sketch of a St. Louis Cardinal, a red bird with a bat over its shoulder. The bombings and uprootings stopped when the ban on the *St. Louis Sporting News* was lifted.

"Allow me to speculate for a moment," said the Wizard. "We have seldom had an American player in our leagues. Oh, we have Courteguayans who have played for a time in the United States, but at the moment no real Americans. What I propose," said the Wizard, smiling deviously, "is that we create our own. El Gato here speaks English of sorts that I have taught him. At least enough to get by. We claim he is from Miami, but born there you understand. And suppose we named him Mantel, just a fraction off the name of the American superstar. Only he pronounces it Man-Tell. We give him an American first name, say Michael, and we translate his nickname to 'The Cat.' We shorten the first name to Mike."

"What we have now, if I am not mistaken is Mike 'The Cat' Mantel, pronounced Man-tell," said General Bravura.

The Wizard glowed.

"Although the idea is at least partially mine, he shall of course play for one of your teams," said the Wizard.

"Done," cried General Bravura, clapping his hands.

THIRTY
THE GRINGO JOURNALIST

When the boys arrived in the Bigs they were not only curiosities because of their youthful appearance; at the time Latin players were few and far between, so they were regarded as both exotic and dangerous. The boys found the large American ballplayers to be rough, crude, mean-spirited and racist.

Tiller tried to take them under his wing; he treated them exactly as he would if they were his own sons, and got along well with them, though that part of their relationship had to be kept secret.

Esteban, whose brow was always furrowed, was an enigma to the other players, but they refrained from razzing him much because his dark countenance gave the impression that retaliation was inevitable. Julio, on the other hand, was slight and vulnerable to physical, but more often to emotional harassment. Cinnamon was the kindest thing he was called.

SITTING IN THE TEAM LOCKER ROOM in Cleveland, listening to the unkind words of his teammates, Julio recalled that as a child he would wake as the first blue talons of dawn pierced the windows in the completely renovated tin-roofed hut, to hear his parents arguing about sex.

"Courteguayan boys are born with erections," his father would say when Fernandella complained about the frequency with which he demanded sex, and the startling positions he insisted on in hopes of producing other offspring as exotic as the twins.

"A true Courteguayan man has an erection from the day he is born until the day he dies. A great man goes to his grave with a bulge in his pants. Those lucky enough to be born in hospitals are no longer virgins by the time their mothers carry them home. There are obvious reasons why hospital nurseries are divided in half with boys on one side and girls on the other."

The twins, Julio and Esteban, would peer across the hut, eyes straining in the bluish light, trying to comprehend what the ghost-like figures of their parents were doing beneath the sugar-sack sheet.

Fernandella, though she often complained vigorously at the beginning, soon became a willing participant in the morning athletics—in fact it was her voice that always awoke the twins. Her cries of pleasure sometimes frightened the yellow-crested cockatoos from sleep and they would walk about on the coral-tiled roof, their feet making tiny music.

Hector and Fernandella almost always managed to keep a thin, sugar-sack sheet over themselves, Hector gripping it fiercely at the nape of his neck with his left hand, as he changed positions, which he did frequently.

Julio sat stiffly on the pocked bench in the locker room, not afraid to meet the eyes of the harassing ballplayers. This is a chance to earn their respect, he thought, even their envy.

"Courteguayan men are born with erections," he said, imitating his father. "In the hospital where I was born, when I was but two days old I crawled from crib to crib deflowering virgins. The parents of the girl babies complained and I was tied by my ankle to my crib."

"You tell 'em Cinnamon," said one of the ballplayers, his tone not entirely unfriendly.

"But that," said Julio, "did not stop the girl babies from coming to me."

The other players laughed.

Julio had noted by watching the players that bravado was not necessarily doing, but always claiming to be prepared to do, and always bragging on past exploits.

Night after night he watched the ballplayers, including his chief tormentors, J. Carroll and Bubba Lee, sally forth in pressed sports jackets and shined shoes, on their eternal quest for beaver. He also noted that about nine out of ten nights they straggled back to the hotel alone, or in groups of two or three, slightly disheveled, slightly drunk, and virtually never accompanied by women.

"The most beautiful nurse on the ward took me into the supply room where she pressed me against her breasts, while her cool fingers explored my manhood," Julio went on, staring straight at the other players. Esteban, in the meantime, had dressed without exploring any part of his body, and busied himself at his locker, his ears burning as if they were outlined in red neon.

"I WILL TELL YOU HOW my parents met," said Julio. "My father was a gaucho, herding cattle high in the barrens above San Cristobel. It was sunset, he had prepared his camp, built a fire, eaten his simple fare, and was sitting on a rock, hunched forward, drinking coffee from a tin cup and stirring the fire, when a young woman rode out of the shadows and dismounted.

"My father peered at her from under the wide brim of his leather hat, saw that she was beautiful, strong and healthy, dressed in cowboy gear, and obviously interested in him. He ignored her.

"The cowgirl looked at where my father had tethered his horse by dropping a heavy rock on the reins. She walked into the darkness, carrying a small hatchet she took from her saddlebag, she cut a small tree, sharpened the point, and, in clear view of my father screwed the stake into the ground with her bare hands, until it was secure enough that she could tie her horse to it.

"My father showed no sign of having observed her feat of strength. He just sat, hat low over his eyes, stirring the fire.

"The cowgirl, determined to impress my father, looked around the gully, her eyes lighting on a good-sized clod of dirt near the fire. She pushed her hat back on her head so my father might see the strength and beauty of her face, picked up the clod of dirt, placed it between her breasts, then standing straight as an Amazon warrior, placed a hand on the outside of each breast, and with a tremendous thrust broke the clod of dirt into a thousand pieces.

"The corner of my father's left eye twitched almost imperceptibly, but he remained hunched over, sipping coffee, stirring the fire.

"The woman who was to be my mother was no quitter. She again stepped out of the firelight, only to return with an almost-round white stone the size of a cantaloupe. She positioned herself in my father's line of sight, making certain he could see her fine shape, her muscular body, the leather chaps she wore over her wrangling pants. She took the rock, which was quartz-like and glittered with fool's gold, placed it between her thighs, applied mighty pressure until the rock groaned, and cracked into gravel.

"Then she stood staring boldly at my father. He raised his head slightly so he could see her with one eye; the firelight skimmed across that eye like lightning. He finished his coffee, set down the cup, but continued to stir the fire with his prick."

The players laughed in spite of themselves. Julio could see he had crossed the line from foreigner to compatriot.

"What do you reckon a preek is, J. Carroll?" said Bubba Wales.

"You ought to know, Bubba, why I heard a girl explain it all to you the other night."

J. Carroll, looked at Julio and smiled, letting Julio know that this story was aimed directly at him.

"We were up in Bubba's room with our dates the other night," J. Carroll said to Julio, "and Bubba and this girl who looked a lot like Casey Stengel, were gropin' around on his bed.

"'What's that I feel against my thigh?' the girl said.

"'Why don't you take it out and have a look at it?' says Bubba in his subtle way.

"Well, there was a lot of rustlin' and zippering going on for a while.

"'Why I declare, what is this thing?' Miss Casey Stengel was saying.

"'That's a prick, honey,' says Bubba, just as sure of himself as you please.

"'Oh, no,' says Miss Stengel, 'it may be a lot of things but it ain't a prick. A prick is a foot long and comes from Courteguay.'"

Even Bubba laughed. Julio and Esteban were seldom harassed again except with good nature.

THIRTY-ONE
THE WIZARD

Let me tell you a story. After the coming of Dr. Noir, the whole complexion of politics in Courteguay changed. Before Dr. Noir the Government and the Insurgents were on quasi-friendly terms even though they were officially at war. The story is actually one of how the women of Courteguay came to be excellent baseball players, something I don't have to tell you, Julio, for as I recall your sainted mother Fernandella was a shortstop of cunning, agility, and also wielded a powerful bat.

I recall the time El Presidente ventured deep into the heart of the jungle for a secret meeting with the Commander of the Insurgents, a certain General Bravura.

When General Bravura was in power he estimated that there were three hundred people in Courteguay wealthy enough to buy a Mercedes-Benz. General Bravura then suggested to his cousin Eduardo that he apply for a Mercedes-Benz sub-dealership, a branch of the main dealership in Santo Domingo, Dominican Republic. General Bravura of course got a percentage on every sale, and the wealthy of Courteguay knew which side their foreign bank accounts were buttered on so to speak. Over three hundred Mercedes were sold each year; the trade-ins were sent back to the Dominican Republic, sometimes to the United States, for low mileage Mercedes sold very well there.

When the Old Dictator, after an appropriate term in exile, overthrew the government of General Bravura, there were accompanying riots, as there were each time a regime was replaced. Foreign photographers captured the sacking of the Mercedes dealership in San Barnabas. But what was interesting about the sacking was that the restless young men who were looting and celebrating were—instead of driving the cars at full throttle down the Avenida Bougainvillea—were pushing the Mercedes by hand because no one but the very rich knew how to drive.

What can we do to make the women of Courteguay worship baseball in the same way as our men? As I see it baseball can only be totally successful as both our national sport and national export if it is beloved by all the population. In Haiti, fort instance, only the men play soccer, and how beloved is soccer in Haiti? Let me answer my own question with another question. How many world-class soccer players has Haiti produced? Let me answer my own question. None that I know of. Now, how many world-class baseball players has Courteguay produced?

"About three dozen," said Julio, interrupting the Wizard's story.

"Please don't interrupt," said the Wizard. El Presidente had ventured into the jungle with a large entourage, including representatives of the local and international press. The spring before, General Bravura had visited El Presidente at the Presidential Palace in San Barnabas, under somewhat similar circumstances.

"Let's not get down to business so soon," said General Bravura who, as always, was dressed in camouflage fatigues, his beard ragged as Spanish moss hanging from a tree branch. "I miss the city," General Bravura went on. "Though we have many amenities." He gestured toward the wall of electronic equipment in his quarters, the television, the air conditioning, all made possible by a huge electric generator, a gift from El Presidente on his last visit. "I miss the restaurants, the excitement of the marketplaces, the parades, and of course the palace. You are taking good care of the palace?"

"Ah, my old friend," El Presidente said, "I'm sure it won't be too long until we exchange places again. In fact I have brought along a small offering to aid you and your conscientious servants in your campaign to unseat myself and the other impertinent brutes, your recent words I believe, describing my regime."

El Presidente smiled broadly and waved his orderly, a Haitian dwarf who cradled a sub-machine gun in his baby-like arms, forward. The orderly dragged a black suitcase to General Bravura's feet, laid down the gun and opened the case, which was stuffed with new American bills in large denominations.

General Bravura's eyes gleamed.

He smiled, but sadly. "I would be less than honest with you, old friend, if I did not mention that certain representatives of the CIA and FBI have recently sent me, as well as two thousand military advisors, an amount of currency that makes your own noble gesture seem cheap by comparison. As we have anticipated, the Americans have become as disillusioned with your regime as they were with mine, and as we also predicted, they now guarantee me unconditional support in seeking your overthrow."

"I have to admit, comrade of my youth," said El Presidente, "that I do have my ear to the earth as it were, and that I have been kept apprised of your secret negotiations with the United States. My gift was indeed a hollow gesture. A test. I wanted to be sure we are still friends, that greed had not come between us. Incidentally, I am keeping the palace in its usual resplendent manner. I am painting and redecorating the east wing—peach and the delicate blue of a baby's eyes. Do you approve?"

The two friends laughed heartily, filled up their brandy glasses and got down to business.

"Ah, the women," said General Bravura, "since you brought up the subject perhaps you have some suggestions?"

"I have been trying to remember what it is that women like so that we might be able to incorporate it into baseball," said El Presidente.

"Well," said General Bravura, "women like clothes. It is my experience that above everything, except their children, women love silks, satins, laces. Well, most of their children, depending on the individual woman and the quality of the silk. My own Lourdes, bless her loving heart, while we are serving our time in exile, wears her cartridge belt and fatigues, but how she longs for the wardrobe she left behind—I trust her gowns and furs are being stored in temperature-controlled vaults." General Bravura stared at El Presidente until he received an affirmative nod.

"If what you say is true," said El Presidente, "then it will be a simple matter to create baseball uniforms made from silks and satins in colors that will cause the flowers to blush. Bats and balls will be painted in alluring pastels. We will plant marigolds and zinnias in the coaching boxes. Women will be allowed to design their own baseball footwear to match their uniforms, which will be unique each and every one; it is important I believe that no two be alike. There must also be a prize for the unglamorous position of catcher, perhaps a mitt studded with jewels which at the end of each season become the property of the catcher?"

"Unfortunately, the soccer players of Haiti, a pox on them and their offspring, tried those very same methods a few short years ago; silk uniforms of a variety of colors, pink soccer balls, a tea dance after each game. Nothing worked."

"Nothing is impossible," said El Presidente. "Think now. What are the fundamental needs of women?"

"Food, warmth, love," replied General Bravura.

"Right," said El Presidente. "We could withhold food until they took up baseball. But that policy would be cruel and would cause, to say the least, a certain amount of resentment. And they would play the game out of fear. We must make them play the game out of love. They must have good reason to strive for perfection."

The two men pondered the situation.

"Warmth cannot be eliminated," El Presidente continued. "The average temperature in Courteguay is 87°F. Neither politicians nor wizards can make Courteguay cold."

They paused again, contemplating.

"Love!" the old war horses cried together. "If skill at baseball makes our women feel loved, if a moving fast ball or a .300+ batting average earns a woman's love, we will have to advocate no further."

"We have overlooked one thing."

"What is that?"

"What is it that a woman values more than love?" said General Bravura.

"Certainly not sex."

"Certainly not."

"I give up."

"Marriage," said General Bravura.

"Of course," said El Presidente, grasping the significance of the moment. "In order to be married a woman must have demonstrable skills as a baseball player."

"We will not even have to take credit for making the changes in the law," cried El Presidente, pacing rapidly back and forth, hands clasped behind his back. "We will blame it on the church. While I am still in power I will, in exchange for a box of Cuban cigars and a flagon of French brandy, have the Bishop of Courteguay notify all the priests that Rome has decreed," and here he paused a long while, composing the encyclical.

"Before a wedding can take place in Courteguay," he began, "there shall take place a baseball game, in which one team shall be composed entirely of women, among the women must be included the prospective bride, her sisters, married or single, also the bride's mother and grandmother, if living. The mother of the groom may be included but only if she is in favor of the wedding."

"You know this could backfire," said General Bravura. "What if the unmarried women were to withhold their sexual favors until their baseball skills improve, something that could take years. This could produce a whole generation of frustrated men who might turn to Haiti for wives and in so doing corrupt our pure Courteguayan blood."

"My friend," said El Presidente, smiling, "how many virtuous women do you know?"

"I concede," said General Bravura. "Now, please continue."

"The other team may be composed of whatever make-up the groom deems advisable, or affordable, amateur or professional. The women must make a responsible showing against the groom's team. We will leave that wording intentionally vague...."

"Good, for a responsible showing might mean that the bride came to bat three times and fouled off at least one pitch in each at-bat. But not for long. If women are going to be forced to play baseball they must also be forced to be good at it."

"Perhaps a panel of three judges in each village to determine when a prospective bride has performed adequately. The groom must not be allowed to vote," said El Presidente.

"True. All grooms suffer from temporary insanity. We will have the priests deliver the encyclical next Sunday from behind their chain-link fences. Speaking of which, you know of course that I have been very lax with the priests, in fact I offered them the option of coming out from behind their fences. They refused. We even took down one or two fences and laid them flat on the ground, but the priests choose to be restrained by flat fences."

"Their lives are so much easier behind the fences, it is obvious why they stay there," said El Presidente.

"There is one other matter I find grave and distressing," said General Bravura.

"And that is?"

"Your assistant, your Head of Secret Police, Colonel Lucius Noir."

"Colonel Noir is overly ambitious, but he is a loner, and loners seldom overthrow governments. He is obsequious, malevolent, unscrupulous, seems to have eyes in the back of his head, qualities I do not find entirely displeasing. Dr. Noir, as he prefers to be called, can sniff out even a hint of disloyalty. He radiates evil, but as long as it is directed towards my enemies...."

"Still, I worry for you, old comrade. As wise men say, Mine enemy grows older. As do we. Be vigilant, my friend. I have attended too many wakes for departed companions."

THIRTY-TWO
JULIO PIMENTAL

The carnival was only a block square; the air was full of the smell of cedar shavings, frying onions, hot grease and French fries. The noise of the compressor generator was deafening. The rides were rattling and dangerous; many of the green neon bars that outlined the circle that was the ferris wheel were burned out.

There were canvas banners bellying out in the wind, each printed in garish colors, advertising the midway shows. One featured the hairy face of a bearded lady, while another showed a torso with seal-like flippers substituted for arms and legs. The head on the torso was that of a boy with slicked back hair, balancing a ball on his nose. The banner read GERALDO THE HUMAN SEAL.

Though she was made up like an old woman the Gypsy fortune-teller was young. Her wrists were circled by tinkling silver bangles; she wore a green bandanna tied about her head pirate-style.

Strangely, it was Esteban the cautious, who was drawn to her. Julio was more intrigued by a girlie show further down the crooked midway, and in a large, barrel-like construction where, inside, motorcycle daredevils, many of them female, rode in circles defying gravity, coming within inches of the top of the barrel and compound fractures.

The Gypsy girl stood behind a narrow counter. On the midway side of the counter a single maroon-topped, chrome-shafted restaurant stool sat unevenly among the shavings, appearing to be mysteriously bolted to the earth.

The girl crooked a finger at the twins as they sauntered by. Esteban angled slowly toward her, as if he were a fish, hooked, and the Gypsy girl held the pole slowly reeling him in.

"For twenty centavos I will reveal the future, analyze the past, delve into the unknown...."

Esteban perched his stocky form on the single stool. He dug the money from his pocket and presented it to her.

Julio stood fifty feet behind Esteban, rocking on his heels, grinning at his brother's gullibility.

"You are not all here," the Gypsy girl said, then seeing that Esteban misunderstood, added quickly, "I don't mean you are stupid, but something about you is strange."

She closed her eyes, seizing one of Esteban's heavy hands with her own long, brown fingers.

Esteban saw that her eyelids were a frosty-red. He wondered if the color was achieved with paint or if it was produced by sheer concentration.

"Your aura is big as a circus tent. I can't quite comprehend it. It reaches all the way to where your friend loiters, scuffling."

"He is my twin," said Esteban.

"Ah," said the Gypsy, opening her eyes. "That explains it. You two share more than you realize."

"We know," said Esteban.

"She's a fraud," shouted Julio. "Come on! Let's go see the dancing girls."

"Your future is like your body," the Gypsy girl said.

"How is it like my body?" asked Esteban.

Julio was edging closer to the booth. A few passers-by were stopping to watch the fortunetelling.

"You will live long, become wealthy beyond your wildest dreams, and die happy in your own bed," said Julio to his brother, his smile wide and infectious.

"Perhaps I should pay you," said the Gypsy girl without a trace of humor.

"Perhaps you should," said Julio, "for my prognostications are as reliable as yours."

The Gypsy girl stared at him, a half-smile on her gaudily painted face. "Your brother's life will be like his body," she repeated, her eyes fastened to Julio's face like insects. "Short and compact," she added.

"Fortunetellers are not supposed to be crepe hangers," said Julio, "you are supposed to lead customers on, entice them to spend more money."

"Short and compact," the Gypsy girl repeated. "If I wished to leech money from you I would stop now and demand more payment." She held Julio's eyes with hers.

Julio, though he certainly didn't wish to admit it, or even think it, felt as though steel rods connected him with the Gypsy girl.

Esteban turned uncomfortably back and forth on the red-topped restaurant stool.

"I like to persuade skeptics of my worth," the girl continued. "You may pay only what you think the information is worth."

Looking straight at Julio she went on, "Your brother will be murdered. By a woman. A mysterious woman who will still his heart with a thin silver knife. The deed will be done far away, in another country, but in the foreseeable future."

"How can we prevent it?" asked Julio, surprised to hear his voice, surprised at the concern it registered.

"You cannot," she replied. "I see what is going to happen. The future cannot be changed."

"Charlatan!" cried Julio.

"I sympathize," said the girl.

"That's all you have to say?" said Julio, his arms raised in exasperation. "You tell me my brother will be murdered and all you offer is sympathy? You are not only a fraud, but a cruel fraud."

"It's all right," said Esteban, standing suddenly. "I am here, remember. And I do not like being talked about in the third person. I am not afraid of death, no matter what its form. We are all going to die, what does it matter if my time is shorter than someone else's?"

"Philosophical rubbish," stormed Julio. "My brother has no sense concerning the urgency of life," he shouted at the fortuneteller.

"And you have," she said, smiling darkly. "What if his future had been yours?"

"If I believed the edict, I would fight it."

"You don't believe it?" said the Gypsy girl.

"Of course not."

"Then why are you so upset?"

Realizing he had been taken in, Julio glowered. The crowd continued to gather. Several people had their money out, hands extended, ready to pay for a prophecy.

"Since you don't believe," said the Gypsy girl to Julio, "then you won't mind hearing what your future holds?"

Before Julio could speak out—his mouth was already open to do so, his tongue touching his top teeth—the fortuneteller silenced him by holding up her hand like a police officer.

"No money," the Gypsy girl said loudly. "A free prophecy for the skeptic."

She beckoned Julio closer, crooking her long, brown fingers, smiling enigmatically.

Reluctantly, Julio took her hand. As he did so he felt as if his body were generating electricity. As the Gypsy girl drew him up beside Esteban, he put his free arm about Esteban's shoulders and the sensation increased as he did so.

"If the generator fails, we can use the power of your combined aura to light the midway," the girl said. She then continued, speaking directly to Julio. "You, my friend, will fly."

She remained silent for several seconds to give the prophecy dramatic effect.

"Like a myth, with the beauty of a rainbow, with the breath of a dragon and a beating of wings, the hissing of a trillion geometrically patterned snakes."

The people in the crowd sighed collectively at the wonder of her words.

"I often travel by airplane; there is nothing miraculous about it," said Julio dispassionately.

The crowd murmured.

"You have so little imagination," said the Gypsy girl. "You do not wonder how a million pounds of metal soars through the air with the grace of a condor. But never mind. You will fly beyond the metal wings of man. You will FLY!"

The crowd squeezed closer, offering their money, eager to be deceived.

"Go in peace," the Gypsy girl said. She leaned across the counter and kissed first Esteban, then Julio on the cheek. Esteban turned away and was squished through the crowd like an orange seed. Julio remained where he was.

"It is both a pleasure and a sadness to be allowed to speak the truth," the Gypsy girl whispered to Julio, kissing him again, this time on the lips, her mouth open, her tongue inflamed.

"Do you have a name?" he asked.

"I am whatever you choose to call me," said the girl.

"In that case," said Julio, "we will christen you Celestina."

"We? I see only you speaking."

"My brother knew your name before I did. We read each other's minds."

As her lips crushed his mouth Julio could smell cinnamon, and sun-warm earth, and he saw that the girl, behind her garish make-up, was probably no older than he was.

He slipped a one hundred guilermo note into her hand. "I will see you in the sky," he said.

Only Esteban, standing stolidly in the background knew that the girl was the same one who had taken him into the jungle years before. A girl named Celestina.

THIRTY-THREE
THE GRINGO JOURNALIST

As they walked through the streets of San Cristobel the Gringo Journalist swiveled his head about, his body reluctantly following. What he had seen was, he thought at first, a movie poster, a cardboard cut-out of a middle-aged peasant wearing baggy black slacks and a loose white cotton shirt. Then the cut-out moved, turned to face the Gringo Journalist and the Wizard as they passed. To the Gringo Journalist's eyes he was no more than half an inch thick.

"What?" said the Wizard. He had smiled at the man; they exchanged a brief greeting.

"What's going on? That man looks like a cut-out. He's less than an inch thick."

The Wizard shrugged.

"You saw it," said the Gringo Journalist.

"Indeed," said the Wizard.

"Do you have anything to do with the way he looks?"

"Hermitio Aquarian was born without a sense of depth perception. Only the most primitive of medicine was known and practiced in his remote village, where, instead of growing up handicapped, Hermitio was considered enchanted," the Wizard began.

"To Hermitio the earth is flat. Trees are flat, rocks are flat, the house of his mother is flat.

"As a child Hermitio Aquarian was in a perpetual state of shock and surprise from bumping into objects that he perceived as flat, that he was about to walk over. To Hermitio a chair looked like a chair that had been stepped into the earth by a giant. But he adjusted, as children with handicaps do. He learned to pull himself up onto things that to him were as flat and uni-dimensional as a crushed cockroach. He learned slowly that his friends and family, each of whom appeared to him like the glossy models on the pages of catalogs, were really upright as he. He is a gardener, to him a lawn looks like a lawn. He has found his place in life, though it took some time to adjust to the fact that a lawn mower was...."

"Not flat," said the Gringo Journalist. "The question is why do I, and I assume everyone else, see him as he sees the world?"

"Handicapped people often develop their other senses to extremes. It is very easy for him to make his way through crowds."

The Gringo Journalist turned and stared at the spot behind them where the cut-out man leaned indolently against a lamp post.

"Have you forgotten you are in Courteguay, where magic does not need an explanation?" says the Wizard. "Besides, it is the least we could do."

THIRTY-FOUR
THE WIZARD

Esteban's hitting was always a problem. He was an adequate if uninspired catcher. But he could not hit, or run the bases. "Tell you how slow he is," said Al Tiller, addressing a gaggle of sportswriters in the dressing room after a particularly humiliating loss, where Julio had pitched a two hitter, but one of the hits was a home run, and where the team had been unable to get a runner beyond first base. Esteban's batting average was a puny .130.

"I seen trees grow faster than he runs. He once started out for second base in the fifth inning and got there in the ninth. He is slower than shit movin' through a long dog."

Eventually, the sportswriters got around to Esteban's hitting. "He's the only player I ever managed with a negative batting average. When he comes up in a situation I've got a special sign telling him to get hit by a pitch."

But humor could only go so far. The owner and general manager could not believe that Julio would not pitch to another catcher. They threatened to send both boys back to Courteguay, if Julio continued to insist that Esteban be his catcher. They agreed. Management withdrew the offer for they couldn't release their star pitcher. They forced Julio to pitch to another catcher. He smiled sullenly, went to the mound and lobbed batting practice pitches to the opposing batters. After seven consecutive hits, rather than take Julio out of the game, word came down to Al Tiller to put Esteban in. Julio pitched a shutout for the remaining innings.

At the All-Star break Esteban consulted a moth-eaten priest behind the chain-link fence. As a side bar, Julio Pimental never played in an All-Star game though he would have been a choice of the National League manager for probably eighteen of his twenty professional seasons. But, since Julio would pitch to no one but Esteban, and Esteban was never a factor in All-Star voting, Julio had to be dropped from the team every year.

"Do you think a holy relic might do the job?" the old priest asked.

"I believe in holy relics," said Esteban.

"Then it is as good as done." The priest retreated to the huts where he and his compatriots existed. Minutes later he returned with an inch-long sliver of bone, which he handed to Esteban. "This is from the arm of Saint Cayetano of San Barnabas, a simple fisherman who, though he had to fish from the Dominican coast, then smuggle his catch back to Courteguay, became lost at sea, landed in Florida and returned to Courteguay in possession of a cathedral-shaped radio which, when properly motivated, spoke in many voices and of many things."

"I will insert this shard of bone into my bat and Saint Cayetano will take pity on my inability to match the round bat with the round ball."

Esteban carried the shard back to America, inserted it into the hitting end of his bat and his batting average for the remainder of the season was .312, while the only Major League Baseball Club in the True South put on a late season rally that allowed them to finish in second place in their division.

Esteban's emergence as a hitter was not without trauma. After a month of hitting over .300 he shattered his bat one night in San Francisco. Pieces of the bat scattered in all directions as if it had exploded from inside. Esteban, neglecting to run out the pop fly he hit, dropped to his knees and began gathering bits and pieces of the destroyed bat. At his urging the bat boy returned splinters of bat and the other players picked up what bits they could find. Esteban struck out in his three remaining at-bats, and on the team bus and later in their hotel room the twins frantically searched for the bone chip from the arm of St. Cayetano of San Barnabas.

Unable to find it they slipped out of the hotel and made their way back to Candlestick Park. They talked a caretaker who recognized them into letting them in, and in the predawn fog and drizzle, crawled about the infield noses to the ground desperately searching for the bone shard.

The search was unsuccessful. Esteban eventually fell into a fitful sleep while Julio slipped out of the hotel and after asking directions several times found a butcher's shop where he explained, with great difficulty, what he was looking for (though Esteban learned to speak grammatically correct and almost unaccented English, Julio liked to give the impression he had a limited knowledge of the language. In interviews he frequently lapsed into Spanish and 'How you say?' were three of his favorite words, though the non sequiturs and malapropisms he came up with were too clever not to have been intentional). Julio held the shard over a gas flame until it dried, then polished it with cloth. On the way back to the hotel he stopped at a hardware store and bought a small drill and a hammer and chisel.

Julio spread the broken pieces of bat on his bed and began dismembering them with the hammer and chisel.

"I've found it! I've found it!" he yelled into Esteban's sleeping ear.

Julio held the shard before Esteban's bleary eyes.

"I will hit again," said Esteban, grasping the bone chip.

Taking a new bat, Julio drilled a hole in the business end and inserted the shard, then he closed the entrance with plastic filler. Esteban, now wide-awake, took a few mighty practice strokes.

THIRTY-FIVE
THE GRINGO JOURNALIST

She was one of the refugees from Courteguay; eighty of them crammed together, scrunched like broccoli, the girl recounted, her eyes wide with the remembered discomfort of it, in an open boat, dilapidated, unseaworthy, the bottom spurting water as a wounded general spurts blood.

Several people were lost when the boat was swamped repeatedly. She told of sharks turning like saws in the bice-colored waters, waiting, told of the agonized screams of those who were swept away, told of the ugly stains on the waves, how blood, like rust, colored the waters.

The boat limped into Miami harbor and promptly sank, losing a few more of the refugees. The remainder were arrested and preparations were made to ship them home to Courteguay.

"We are political refugees," they cried.

"Courteguay is not considered an unpleasant place to live," countered the US Immigration Service.

"But Haitians arrive in America daily, by the boatload."

"If Courteguay was to become part of Haiti we might consider you."

"We are poor."

"So is most of the world."

"The priests live behind chain-link fences."

"By their own choice. We are sorry, but unless your life is in danger in Courteguay, or unless you have relatives in the USA."

"I am not from Courteguay," said the girl.

"Where are you from?" asked the immigration official.

"I am from the sky," she replied.

"Mentally unstable," the official scribbled on a note pad.

"I have relatives," the girl said cunningly. "The Pimental brothers, who pitch in the President of the United States Baseball League are my cousins."

She looked deep into the eyes of the immigration officer. He stamped each application "refused" and the would-be immigrant was led away. He used the same stamp on her application but what appeared on her application was "APPROVED."

She was waiting outside the ballpark when Esteban and Julio emerged.

"She is the girl from the sky," said Esteban, not at all surprised by her appearance.

"She is the Gypsy fortuneteller," said Julio, also unsurprised.

Esteban took her to dinner where she ate nothing but stared at him with large starving eyes. Back at his hotel room her lovemaking made Esteban forget, possibly for the first time in his life, the mysteries of philosophy and religion.

"I was very lonely," Esteban said, her head on his shoulder, her perfumed hair spread across his chest. She accompanied him on the remainder of the road trip. Back home she moved into Esteban's room in the apartment he shared with Julio.

"Nothing good can come from this," Julio prophesied ominously.

"You have more than your share of women. Allow me a little pleasure," said Esteban.

"There is a difference between pleasure and enchantment. She has attached herself to you. It spells trouble."

"Nonsense," said Esteban, who, even after he had showered carried the odors of the strange girl on him.

THE WIZARD ARRIVED UNEXPECTEDLY, his balloon landing roughly on the roof of the hotel, jarring the plaster off the roof in the penthouse. The Wizard was not in top condition, his balloon having been caught in Tropical Storm Carlotta, one of the first hurricanes of the season.

Looking like a drowned rat the Wizard knocked on Julio's door. He clutched a very wet sack of pheasant burritos sent by Fernandella.

"I need some sleep," he said. "I've been drifting in this hellacious storm for several days." Esteban peered at him from behind Julio.

"You may share my bed," said Esteban. "Later, Julio will go down to the lobby and take his choice of the slim, beautiful young women who scatter themselves about like flower petals. My girlfriend, who interestingly enough tells me her name is Carlotta, will not be joining me tonight."

The Wizard, taking only enough time to toss his wet caftan into the bathroom and cover himself in a white terrycloth robe supplied by the hotel, collapsed into Esteban's bed.

Esteban read for a while in the sitting room between the two bedrooms, finally retiring when he tired of hearing the amorous moans coming from Julio's room.

He was soon sound asleep.

Deep in the night the woman, Carlotta, appeared in the hallway as if somewhere a magician had gestured hypnotically and sent her there. Though Esteban had given her a key, she opened the door without using it, and crept into the foyer, hearing the lustful sounds emanating from Julio's room. She smiled and entered Esteban's room. She sensed something wrong, but waited until her eyes adjusted somewhat so she could see the slumbering lump that was Esteban, and beside him a petite form in a hotel housecoat with a pillow strategically over her head. Carlotta drew a thin stiletto from her purse and pierced Esteban's heart with one flick of her wrist. As she moved a step closer in order to lean across Esteban's body and dispatch the woman, the stiletto in her hand turned to a delicate orchid, and the wild-eyed Wizard sat up and stared at her.

"What have you done," he croaked. "I smell blood."

UPON THE ANNOUNCEMENT of Esteban's death there followed national mourning in Courteguay. Only President Kennedy's assassination had triggered greater consternation.

Within hours of the announcement, the Wizard, like the angel of death himself, hissed airward in a black balloon with a black gondola. He was dressed in a black satin cowled cape with a single silver star over the heart.

"I knew it," wailed Fernandella, throwing a plate at her husband, Hector Alvarez Pimental, "your evil ways have come home to roost. I predict that the stream will dry up, the fish will rot in the sun, the stench will cause the cockatoos to fly away. Everything will return to the way it was before the twins became famous."

Hector Alvarez Pimental calculated that with one son dead his allowance would be cut in half, might disappear altogether, for it was Esteban who suggested the allowance, cajoled Julio into going along. Now, if Julio refused to hurl the ball to another catcher....

He wondered if he would be able to sell seating at Esteban's funeral. As he ate a breakfast of pheasant burritos and a large glass of passion fruit juice, Hector Alvarez Pimental pictured ten of thousands of plaster of Paris catchers each in the image of Esteban Pimental, each scrunched in a crouch, each with red cheeks, blue eyes, chest protectors and shin guards. After breakfast he phoned a wholesaler in San Barnabas and ordered a hundred thousand to be ready the day of the funeral, or before if possible.

The funeral, of course, would be held at the former Jesus, Joseph and Mary Celestial Baseball Palace in San Barnabas, renamed Dr. Lucius Noir Soccer Pitch when Dr. Noir came into power, renamed Juarez Blanco Baseball Megatropolis the last time Dr. Noir was deposed, renamed Esteban Pimental Memorial Stadium, less than eight hours after Esteban's death was announced.

Photographs, Hector Alvarez Pimental thought, were another matter entirely. He found a signed 5×7 of Esteban in full baseball regalia, and ordered half a million copies. He would wholesale them for twenty centavos each, let the vendors sell them for whatever the traffic would bear.

THIRTY-SIX
THE GRINGO JOURNALIST

Pete Hasslewaite, the Mets twenty game winner, was beaten the first two times he faced Julio, 1-0 and 2-1. The third time they faced each other, every time Julio came to bat Hasslewaite threw at him. The first pitch merely brushed him back, the second made him step out of the batter's box, the third missed the bill of his cap by half an inch and sent him sprawling in the dirt. Hasslewaite then struck Julio out on three pitches.

"Live in fear, greaser," the catcher rasped, "you ever seen a baseball hit a melon?" He laughed, tobacco juice spraying through the bars of his mask.

Though tempted, Julio did not retaliate. Instead the next time he came to bat, he stepped back and hit a brush-back fastball cleanly up the middle for a single, batting in a run to give his team the lead.

The third time he came to the plate, the catcher spat contemptuously an inch from Julio's shoes.

"You ever played in pain, greaser?" the catcher, who would one day be elected to the Hall of Fame, growled. "The Chief," for Hasslewaite, a swarthy, raw-boned Oklahoman, claimed to be one-quarter Cherokee, "is gonna give you a horsehide lobotomy, greaser." The catcher grinned evilly and spat again.

The first pitch was aimed for Julio's crotch; by springing backward with a panther-like quickness he avoided it. His manager stormed from the dugout and jawed with the umpire for several minutes, all the time pointing accusingly at Hasslewaite, while the Mets fans booed and brayed, and Hasslewaite stood insolently on the mound exuding innocence.

Hasslewaite pitched two strikes, then zipped a fastball toward Julio's head. Julio moved back only an inch or two; the ball passed under his chin.

"The Chief has great control, greaser. He's gonna stick the next one in your ear," and he laughed again, tobacco juice gurgling in his throat. They'll be refried beans all over home plate...."

Instead of going for the head, Hasslewaite used a curve ball that sliced in and hit Julio on the pitching arm, just above the wrist. By the time the manager and trainer reached him the wrist was swollen and greenish.

"Tough luck, fella," said the catcher, mask in hand, grinning from yellowed eyes.

"Very unwise," was all Julio said to the catcher, as he was escorted from the game. In spite of the burrito poultices his mother sent from Courteguay and the ministerings of the Wizard, Julio was out of action for six weeks. But Hasslewaite never pitched again. His rotator cuff mysteriously ground to a halt. He was unable to raise his pitching arm above shoulder height.

Ten years later, at a small, seedy carnival in Baltimore, Julio saw Hasslewaite for the last time. Among a crooked ring-toss game, weighted milk bottles, and a sinister puppet show, was a grimy freak show featuring a gorilla-baby, a bearded lady and a ruptured strong man. Also on the program was Hasslewaite; Julio recognized him from his portrait on the garish canvas banner in front of the freak tent. A beady-eyed man in a pinstriped baseball uniform, with yellow daffodils growing from his right wrist where his pitching hand should have been.

THIRTY-SEVEN
THE WIZARD

Magic is only something you haven't seen before, the Wizard told Julio. Some things that happen to us every day, people on the other side of the earth might call magic. While we might be equally impressed by what they consider ordinary. For instance, I have heard that there are places where the wizards can make it so cold men turn to marble before your eyes.

Julio recalled the wizard's words the first time he saw the butterflies darken the sun.

High in the sand hills above San Barnabas, where the cane fields petered out to rock as the elevation increased, where stubborn evergreens stood hunched over like seraped old men, was the place where the monarch butterflies spent the winter in hibernation. It would be many years before the outside world would discover the wondrous event, though it was known and ignored by the Courteguayan hill people since the beginning of time.

The monarchs, large black-and-orange butterflies, with wingspreads of up to four inches, migrated each fall from as far away as Canada. Some years a hundred million of them made the dramatic journey across the USA, lines of them intersecting, the main stream becoming larger and larger, vibrating like Halloween streamers. Pulled by some invisible magnet, they crossed the continent, eventually forming a Mississippi of butterflies that flowed like an endless pipeline over the ocean to Courteguay and to the evergreens high in the sand hills.

Once they arrived, the black-bordered monarchs folded their wings, attached themselves to a needle of evergreen, and rested until spring when they awakened and again formed a fluttering, thousand mile conduit back to North America, an undulating, whirling skyride of color.

From the base of the hills, the butterfly-saturated trees looked dead, as orange as if they had been singed. Travelers from San Barnabas stared up at the pale orange trees and remarked that they must suffer from dry rot or blight. Then the trees passed from their minds. The hill people knew the truth of the butterflies but considered the phenomenon unremarkable.

The residents of San Barnabas were used to the whirling tunnel of butterflies passing over the city each October and April, but only the Wizard had ever had the curiosity to follow the golden horde to its resting place.

The first year the Wizard was rich enough to own a hot air balloon, he hovered high above the endless orange tube of life, which from above appeared to be full of jittering orange smoke. The Wizard knew that butterflies were so named because early peoples thought that witches took on the colorful, mysterious form in order to steal milk and butter.

The Wizard, ever avaricious, fantasized that these butterflies took their color from gold, and that wherever they came to rest he would find a mine stuffed with indescribable wealth. The butterflies, he decided, restored themselves by bathing in gold dust. What he did not expect to find was the most tranquil spot on earth, a fairyland of sleeping orange evergreens.

The few peasants in the area respected the butterflies, did not even cut firewood in "the season of the sleeping sunshine," which was how they described each butterfly winter.

Local farmers stock their wood in the early fall, the Wizard reported back, for they've found even the sound of an ax will cause some butterflies to fall to the ground. And those that fall from the evergreen needles die. If a tree is actually cut, the ground around it is papered with the silken wings of monarchs.

When Julio Pimental returned to Courteguay, after another season of baseball in America, he was heavy-hearted and arm-weary. He sat for days next to Fernandella's cool stream, the only movement about him his eyes, which twitched involuntarily when the brilliant blue fish tossed themselves in the air like coins.

Fernandella tempted him with pheasant pie, pickled pheasant, pheasant burritos, as well as something indescribable, a dish she had seen illustrated in an American magazine Julio had sent to her. She carried the recipe down to the fenced compound, where the eldest priest translated for her, his face pressed against the chain-link fence that confined him. The translated ingredients included lampblack, and a small electrical appliance. The dish, which was supposed to be Chicken Alejandro, though Fernandella used pheasant instead of chicken, turned out less than satisfactory.

"I am not going back," Julio sighed. "Baseball players in America may be well paid, but they are not idols; they are traded like goats from one farmer to another."

But by now even Fernandella was used to luxury. And Hector Alvarez Pimental, with the Wizard acting as a commissioned broker, had just ordered a chartreuse BMW with white leather upholstery.

"With home cooking and a few days rest you will soon be good as new," said Fernandella.

"Have you considered playing winter baseball in Mexico?" his father asked, feeling the biceps of Julio's pitching arm.

Julio mooned by the crystal stream for another week, while his twin, Esteban, studied Latin texts at the San Barnabas Library, conferring frequently with the moth-eaten priests in their chain-link enclosure.

Early one morning Julio heard children screeching in the hills high above the house; he looked up to see several silhouetted against the sky like stick drawings. Each child's arm was extended upwards. They ran along the crest of the hill, pointing, as if flying invisible kites.

Curiosity overshadowed his torpor, and he languidly climbed the hill.

"The butterflies are coming," the children chanted.

Julio scanned the sky; it was pale as ice. The short grass on the hill was scorched yellow; the day would be white hot in an hour or so. The sky was blank as water.

"How do you know?" Julio asked the children, who stared back at him with the contempt the very young have for adults who do not share their intuition. Though Julio was scarcely a year older than the oldest, his clothes and manner tagged him as an adult, and they automatically mistrusted him.

"Everyone knows," a sullen-eyed girl in a sugar sack dress finally replied.

"I can't see a thing," Julio replied.

"It is sad to be blind," said the girl. "My grandfather is blind."

"I mean in the sky," said Julio.

"The sky. The land. Blind is blind."

"I can see," said Julio, raising his eyes to meet the girl's dark stare. She was perhaps a year younger than he, with a colt-legged vitality. Julio could see her tiny breasts pushing like shadows against the white sackcloth.

"Really?" said the girl, Quita, a mocking smile on her lips.

"I see a terrible beauty in front of me," said Julio. As he said it he felt his chest tighten; he was unable to take a full breath; it was as if his ribs were taped. His statement had not emerged in the bantering tone he intended. The girl, her lips slightly parted, continued to stare at him with sad, dark eyes.

Julio, who had learned to joke in blighted English, outside baseball stadiums, with fans, groupies, Baseball Sadies, could think of nothing to say to this girl in his native language. He felt as he did when the bases were loaded, the winning run dancing yo-yo-like off third base. Reacting accordingly, he breathed deeply, clearing his mind of everything. He pretended he was on the mound, the translucent batter glowing dimly to one side of the plate, his only thought to hurl the ball to his brother, Esteban. Hurl it without interruption.

Moments passed. The other children raced on across the spine of the hill, arms still spearing skyward, while Julio stood as if in a trance. The girl sat down in front of him, pulled up her knees, locking her long fingers in front of her ankles. Julio blinked, stared up at the sky that was still blank.

"You look as if you're in prayer. Are you one of the religious ones?" asked the girl.

Julio gazed down at her as man must first have gazed at fire.

"No," he said. "But I am rich enough to buy you your heart's desire."

"No one is rich enough to buy anyone's heart's desire," said Quita, "especially mine. I want to fly in the body of a white heron, sleek and smooth as soap, piercing the sky; I want to see my moon shadow dark on the water below me. Are you rich enough to buy me that?"

"No," sighed Julio, his own lips parting as he watched Quita's face. He would have traded his career for one kiss; he was terrified he would frighten her away.

"The religious ones talk of going to meet their leader in the sky. He walks on water and converses with oxen, at least so they say."

"I am not one of them," said Julio. "The priests are kept in corrals like cattle; the militia has orders to shoot the missionaries you speak of."

"I'm glad on all counts," said Quita. "The religious ones are not interested in now. They claim to wait for their pleasure in another world. I seek pleasure now, and in the next world, if one exists. Are you really rich?"

Julio breathed deeply, exhaled, letting the air and tension float from him. He noticed that Quita's eyes were set wide apart. She would make a great pitcher, Julio thought. She could watch base runners while facing the plate.

"Yes. I am rich. I have just returned from playing baseball in America. I am a pitcher."

"If you are rich why are you unhappy?"

"Because I am lonely. My life in America is like being locked in an empty room for months at a time. And, as a baseball player, I am expected to perform miracles."

"With loaves and fishes like the leader of the religious ones?" asked Quita. And though Julio met her straight, innocent gaze, he could not tell if she was making fun of him or sympathizing.

"With my right arm and a baseball."

"I know about baseball," said Quita. "My father was Milan Garza. He has been honored by El Presidente as a Courteguayan Baseball Immortal. He died when I was very young. El Presidente would not allow my mother to bury him: his body was taken away and is preserved in a glass case in the Hall of Baseball Immortals in the Capitol building. I have never been there, though I am told my father stands as he did in the outfield, in his Cardinal of St. Louis red-and-white uniform, his glove on his hand, a holy aura about his head. I am told too, that his eyes glow in the dark."

"I have never been to the Hall of Baseball Immortals either," said Julio, "though I am rich enough to go any time I wish. Rich enough to take you with me. But Milan Garza is a national hero. In America I am often asked by reporters if I knew him. He played for years in America. As his daughter you should be rich beyond your dreams."

Quita stood up and moved closer to Julio. As she did so he caught the first odors of her: sun-sweet earth, but behind that something darker, muskier, like the scent of the deep-colored nasturtiums that bloomed on the shady side of Fernandella's new home.

"You have been away for years. Have you not heard of Dr. Noir? My father decided to run for the Presidency of Courteguay. It was the one thing he wanted that he could not have."

"But what of the honors your father received? El Presidente named Milan Garza a Knight Commander of the Blue Camellia. I read about it."

"One cannot eat titles, or praise, or adulation, as you must well know. For I recognize you now, one half of the The Battery,

Courteguay's most famous export. El Presidente used to say you and your brother were worth more to Courteguay's economy than one million pounds of mangos. Is that true?"

Julio smiled, trying to imagine one million pounds of mangos.

"My father was murdered," Quita continued. "Poisoned so he could be displayed forever in a crystal coffin at the Hall of Baseball Immortals. 'A dead idol is much safer than a living one,' Dr. Noir told my mother in a supposed note of condolence. 'A dead hero can never disgrace himself in his old age, can never support unpopular political causes, disclose unacceptable sexual preferences, become falling-down drunk in public, or display an aging and ill-conditioned body.' You should become familiar with such quotes. You should also know that if you become rich and famous through baseball Dr. Noir will see to it that you have a short life span. Has no one told you that?"

But Julio was barely listening. He breathed in the sweetness of Quita Garza, though far in the back of his mind he recalled the fortuneteller who predicted his brother's early death. No, no one had told him anything. But Julio was not very interested in death, or warnings of death. He was in love. The white sky made him dizzy.

He took Quita Garza in his arms and the heat she radiated through her thin clothing disoriented him even more. Her lips were soft and easily parted, and as they kissed she clung to him with a ferocity he had not anticipated. He thought of easing her down onto the scorched grass of the hilltop, imagined the silhouette their bodies would make against the declining sun.

BUT THEIR PASSION WAS INTERRUPTED by the softest of sounds: birds seemed to hush, the wind surrender. The sky darkened even more as the wild spiral of golden and black butterflies came into view, an onrushing endless train hurtling overhead, hundreds of feet in the air.

"I want to follow them," whispered Quita, staring up into the velvet movements of a million wings. And Julio, gazing with love into the girl's long face and luminous eyes, could deny her nothing. She took his hand and they trooped along the spine of the hill. The river of butterflies soon arched from horizon to horizon.

All the remainder of that day, and all the next, the conduit of butterflies flowed over Courteguay like an orangeade rainbow.

On the ground, Julio and Quita followed along; they left the city behind, crossed the flatlands to the foothills, and began a slow climb toward the timberline, where the air was calm and sweet.

When they arrived at the butterfly forest, millions of the silken-winged creatures were already covering the evergreens on the edge of the timberline. Millions more were arriving, seeking rejuvenation after their long flight over the ocean. There was such a profusion that their wing beats could be heard; the draft from these fluttering snippets tousled Quita's long, reddish-brown hair.

Julio and Quita watched, enthralled.

"The wings of those on the trees are closed like hands at prayer," said Quita.

"Do not give them so much credit, said Julio.

"Can you fly home from America on your own wings?"

"I cannot," he admitted. "Can you find it in your heart to love a man who cannot fly?"

When she didn't answer, Julio took her hand, which was dry and cool, and pulling her close to him kissed her. She responded, her tongue sweet and warm, exploring his lips and teeth, like a butterfly itself.

The arriving butterflies blotted out the sun as they hovered, searching for a place to land. Though it was mid-afternoon, their gentle shadows dispelled the violent heat of the day, and it became comfortable as evening. Julio undid the single button at the back of Quita's dress, and she helped him pull her arms out. She unbuttoned Julio's shirt, and suddenly her tiny breasts were against his chest, burning like hot coins. Julio bent his head and her nipples tasted salty; she smelled of new rope, of tanned leather, and of the dark nasturtiums.

"I want you to know that I am not a virgin," Quita said, as Julio pulled her down beside him in the sun-sweet grass beneath the butterfly trees.

"Unimportant," said Julio.

"Whenever he feels it necessary, my stepfather sells me to his friends, or to strangers," she insisted.

Julio covered her mouth with his. Swallowing the last of her words, he fitted their bodies together, locking them in passion, two puzzles completed by a single action.

"I have never made sex for love," Quita whispered, much later, their bodies still deliciously entwined. "I never thought I would. Now I know why couples moan in the night."

"I am glad my father did not have daughters when he was very poor. He would have been tempted, I'm afraid," said Julio. "But I am rich, and at home for four months, and I promise you will never be touched again, except in love...."

"Oh, look," said Quita, for a butterfly had landed on her right arm near the elbow. Both her arms were locked about Julio's neck. He was still inside her, their bodies sleek and sweet with their blended sweat, their mouths ripe with the tastes of each other.

Then another, and another of the gentle butterflies landed on Quita's arm. Wings closed, they were no thicker than two thin swatches of silk.

"My back," said Julio. "I can feel them on my back."

Quita raised her head and peeked over Julio's shoulder.

"They have woven us a blanket for the night," she said. "There must be ten thousand of them on your back. Feel their warmth."

As she spoke, thousands more butterflies covered the couple with their gentle color.

"Do they have hearts?" whispered Quita.

"I feel them beating like a million pinpoints," said Julio.

All that evening the shimmering butterflies continued to arrive until they had covered every inch of the lovers; only the places where they were joined in passion and in love were not cloaked in black and gold. They looked like a burnt-orange sculpture in some erotic museum.

"They will fall and die if we move," said Quita.

"Then we won't distress them," said Julio, as again he covered her mouth with his, and as he did, butterflies settled on their closed eyelids.

And there they stayed, down all the long, silken days of their butterfly winter, Quita and Julio, entwined in love, secure under the sleek blanket of butterflies, waiting for spring.

THIRTY-EIGHT
THE GRINGO JOURNALIST

Did Octavio Court actually exist? This was a question the Gringo Journalist asked himself many times. Courteguayans could be appallingly vague when asked questions they didn't want to answer. "Ah, yes, Octavio Court," they would say. "A great man." Then, they would ramble off on some tangent or other and the Gringo Journalist would find himself being told the history of the mango, or how a mysterious American brought baseball to Courteguay.

History books, he discovered, were less than helpful. The Gringo Journalist knew that history is written from many different perspectives, none telling the whole story, most imparting only biased half-truths at the best.

Translated from the *Encyclopedia of the Republic of Courteguay*:

> COURT, *OCTAVIO JUAREZ*. Founder and First President of Courteguay. b. *c.* 1831 in Santo Domingo, D.R. Education not known. Joined the army of the Dominican Republic as a young man. Rose to the rank of General. He was in command of the Border Patrol, charged with keeping Haitians in Haiti. Court did not like the constant change of governments in the D.R. and with a vision of a more stable

> government planned, along with his comrade General Jose Maria Bravura, to overthrow the government. The coup was unsuccessful and Court and Bravura fled to the jungle. Through diplomacy, threats, and the wish of the government to be rid of him, Court persuaded both the Dominican and Haiti to grant him a number of acres of useless land, and the Country of Courteguay was formed. What had been General Court's outpost became San Barnabas. Octavio Court is known as the Father of Courteguay.

THERE FOLLOWED TWENTY PAGES of what the Gringo Journalist thought of as speculative fiction. He had once read a supposed biography of St. Ann, the supposed mother of the Virgin Mary, a 200+ page book that contained no facts, nothing to substantiate that such a person as St. Ann ever existed. The remainder of the information on Octavio Court was much the same. *Octavio Court probably* was a favorite way of beginning a sentence.

The Gringo Journalist consulted other sources.

Translated from the *Encyclopedia of the Dominican Republic*:

> COURT, *OCTAVIO*. First President of Courteguay. b. 1825 in Santo Domingo, Dominican Republic. Education unknown. A traitorous general in the Dominican army, Court and an accomplice attempted to overthrow the government of General Juan Garcia Melendez, and was soundly defeated. He fled to the jungle where he and his bloodthirsty followers began a campaign of intimidation and guerrilla warfare. Since they were so firmly entrenched in the jungle the governments of the Dominican Republic and Haiti agreed to cede to General Court a few sections of worthless land in return for an end to the attacks. Thus was the miserable little country of Courteguay born. Though General Court must be long dead there is no record of his death.

From the *Book of Haitian History and Religion*:

> COURT, *OCTAVIUS JUAREZ*. Oppressor of Haiti. b. *c.*1830 in the Dominican Republic. Court rose to the rank of general in the Dominican Army where he was assigned to persecute Haitians who accidentally strayed across the border into the Dominican. Court

and another general attempted to overthrow the government of the Dominican and failed. While in exile they raided villages in both Haiti and the Dominican, leaving behind a trail of bloodshed. Emissaries of both counties agreed to give General Court a section of land in return for peace. Not surprisingly he named his land Courteguay; half of which still truly belongs to Haiti. Late in his life General Court vanished from his presidential palace and was never heard from again.

An ambiguous statement if the Gringo Journalist ever heard one.

THIRTY-NINE
THE WIZARD

Like a true Wizard I am able to be in more than one place at a time. Being omniscient is one of the first requisites for being a Wizard, though it has taken years of practice and I have not always been so endowed. I am what is known in literary circles as an unreliable narrator. I will tell you the truth and history of Courteguay, but it is your ear that hears my tales, your mind that must decide which is truth and which is history. The people of Courteguay, if they are anything besides baseball fanatics, are liars. It is in the blood. This Gringo Journalist who follows me around like flypaper heard the tale of my being murdered by a perpetual loser named Cecilio Escadero, but since he had interviewed me before he heard the tale and found me quite alive he discounted it. He forgot that he was in Courteguay.

The visiting journalist has good intentions. I give him full credit. He has made a valiant attempt to ascertain the facts. He is at this very moment in San Barnabas, ensconced in a second-class hotel sorting through his notes and tapes. He has spent four months in Courteguay researching the History of Courteguay, in spite of the fact that his home country, the United States, where he is considered a successful author and is revered as much as a writer can be in a country that does not value its artists, has refused to fund his visit to Courteguay. During his stay he has researched (a) the History of Courteguay (b) the history of baseball in Courteguay (c) my life story (d) the story of Julio and Esteban Pimental the most famous baseball players exported by our country (e) the life and times of Dr. Lucius Noir.

He thinks he knows what has happened. He has conducted interviews with anyone who will talk with him. He has tried to hire someone to guide him into the wilderness to a camp where it is rumored that a group of insurgents led by the late Dr. Lucius Noir are holed up. I personally have prevented him from doing so. He is a nice young man, more than a little naive. And though I am certain Dr. Noir is dead, what if I am wrong? Dr. Noir might hold this young man against his will, or worse.

The Gringo Journalist, unfortunately, has university training. He looks for things that do not exist, in places that hold no secrets. Explanations are usually simple. Take my murder. I owed Cecilio Escadero one thousand guilermos.

I didn't have it. I would probably never have it. Wouldn't have paid him if I did have it. I have an undeserved reputation for welshing on bets. What I told Cecelio was: "If there is any blame here it lies with you for being gullible enough to bet with someone who is a self-admitted liar and cheat."

One thousand guilermos was a fortune to Cecilio Escadero. To me it was nothing. I didn't have it to begin with so it meant little to lose it.

"It is all a matter of attitude," I tried to explain to Cecilio. "If I had won I would immediately have bet again and probably lost. And I would have had no money to pay my debt. Instead I lost my first bet so I saved myself a lot of trouble."

Cecilio Escadero took out a revolver and shot me three times in the chest. He was so literal-minded and so lacking in humor. Especially after I came back to life.

THE FIRST TIME THE WIZARD was murdered he was unprepared for the event. He was shot after declining to pay a gambling debt. His body was packed in cloves and his coffin displayed at the baseball grounds in San Cristobel for two days. On the third day, just before Esteban Pimental was to conduct the service and his body was to be carried to San Cristobel's largest cemetery, the Wizard willed himself back to life. When he sat up in his coffin he frightened the entire student body of St. Vagabond Primary School, who had just finished singing a song mourning the Wizard, praising baseball, and guessing the numbers for that day's pick-three lottery.

YOU SEE HOW IT IS with us wizards. Reputation is everything. One resurrection and your credibility in the gambling community rises like a balloon.

FORTY
THE WIZARD

When Julio and Quita woke from their long, loving, butterfly winter, they walked hand in hand, down from the foothills and across the plain to San Barnabas, while the tunnel of butterflies spiraled above them.

"First I have something to show you," Julio said to Quita. "I discovered it as a child exploring the hills by myself. Esteban was never much company except when playing baseball. He preferred to spend his time down at the compound discussing philosophy and religion with the priests behind the chain-link fences."

Julio held Quita's small hand in his and guided her between the banks of wild morning glories and plumeria toward what looked like a small swamp. The oval area was a bleak, bleached ivory color in contrast to the vivid green foliage and the startling reds and purples of the flowers.

"What is it?" asked Quita. She studied the scene for a moment. "It looks dead and scary." The area in front of her might, in another less tropical country, pass for grass or grain, pale, unearthly stalks topped by gray, claw-like appendages, that could be mistaken for roots.

"This place looks like what I imagine death must be like, grey, dry, grasping, so everlastingly dreary." She turned toward Julio, pressing her radiant belly against his. "Why would you want to show me this deathly place?"

"Because there is a beautiful surprise," said Julio, grasping a pale stalk with both hands as he braced his feet and pulled mightily and sharply upward. There emerged from the earth a purple and yellow flower of intense beauty. He turned the stalk over, shaking off grains of dark earth, exposing the flower to sunlight. Under the heat of the sun the mucous-like gel that covered the petals evaporated like steam, and the petals seemed to expand as well as unfold in a glorious bloom.

"That plant was in the earth upside down," said Quita, laughing delightedly.

"As are they all," said Julio, extracting another plant from the earth, this one unfolding into a magnificent bell of the deepest gold and wine colors. Julio continued extracting the upside down flowers and stacking them into Quita's arms until she all but disappeared and begged him to stop.

"Isn't it wrong to pull so many?" asked Quita.

"A conscience," said Julio, "is to make you feel bad about things that make you feel good."

THEY ARRIVED AT FERNANDELLA'S, both laden with flowers, peeking from behind them like overworked florists, to find that Julio was due to report to Florida for spring training in three days. Esteban was already packed, sitting on his suitcase on the patio reading a Latin translation of *The Stranger* by Albert Camus.

"My season is like that of the butterflies," Julio said. "When they leave, I leave. When they return, so shall I."

Before Julio flew off to the United States for spring training he ensconced his love, Quita Garza, in one of the lavish bedrooms in the east wing of his mother's mansion.

"I am in love with Quita Garza," he told his mother. "She is now part of the family. Protect her as you would your own."

"You are too young to be in love," Fernandella wailed. "You are only ... what ... sixteen?"

"I am an adult of twenty-two," said Julio, grinning, "and I have a birth certificate to prove it."

"Fake though it may be," countered Fernandella. But she did not argue too strenuously, for she knew her prosperity came from the money Julio and Esteban earned from playing baseball in the United States. If Julio was in love, so be it.

He and Quita located themselves in one of the many bedrooms, gorged on fried pheasant, grits, and passion fruit. They made love hour upon hour, for Julio knew he must soon fly away to America for another baseball season. Julio hated the thought of gathering together his few belongings, for packing meant parting from Quita.

"I will return just before the butterflies," Julio told Quita as they lay tangled deep in their bed, kissing her parted lips. "If we are fortunate you will be splendid with our child when I return."

"I will try," whispered Quita, as Julio kissed down her belly, licking the insides of her thighs, savoring the sweet odors of her, the tartness of their mingled sweat.

THE FIRST QUESTION FERNANDELLA asked Quita was, "Do you play baseball?" The second was, "Do you have any idea how old my son is?" And the third, "Are you pregnant?"

Quita, staring at Fernandella with an open, almost insolent gaze said, "No. No," and, "I hope so."

After years of dealing with the deviousness of her husband and the Wizard, Fernandella had come to appreciate candor of any kind. Fernandella quickly came to admire Quita's independence of spirit and her unforced industry around the house. Quita plumped up quickly on a diet of pheasant burritos, and plates of the tasty fish, filleted and fried, directly from the sky-blue stream. A little too quickly, Fernandella thought.

"You are nothing but a girl," Fernandella said to Quita one evening, but though she intended some disdain in the statement, her tone emerged as sympathetic, and she found herself putting her arms around the wild, ragged girl, who allowed her head to rest on Fernandella's shoulder, and whose heartbeat Fernandella could feel through the thin layers of clothes that separated them.

"I have seen terrible things," the girl whispered, as if Fernandella had asked a question. "I am like one of the princesses from the fairy tales of my childhood. I have fallen from grace, been cast under the spell of a wicked witch, where I have gone from princess to peasant in a matter of seconds. Though the spell I have fallen under was cast, not by a witch, but by the wicked Dictator for Life of Courteguay, Dr. Lucius Noir.

"I was indeed a princess. My father was Milan Garza, the most famous baseball player ever to come out of Courteguay, until perhaps Julio. My father's wealth was unimaginable. Comprehend that the average Courteguayan earns just over four American dollars per month. An American twenty dollar bill is a fortune in Courteguay, where the centavo is worth 1/64 of a cent, or less than nothing, and our regular currency, the guilermo, almost as little. Though I was too young to remember clearly, I am told that my father earned one million American dollars, and sometimes even more, for the many years of his career which ended when I was six.

"We lived in a fifty-room mansion on the top of a hill from which we could see the lights of the capital city, San Barnabas, burning like scars across the beautiful night sky. We had other residences. Land. My father was said to own one-quarter of all the acres in Courteguay, which would still be a small holding by American standards, for Courteguay would fit inside Delaware, one of America's smallest states, with room left over for the city of San Barnabas. I was educated by a tutor. I learned to speak five languages before I was ten. My father had a fleet of cars, Mercedes, Rolls Royce, Maserati. Gasoline in Courteguay is over seven dollars a gallon, and only the rich own automobiles, and then only one to a family. A motor scooter in Courteguay holds more prestige than an acre-sized Cadillac in the United States. But in Courteguay my father could have anything he wanted, so he built his own gas station, had the gasoline shipped in on a special boat from Miami.

"Unfortunately, my father decided to want the only thing unavailable to him in Courteguay, political power."

FORTY-ONE
THE WIZARD

The Wizard, who had not always been a wizard, remembered the first village where he had taken up residence. It was a village where desire was visible. At first the Wizard had not realized the significance of the swarm of deep red, firefly-like stars that flowed from the sweet thighs of a passion-seeking woman.

The fire is always there, an acquaintance explained. Desire just makes it visible. A man must always be ready. A man of this village is excused from the cane fields, from the army, even if it is in battle, if word reaches him that his woman's thighs are on fire.

Unattached men walk the streets of the village late into the night, studying the windows of houses where widows or single women live, ever watchful, ever hopeful.

Sometimes the stars gather like a Christmas wreath in the window of a married man's home, pulsating, the molecules rearranging themselves, seeming to dance against the upper panes of glass, seeking escape. But they do not escape. They only throb brightly.

"Ho! Edwardo Gonzales!" the wandering men would shout. Someone would bang rhythmically on a tin can drum. "Wake up,

Eduardo! Your good woman calls!" The men would dance in the street, their feet raising puffs of dust in the moonlight. They would clap and hoot until, inside the house, the husband wakened to the desire that filled the air, reached out to his willing partner and gathered her in his arms. As that happened the stars would retreat from the window in the wake of the soft groans of passion, and the gentle scufflings of love.

Many married men considered it a sign of prowess for their windows to always remain dark. They considered it a sacred duty to satisfy their wives before sleep came so the signal of passion never wandered their house like a spirit, preening in the window like a conceited bird.

These same men were sometimes the object of teasing, usually good-natured, but sometimes not.

"How do we know Ignatio's woman has any passion to offer?" they would cry. "Ignatio tells us, but we have all heard his hunting stories, and seen the gigantic fish be bragged of, fish I would be ashamed to hang between my legs in place of my instrument of pleasure. We have heard his fish described as five feet long, and heard how Ignatio staggered under their weight."

The more prudent let the fires burn in his window occasionally, sometimes let them burn a long time, enjoying the ruckus in front of his house.

A woman who wailed with passion was a prize to be treasured. A man who could extinguish the fire slowly, a star at a time over a long period, until the fiery orb of stars diminished to a few pinpricks of lust, then to nothing at all, could walk the streets of his village the next day with his head held high and his chest expanded. At the communal washtubs his woman would feign tiredness but with a sly and enduring smile.

"It is an embarrassment and also a great blessing," an old woman told the Wizard soon after his arrival.

"There is much rejoicing in the village when a girl is old enough for the colors to fly from between her thighs. When a girl comes of age, when the stars of fire first roar from between her thighs, it is a cause for much celebration and ceremony in the village. And for one old as me," and she bobbed her turbaned head, and eyed the Wizard with what he was afraid was a leer, "alone, and long-widowed, it is a sign that I still possess life's juices. The stars have nothing to do with the ability to reproduce, and everything to do with passion itself. For me they are an advertisement, and there is always someone willing to answer an ad."

She cackled and pulled at the Wizard's sleeve, while he couldn't help but eye her faded yellow caftan where he thought he detected a few pricks of light, like blood-colored gnats, dart across his field of vision. Excusing himself he practically ran away from the old woman, though he gathered he was under no obligation to assuage her passion.

It is said, the Wizard learned, that the stars of a virgin's desire are silver trimmed with crimson. After such an event the young men of the village would gather to preen and dance, roughhouse and joke, display their finest clothes, their hunting trophies, their guns. They would also bear presents, dresses and serapes, scarves, carvings, baseball bats with the girl's name burned into the wood a half-inch deep. Sacrifices were prepared. Acts of heroism attempted.

FORTY-TWO
THE GRINGO JOURNALIST

Julio asked the Wizard about the Hall of Baseball Immortals.

"Some think it disrespectful that The Courteguayan Hall of Baseball Immortals holds the taxidermied bodies of past baseball heroes," said the Wizard. "It was the Old Dictator's idea, though I admit I had some input. The Hall put a stop to some very odd goings on."

"Odd even for Courteguay?" asked Julio.

The Wizard smiled. "Even for Courteguay. You are too young to remember Barojas Garcia."

"I know who he was. A great pitcher for the Boston Red Sox. But he died young, in a car wreck?"

"His car hit a bus head-on."

"Now I remember."

"I can still hear the voice of the Old Dictator crying out, 'Bring me the arm of Barojas Garcia.'"

"Dr. Noir would have made such a request while Garcia was still alive." Julio chuckled at his cleverness.

“There was some terrible confusion,” the Wizard went on. “Those sent to retrieve the appendage were not baseball fans. They brought the right arm to the Old Dictator.”

“Fools!” he shouted at them. “Barojas Garcia was a left-handed pitcher. What could I possibly want with his right arm?”

“What could you possibly want with the left arm of a dead man?” one of the procurers asked. He is still, to the best of my knowledge, cleaning latrines. What happened next, and this is a secret between us, resulted in Milan Garza’s finest year in the Major Leagues, the year he won thirty-five games.

“Milan Garza used to carry the arm in a tuba case. There was a lot of speculation by the media that year, a lot of television gone over frame by frame looking for something odd. Some batters claimed they saw two arms coming toward them, one attached to Milan Garza, the other one free in the air. But nothing ever came of it. Milan Garza told the Old Dictator that he pitched until he got tired, or was being hit too hard, then he let Barojas Garcia pitch for a while.

“A portable relief pitcher?” asked Julio.

“The thing was Garcia had a knuckle ball that dropped off the table, and it would come as a complete surprise when Milan Garza threw it.”

“Is that how it happened? Julio asked.

“If it isn’t, it’s the way it should have happened,” said the Wizard.

FORTY-THREE
THE WIZARD

As soon as he arrived in Florida for spring training, Julio brought up the subject of bringing Quita to America.

"If I understand what yer saying," a phrase the manager, who had replaced the boys' beloved Al Tiller, always used to preface any discussion with his Spanish-speaking ballplayers, "this little girl you're talkin' about ain't even yer wife. What are you, some kind of immoral, godless, heathen-communist?" he thundered. "Baseball is a clean game. We don't allow nothin' dirty or immoral like that."

"Would it make any difference if we were married?" asked Julio. "We could get married."

"Of course it wouldn't, in so far as you draggin' her along, except that y'all would be sanctified in Jesus. It's baseball tradition that we leave our women at home. If one woman got to come along why soon a whole passel of them would want the same, and the game would be on its way to hell in a handbasket before you could say Strike three!"

It had never occurred to Julio before that even the manager and the American superstars all traveled alone during the season. He had slowly come to realize that baseball players were chattels, slaves, but being single he had never noticed that all the players traveled alone, never with their families, and that those wives and families usually lived in the player's home town, not in the city where he spent six or seven months as a player.

"These Americans are of a very strange morality," Julio remarked to Esteban. "They insist for some reason on being married, then can't wait for the game to end each night of the season so they can rush out and break every marriage vow they have ever made as well as several of the Ten Commandments."

"In most cases the flesh is weak," said Esteban, scarcely looking up from the Latin text he was reading.

"But it makes no sense," said Julio.

"What makes you think religion is supposed to make sense?" said Esteban. "Those who insist on sense, logic, or justice in religion, must of necessity be nonbelievers."

"Then why do you choose to affiliate yourself with something that lacks sense, logic, and justice?"

"Faith," said Esteban. "I believe that God is good. It makes my life easier."

"But how can you believe God is good, when the world all around you is brimming with unnecessary suffering, that makes your very statement a lie?"

"Faith," repeated Esteban dreamily.

"I can't argue with that," said Julio. "I don't mean to imply that you are right, only that I can't argue with what you say."

But Julio, who was born with intelligence instead of faith, couldn't accept that it was all right for the God-fearing American ball players to whore, and drink and gamble in their free time, while their families languished at home, while it was unacceptable for him to bring his true love to America to live with him.

He remembered a discussion he had had with a thick-boned, brawny outfielder.

"What are you, some kind of heathen?" the man had said, parroting the manager, when Julio mentioned his longing to hold Quita in his arms, after he had managed to get a phone call through to Courteguay and found out that Quita was pregnant.

"So, when are you gettin' married?" the outfielder had said.

"We have no plans to marry," said Julio. "I will stay with Quita forever. While you ... how many times have you been married?'

"Four times," said the outfielder, "and every last one sanctified by the Lord. I should introduce you to the Rev. Queeg. He's pastor of the One True Church of God's Redemption and Reaffirmation in my home town of Dothan, Alabama. Five minutes alone with you and Rev. Queeg would have you givin' up your godless ways and on your knees praying to the Lord for forgiveness."

"I think not," said Julio. "When do you pray for forgiveness? It seems to me you manage to break most of the tenets of your religion every day."

"Hell," said the outfielder, "God's a good ole boy. Long as you ain't a heathen He ain't about to give you any trouble. Hell, God knows a man can't go short for but a day or two without it doin' him serious physical damage. Nobody's goin' to fault a man for keepin' the temple of his body in first class physical condition."

The outfielder smiled piously, showing that he actually believed everything he had just said.

FORTY-FOUR
THE GRINGO JOURNALIST

Shortly after Julio left for the United States and the new baseball season the political stability that Courteguay had enjoyed for several years came to an end. The Old Dictator, who had been in power so many years people had forgotten his name, was overthrown by the head of his Secret Police, a Dr. Lucius Noir. The Old Dictator's name and his official title El Presidente had become synonymous. Some history books explained that he had been born Juan Barrios, become Col. Barrios, then General Barrios, and finally El Presidente.

To Courteguay as well as the outside world, Dr. Noir was an unknown quantity. The international press barely noticed or acknowledged that the government in Courteguay had changed. Courteguay was poor and not strategically located militarily. The Old Dictator had been in power long enough that Courteguay had become one of the most stable unstable minor nations in the world. But the press barely commented on that either.

In a statement issued on Courteguayan radio, which began as a 500 watt station in San Barnabas (after someone had pointed out that there were perhaps one thousand radios in Courteguay, and

American intelligence couldn't pick up such low wattage, the CIA in the guise of foreign aid increased the wattage to 2,000 so they could freely monitor every word) Dr. Noir said that, "El Presidente grew tired of the burden of leadership and called upon me, as his closest advisor, to form a new government, which, after due deliberation, I have agreed to do.

"The transfer of power has been accomplished peacefully. El Presidente, who served Courteguay with wisdom and distinction, now plans to spend his declining years in retirement on his country plantation.

"El Presidente has asked me to convey his gratitude to the members of the International Press, and to the people of Courteguay, and asks that you wish him well in his retirement."

Dr. Noir was dressed in enamel-white military garb accentuated by an ice-blue, diagonal sash, and many medals. He also wore a white surgical mask, which made his speech difficult to understand.

"The mask," an aid in equally beautiful costume explained, "is necessary because Dr. Noir suffers from chronic asthma, and has, at last count, forty-seven allergies. He is, unfortunately, severely allergic to all eleven national flowers of Courteguay: bougainvillea, hibiscus, red and white plumeria, bird of paradise, orchids, poinsettias, Anthurium, lehua, vanda orchids, and ginger. The very touch of these flowers makes welts rise on Dr. Noir's skin as if he has been scalded."

The International Press was not very interested in the new President's medical problems, though the fact that he had once attended chiropractic college in America did raise a few eyebrows. But that was about all. The International Press Corps in Courteguay were made up of reporters with serious personal and attitude problems, ones who had perhaps attempted to organize unions, or had refused to take early retirement when requested, or had an inordinate fondness for alcohol and drugs that went beyond the usual.

Noting the round, white mask which covered Dr. Noir's face from chin to just below his eyes, a Syrian correspondent suggested to an Israeli reporter that perhaps the good doctor was wearing a yarmulke on the wrong portion of his anatomy. They were separated by a three-hundred pound reporter from Gambia who had once played tackle for Notre Dame.

The old dictator had indeed been in failing health. His last year in power he did away with the Republic Day Parade, when the military marched smartly through San Barnabas, machetes flashing in the sun, to Bougainvillea Square in front of the Presidential Palace, where El Presidente traditionally delivered a rousing speech praising the workers, freedom, baseball, motherhood, sugarcane, and mangos, while condemning the guerrillas in the hills, Haiti, capitalism, and, depending on how much military equipment had or had not been received in the last year, the United States.

WELL INTO HIS FINAL TERM of office El Presidente married the woman he had lived with for twenty-seven years, and after the marriage remained more and more in the palace with his wife, who now wore housecoats and let her greying hair hang loose, quite unlike the days when he was guerrilla leader and she stood by his side dressed in army fatigues, a bandoleer's hat at a rakish angle, ammunition belts forming a heavy cross on her chest.

El Presidente ate custards and worried about his bowels, the loyalty of his staff, and his personal safety. He distrusted his generals and had heard rumors of the ambitions of Dr. Noir, the American-educated colonel who wheezed like a cold wind whenever he breathed.

"Colonel Noir will at least not be able to sneak up on me and murder me in my sleep," the Old Dictator joked.

DR. NOIR DID NOT SNEAK into the Old Dictator's bed chamber himself. He spotted a fourteen-year-old boy in the palace who had a certain gleam in his eye—the same gleam Dr. Noir saw when he stared into the mirror of a morning. The boy's job was to feed the cockatoos, parrots, and birds of paradise and clean their cages.

He had the boy brought to his office in the palace annex.

"If you had three wishes, what would they be?" Dr. Noir demanded. "Quickly, now, I will give you only one minute to answer."

The boy, who had a stocky body with bow legs, and a wide, stupid face the shape of a pail bottom, blurted the first things that came to his mind.

"A washing machine for my mother; a green felt hat; a silver portable radio this big," and he spread his stubby hands to indicate a length of thirty inches or so.

"Be here tomorrow night at 10:00 P.M.," said Dr. Noir. "Speak to no one of this, not even your mother. If you do I'll have you both killed." The boy stood stupidly in front of Dr. Noir, but his eyes glowed.

"Are you right or left handed?" asked Dr. Noir.

"Right," the boy stuttered, after considering the question for several seconds.

Moving from behind his desk Dr. Noir seized the boy's left hand and with one deft motion, first dislocated, then fractured the boy's left little finger.

The boy screamed in pain.

"If you speak even one word of our meeting I will personally treat every joint in your body the same way," hissed Dr. Noir. "Now get out!"

THE BOY APPEARED AS SCHEDULED the next evening. A marvelous snow-white washer sat in front of Dr. Noir's desk; it was round and chubby as a baker, and its chrome parts sparkled under a white light bulb Dr. Noir had had installed specifically for this occasion.

The hat, furry as a caterpillar, and parrot-green in color, rested on the machine lid.

The radio, cheap and garish, gleamed brighter than any thirty pieces of silver. Dr. Noir turned the radio on. It brought in a Miami station playing something that sounded like garbage can lids being slammed together, while in the background a chorus of demons wailed in everlasting pain.

The boy stared rapturously at the items.

He reached out to touch them.

"No!" shouted Dr. Noir, then coughed furiously because of the sudden expulsion of air.

"You must earn these gifts," he said.

"I will do anything," said the boy.

"I know," rasped Dr. Noir, smiling, his cheeks expanding on either side of his mask. He reached under his desk and produced a machete, the blade thin and blue as a razor, sharpened until it could cut a sheet of paper as it floated mid-air, silently, as if the paper were part of the air itself.

"You know where El Presidente and his wife sleep?"

The boy grew pale, but nodded, his eyes enlarging.

"Two swings of your weapon will do it. Then all this is yours," and he smiled again, one of the few times Dr. Noir had smiled twice in one day, the white orb of his mask seeming to wear an expression of cunning.

Years later a young American movie producer would remember stories he had read of Dr. Noir, and use him as the model of a harsh-breathing villain extraordinaire, in a series of space-adventure movies which made the young American producer's name, and the actor who portrayed him, into household words.

"I can't," the boy stuttered. "I do not need these," and he backed a step away from the gleaming presents.

"You have no choice. You have no reason to be here at the palace tonight. I'll simply call my guards, say you made an attempt on my life with this machete, and they will kill you. But not of course until I amuse myself a little," and he stared at the boy's swollen and bandaged finger.

"After the deed is done," he went on, "go home and rest well. These prizes will be on your doorstep in the morning," and Dr. Noir waved the boy from the room.

The boy picked up the machete. He swung it once, half-heartedly. It made no sound as it sectioned the air.

The boy and Dr. Noir each kept their bargain. The bodies of El Presidente and his wife vanished, the way bodies tend to do in unstable political climates.

The boy, after being unable to eat for a couple of days, and after awakening in the night screaming like a loon on more than one occasion, took pleasure in how his mother adored her washing machine, donned his green felt hat, shouldered his wailing radio, and, in his first full day on the street convinced three girls, none of whom had ever given the hatless, radioless boy a second glance, to have sex with him.

Dr. Noir, after announcing El Presidente's retirement, observed a three-day period of personal mourning for El Presidente, after which he announced his first official edict as new president of the Republic of Courteguay. He banned baseball as a subversive, capitalistic, non-productive pastime, and proclaimed soccer as the National Game of Courteguay.

FORTY-FIVE
THE GRINGO JOURNALIST

Shortly after Dr. Noir seized power in Courteguay, after those in government most loyal to El Presidente, the Old Dictator, had vanished as if they had never existed, after Dr. Noir had promoted each member of his elite group of secret police to lieutenant and given them dazzling uniforms of ebony and white, an emissary was sent to the jungle to deliver a message to General Bravura, the exiled guerilla leader.

> My Dear General: In view of El Presidente's retirement and his relinquishing power to me, I feel that a summit meeting is called for. You were the enemy of El Presidente. If I have acted against you, it was only because as a military man I follow orders without question. I have always admired your courage and your skill as a commander and your brilliant military mind. As disloyal as it may sound I have always felt that Courteguay was in better hands when you were in power than when the country was ruled by El Presidente. I see no reason why we could not iron out an agreement that would allow you a major say in establishing government policy. I foresee making you my closest advisor, and second in command. It only remains to establish what title you would hold, though Vice President of Courteguay sounds well to my ears. I sincerely want to end civil

strife in Courteguay and believe that by meeting we can bring that worthwhile goal to fruition. I suggest that at the earliest possible moment you and your closest advisors come to San Barnabas under a flag of truce, and that we set talks in motion to forever unite our beloved Courteguay under one stable government.

Respectfully,
Dr. Lucius Noir
President of Courteguay

"I DO NOT TRUST HIM," General Bravura said to his followers in the jungle. "I only wish I could be in touch with El Presidente in his retirement, but his country home is surrounded by soldiers who state El Presidente is resting and no longer wishes to be involved in state matters."

"I think we should attempt an assassination," said his second in command. "He has only been in power a few days and cannot possibly know what dangers lie ahead. He will be more vulnerable now than in the future."

"We should at least talk with him," said General Bravura.

On his second week in power Dr. Noir stood on the steps of the presidential palace and watched as three dilapidated Jeeps approached the gates. General Bravura and eleven of his lieutenants and advisors accompanied him. Dr. Noir welcomed them, said that a banquet had been prepared, and led General Bravura and his entourage into the palace.

Once they were in the semicircular foyer of the palace, an armed soldier appeared from behind every marble pillar, rifle at the ready.

"Surrender your weapons, please," said Dr. Noir.

One of General Bravura's lieutenants attempted to draw his side arm and was shot dead. General Bravura was taken through a side door to the sun-bright garden full of blazing bougainvillea growing against the white coral of the walls. General Bravura was handcuffed and forced to stand between two swaths of bougainvillea. A few seconds later he was shot. The remainder of General Bravura's associates were marched to the basement of the palace to a section Dr. Noir liked to refer to as the wound factory.

BECAUSE OF DR. NOIR the baseball fields of Courteguay lay abandoned. In smaller towns or in small parks in the cities, the infield was sodded, home plate and the pitcher's rubber uprooted like large vegetables. All across the nation backstops were scrapped. On the outskirts of San Barnabas was a dump full of a tangle of mesh backstops, deposited at odd angles, rusting, grating eerily in the night wind, sections rubbing together squeaking and creaking as if among them metal rodents clacked and scuttled.

The larger baseball parks, the St. Ann Mother of Mary Stadium and the Jesus Joseph and Mary Celestial Baseball Palace, the Stations of the Cross Ballpark at the north end of the country, and two other major parks were totally off limits, left to decay in silence. Armed guards were placed at each entrance with instructions to shoot intruders first and ask questions later; it became an imprisonable felony to photograph either the stadium or the guards.

The grasses grew tall and wild, cowlicked, seeming to sense their new freedom. Berry vines appeared, delicate and green at first, but soon grew bolder, their spines fiercer, their stocks big and round as fingers. Weeds fought their way up through the shale of the bullpen. Small flowers peered jauntily through cracks in the asphalt in front of the concessions. Birds found sanctuary in the uppermost corners of the grandstand, their nighttime flutter and daytime squawking and squalling became the ballpark's only sounds. Wind pried at the heavy shingles on the roof, and with no one to listen the shingles seemed to give up their grip easily, making flapping sounds in the night like travelers demanding entrance, then spinning crazily downward to lie in among the tangled grasses, or land like kites in the parking lot already inundated with weeds, vines, and flowers, sprinkled like croutons in a salad.

Dr. Noir imported fifty thousand soccer balls from Haiti.

FORTY-SIX
THE WIZARD

A group of boys on a spring day after school headed to a vacant lot where a ball appeared, not a baseball at all, but a tennis ball, worn, hairless and weathered to the color of a mouse. A fence picket became a bat, dandelions were pulled and stacked to use as bases.

The voices of the boys rose on the scented spring breeze, shrill as starlings.

"Stee-rike," a sweet voice shrilled.

"Burn it in there, Ernesto," cried another.

The ball rose in a long arc to the outfield, a dark-skinned boy glided under it, pounded an imaginary glove, caught the ball on the move and fired to home, though there was no runner.

Again the bat met the ball with a resonant thump and the forbidden sounds of baseball echoed over a little corner of Courteguay, until a jeep growled down the street and stopped outside the school fence. Two soldiers leapt from the rear of the jeep, each brandishing a submachine gun.

"Ho!" the leader called. "The ball. Give us the ball."

The boys bolted and ran, scurrying across the vacant lot and the school yard and disappearing into the cherry-colored bougainvillea. The soldiers loped slowly across the yard, joking easily, for they had both played baseball when they were children.

At the edge of the lot, the tallest soldier, not with rancor, but because of boredom, sprayed the bougainvillea with machine gun bullets. The soldiers walked back across the lot. One of them kicked the pile of dandelions that was second base. They climbed in their jeep and drove away, the odor of green grass clinging to their uniforms.

The children crept slowly back to the lot, emerging from the bougainvillea like rabbits, nose first, testing the air. At first they thought that one of their friends was playing a trick on them, that he was lying face down on the edge of the bougainvillea feigning sleep, that bougainvillea blossoms had dropped onto the back of his grey T-shirt.

The boys became serious and silent, exchanging frightened glances. One of them nudged their friend with a toe. One of the death flowers on his back burbled audibly. The boys ran to find some adults. Their dead friend, nine-year-old Trinidad Munoz, became the first baseball martyr.

FORTY-SEVEN
THE GRINGO JOURNALIST

"The deeds of a leader are relatively unimportant. What is important is that he look the part of a leader. Unless he is a thoroughly despicable tyrant or a mewling coward his actual performance matters little so long as he looks the part, appears often enough in public, dresses in a manner appropriate for a person in a position of power, and displays the proper amount of eccentricity, enough to make him remarkable and audacious, without being a zealot or a fanatic," said the Wizard.

"It is quite the opposite in baseball," said Julio. "A Greek god in a diamond-studded uniform who cannot hit or field or pitch is gone in a day. Audacity must be accompanied by talent. Everything must be accompanied by talent. Talent is everything."

"True," said the Wizard. "A sports hero is paid to perform. If he can perform with panache, if he can elicit sympathy, he will become an idol. The same is true for a politician."

"Not true," said Julio. "It is that a politician has more tricks available to him. If he is in a slump he gives the people the spectacle that they crave: a parade, a show of strength, bribing the Olympics to come to his country, something, anything to make the rabble feel good about themselves, though billions of public money are wasted, and the country becomes hugely poorer."

"Being a Wizard is the perfect preparation for leadership. A perfect leader must continually pull coins out of noses and make flowers rain from the sky," said the Wizard.

"A plodding leader may be more capable than a wizard, for a wizard has no illusions. A wizard knows that there are no wizards, that coins come not from amazed noses but from between the wizard's fingers, and that the flowers that rain from the sky were in his pockets first. I agree with you that talent is essential, but ... look at Roger Maris, a great baseball player but a plodder. He lacked panache, and unfair as it was, he has never been given his due, probably never will. The fans and the press long for the perfect combination, genius and eccentricity. Look at The Bird ... Detroit's Mark Fidrych."

"But The Bird is the perfect example," cried Julio. "It doesn't matter how much you talk to the ball, tend the grass, or stalk about the mound, when your fastball is gone so are you."

"Oh, but The Bird, if only I could have worked with him. He was born to be a leader. He should have become a politician for he was already a wizard," the wizard continued.

"Politicians suffer similar fates. Those who do not provide bread and circuses do not fare well. President of the United States Carter was probably the most compassionate, honest, genuinely decent man to be President in a century. But he did not look the part. He did not act aggressive when aggression was called for, he did not supply spectacle when the nation cried out for spectacle.

"Now, Dr. Noir. I must give the Devil his due. On the day Dr. Lucius Noir seized power in Courteguay he decreed that as long as he was dictator all the mirrors in all of Courteguay would reflect only his image.

"Children screamed. Women fainted. Mirrors were a scarce commodity in San Barnabas. A hubcap or a piece of chrome from a wrecking yard often served the purpose. People who had mirrors or make-do mirrors gasped in horror the first full day of Dr. Noir's regime for when they went to brush their teeth, there staring back at them was the dictator of Courteguay. Even the rivers, lakes and ponds carried his reflection, so that even the peasants of the fields when they went for a cool drink or to wash the sweat from their brows in a stream or rain puddle were confronted by a strange man, one many peasants did not know. *Haitian voodoo!* people screamed. The military along the border to Haiti were increased ten fold."

SECTION THREE

THE WOUND FACTORY

"When a book is published, some characters get a life of their own."

—W. P. KINSELLA

FORTY-EIGHT
THE WIZARD

The Gringo Journalist, who would one day win the Pulitzer Prize for his collected writings about Dr. Lucius Noir's time as Dictator of Courteguay, was born in Onamata, Iowa, a somnolent farm town of forty frame buildings located on the banks of the Iowa River, in Johnson County, just south and west of Iowa City. He graduated from journalism school at the University of Iowa, qualified for a four-month internship program sponsored by some of the nation's major newspapers, and was assigned to the *Washington Post*, as the most junior of junior reporters.

The Gringo Journalist had no interest in Courteguay. He had never taken a geography course in university, and, until he was assigned to visit there as part of a tourism promotion sponsored by the new Courteguayan government, he had always thought Courteguay, if he had given it any thought at all, was in Central America.

At the University of Iowa, he had been entertainment editor of *The Daily Iowan*, the university's student newspaper, and during his four years with the paper had written several hundred theater, movie, and book reviews. His fondest hope was to review theater productions in Washington, D.C.

The tourism assignment was refused by several senior reporters because they felt Courteguay was so small and so close to Haiti, at that time controlled by the ruthless Papa Doc Duvalier, that it might be overrun at any moment. There is nothing reporters like better than free trips to exotic foreign lands, but they prefer free trips that don't involve danger or inconvenience, unlike congressmen who are not smart enough to sense danger, hence, years later, the fools who visited the Jim Jones compound in Guyana.

"I don't think they have indoor plumbing in Courteguay," said one reporter who declined the assignment. "In order to eat, you probably have to pick mangos off the ground and wash them yourself, besides haven't they just changed governments again? There are likely to be mortar shells exploding in the streets, and excitable snipers in the palms. Send someone who's feeling suicidal."

Though the Gringo Journalist was not feeling suicidal, he was the lowest of the low; he didn't have the luxury of refusal. He took whatever assignment was thrown his way.

The actual trip to Courteguay turned out to be a disappointment. The Gringo Journalist, and the dozen or so press people on the tour, saw virtually nothing of interest. They were housed at an adequate beachfront hotel, the beach being on Lake Verde, a man-made lake that was filled with trash and smelled putrid. They were taken on tours of downtown San Barnabas, shown the Presidential Palace, from the outside only, taken for a drive through sugarcane fields, shown through an evil-smelling sugar processing plant, given a souvenir bottle of El Presidente Pure Cane Syrup, and taken to a night club featuring a marimba band, limbo dancers and a fire-baton twirler. They were not allowed to go anywhere unescorted.

While the other reporters enjoyed the holiday and the free liquor, the Gringo Journalist was observing everything carefully. He concluded that things were not as tranquil as the ever-smiling Director of Tourism would like them to believe.

The only interesting information he had learned before the excursion came from a senior sports reporter at the *Post*.

"For the size of the place," he said, "they produce a hell of a lot of good baseball players."

The Gringo Journalist asked the Director of Tourism if he might take in a baseball game. He had seen a baseball stadium in downtown San Barnabas, although the tour had passed by it without a word from the tour guide; he had been able to translate the sign in front of it as St. Ann Mother of Mary Stadium.

"I'm afraid that will not be possible," the white-suited Director of Tourism told him, "the baseball season is not in operation at the moment."

The Gringo Journalist noticed too that the Courteguayan coat of arms, which featured crossed baseball bats, one filed to the thinness and sharpness of a sword, had been removed from the crown of the pith helmets of the stoic, white-uniformed palace guards. His questions about the fatigue-clad, submachine-gun-toting soldiers who seemed to always lurk on the edges of the tourist areas went unanswered.

"Leave well enough alone," a colleague told him. "We're on a freebee. Drink the liquor, enjoy the women. Keep your nose clean."

HE HEARD A PERSISTENT RUMOR that a wizard with many names had written a novel in which a certain Dr. Lucius Noir was a character, the incarnation of evil, and that eventually the character had come to life and was now wreaking havoc in Courteguay. When the junket returned to America, while his colleagues wrote puff-pieces for the travel page on Courteguay the Beautiful, the Gringo Journalist begged a senior editor for travel money to investigate Dr. Noir's American school days.

By agreeing to relieve a senior editor of a particularly repugnant feature on an aging movie star's latest marriage, this time to a sixteen-year-old pool boy, the Gringo Journalist was rewarded with a travel voucher and expense money to visit Davenport, Iowa.

He had to change planes three times to get from Washington, D.C. to Davenport, Iowa, but the trip proved to be well worth his while.

The first thing that the Gringo Journalist learned was that Dr. Noir did not graduate from the chiropractic school there.

"He was a difficult and only marginally motivated student," the public relations director of the school said, choosing her words very carefully.

She was able to produce a photograph of Dr. Noir as an undergraduate, his shining black face centered by the slightly convex surgical mask.

"He seemed more interested in perfecting his English than in learning the intricacies of chiropractic treatment," the public relations person went on, fingering Dr. Noir's file, keeping it well on her side of the desk where the Gringo Journalist could not peek at it, even though, as a reporter, he had taught himself to be an expert at reading upside down.

"Exactly how close did he come to graduating?" asked the Gringo Journalist.

"He was only here for two semesters."

"Then he has no right to call himself Dr. Noir?"

"Not insofar as this school is concerned. I imagine that in Courteguay he can call himself anything he wishes."

"How were his grades?"

The public relations person shifted the file closer to her body.

"They were somewhat less than satisfactory," she said.

"I wonder if I might get the names and addresses of some of the students who attended at the same time as Dr. Noir?"

"Since that information is a matter of public record, I see no harm in it. I'll have our alumni center provide you with a list of current addresses."

The Gringo Journalist found that most of his other inquiries drew blanks. Senior staff members were unavailable for interviews, or simply referred him back to the public relations person.

"Well, now, the black boy with the breathing mask," said a retired professor of about seventy, with a fringe of white hair like frosting. The Gringo Journalist had tracked him down at his home.

"Lucius was what he called himself. Always alone. Not many blacks in Davenport. Folks don't know what to make of them. Ordered his hamburgers raw. 'Toast the bread, please,' he'd say real polite like, 'but leave the meat uncooked. Fried meat is very bad for my asthma, please.' He was always polite, kind of bowed when he spoke, but his eyes were bubbling. I never saw so much hate in one man's eyes."

One of Dr. Noir's classmates who had gone on to graduate, was, the Gringo Journalist discovered, employed at the University Hospital in Iowa City, some sixty miles west of Davenport. He bought her lunch in the hospital cafeteria.

"I remember him well," said Patsy Akimoto, "since we were both foreign students we were teamed together on a lab project in our first year. The main thing I discovered was that Lucius was not a humanitarian."

"How do you mean?" asked the Gringo Journalist, dipping into some pale gruel that was supposed to be corn soup.

"I think virtually all of us in chiropractic school were there because we wanted to help people, use our knowledge to relieve pain. Some of us wanted to make more money than others, but regardless, to be in medicine one has to have certain humanitarian instincts.

"Lucius Noir was there because he wanted to learn to hurt and cripple people. He told me he couldn't wait to get back to his homeland and start dislocating joints and snapping vertebrae."

"He was a rolling ball of butcher knives," said a student who had known him slightly, "with a neck size that would qualify him for the Guinness Book of Records. He was smart when he wanted to be. Told me he'd read his file in the registrar's office and that his IQ was 131, which put him in the top two percent of the world population. But he was the meanest son of a bitch I've ever known.

"When he wanted something nothing could stop him from getting it, but if he didn't care he'd fail a course without a second thought. There is a story I heard from a Haitian who was a patient here for a few days, a story of Lucius Noir entering some kind of footrace, maybe in the Courteguayan military, a race it was very important for him to win. They say he was losing by a few strides, but at the last second he pulled a razor-sharp knife, or a small machete and sliced off the tip of his left little finger and tossed it across the finish line. After a lot of debate he was declared the winner."

The Gringo Journalist imparted what he had learned in an article titled "The American Education of Dr. Noir." The article earned him an audience with an associate editor, who stated that the Gringo Journalist would be hired on a full time basis when his internship was completed. The associate editor also presented the Gringo Journalist with an American Express card in the name of the newspaper, and gave him ninety days to continue his research into the life and times of Dr. Lucius Noir.

FORTY-NINE

AN EXCERPT FROM A CHAPTER OF A NOVEL WRITTEN BY THE WIZARD

"Anyone can write a novel," said the Wizard. "Especially me. If I can turn myself into a dewdrop, see the world through the eyes of a yellow-tufted cockatoo, inhabit a bullet as it speeds death toward enemy lines, why should I not be able to tell a simple story?"

The excerpt:

> In a fetid alley in Port-au-Prince a wild-haired whore, smelling of sweat, cheap perfume and rum, locked her legs about the huge longshoreman who clasped her buttocks in his great hands and thrust himself into her. The longshoreman had a head big as a pumpkin, and a machete scar from eye to chin on his left side. The whore's eyes glinted like broken glass in the moonlit alley.
>
> When he was satisfied, the longshoreman, who wore a permanent and ferocious scowl, pushed the whore against the wall, ripped off her flimsy top and reclaimed the small fee she had charged for her services. When she shrilled curses at him, he slapped her hard, leaving her sitting dazedly in the filth of the alley. The longshoreman lumbered drunkenly away.

An appropriate time later the whore, Regalia Noir, gave birth in a charity ward to a baby boy she named Lucius. She didn't want the baby, but it was her lot in life. She stared down at the baby's stolid, frying pan face. She saw nothing there; she no longer remembered the longshoreman. Worse things had happened to her since she became pregnant. The baby's black pupils stared up at her, hatred boiling like eels in those wounded eyes.

MEANWHILE, IN A FETID ALLEY in Port-au-Prince, a wild-haired whore smelling of sweat, cheap perfume and....

FIFTY
THE GRINGO JOURNALIST

In a story done by *60 Minutes* on Dr. Noir, the opening lines spoken by correspondent Ed Bradley were, "Many people surmise that it would take a fiction writer to create a character like Dr. Lucius Noir, Dictator of Courteguay, so strange is his story."

What Ed Bradley didn't know, and *60 Minutes* didn't find out, was that Dr. Noir was indeed created by a fiction writer. That writer, using the name Jorge Blanco, had submitted a manuscript to a well-known Spanish publisher in Florida. The publisher rejected the manuscript, praising the quality of the writing but stating that the idea of such an ugly, deformed, evil villain, a man who, trained as a chiropractor, used his talent to torture and maim his enemies, would not be accepted by readers. They said that Mr. Blanco had a wild and violent imagination, as well as genuine talent as a storyteller, and that they would be happy to look at any future novels he might care to submit.

FIFTY-ONE
MILAN GARZA

It is very quiet here inside my crystal-domed coffin. Not that I cannot move about freely. Although I am very dead it is not as terrible as it ought to be. I spend a great deal of my day in the gardens of the Hall of Baseball Immortals. The eleven national flowers of Courteguay bloom in abundance. Of course no one can see me. I too always assumed, when I was alive, that while the dead are buried in coffins, or stuffed in drawers at mausoleums, or burned to a crisp like the Sunday roast, that their essence does not move about at will.

On the flagstone patio, I sit across the table from the Director of the Museum while he enjoys his morning coffee. I would like coffee too, but the essence of me can do little more than inhale the beautiful fumes. I always drank my coffee black. I hate to see the Director stir three spoons of sugar into perfectly flavorful coffee. I often tip his hand, sending a spoonful of sugar into his saucer or across the table. This has happened often enough that the Director thinks he is developing a weakness in his right hand. Often, as he is about to take a drink, my will pushes against his elbow and coffee spills down his chin splattering onto his expensive suit and camellia-white shirt.

There are barriers, like electric fields that keep me from exiting the Hall of Baseball Immortals. I cannot get to my enemy, Dr. Noir. I cannot even do much to him when he visits the Hall, as he does on ceremonial occasions. I can tell that in his heart he hates baseball, though he mouths platitudes, smiles his oil slick smile, as some anniversary is celebrated that has brought American media to Courteguay, perhaps someone new inducted for their exploits on the field.

Once, as he was cutting a crimson ribbon to inaugurate a new addition to the Hall, I tried to influence the cutting of the ribbon, hoped to make him amputate a finger or two, or at least wound himself. But his bulk was like iron, my pressure on his elbow went unacknowledged, even if it was felt, which I believe it was, for he glanced at the arm that was experiencing a life of its own, frowned, stiffened his arm with resolve and went on with the dedication.

FIFTY-TWO
QUITA GARZA

"I want to see my father's grave," Quita said one evening. "Until now I have been unable to afford travel to the capital, or admission to the Courteguayan Hall of Baseball Immortals, where, it is said, lie the taxidermied bodies of many baseball heroes. But with the money Julio sends me I cannot only afford admission but bus fare to San Barnabas and a new dress." She tossed her wild hair back from her face, and smiled at Fernandella, daring her to oppose the plan.

Quita's memories of Milan Garza were vague, she had trouble distinguishing her actual memories from events she had been told about. She recalled a large, lovable stranger who took her by the hands and swung her in ever widening circles in the magnificent garden behind their many-pillared home. In those childhood days Milan Garza had been a baseball superstar in America, revered like a god in Courteguay, wealthy beyond imagination. But had that giant of a man who disappeared for months at a time been the same man who had cuddled her in his arms and played dolls with her in that same riotously beautiful garden, pouring tea for them, eating pretend cookies, and helping her tuck her dolls in for an afternoon nap?

Why had Milan Garza, one of the richest men in Courteguay, soon after his baseball career ended, decided to oppose Dr. Lucius Noir for the Presidency for Life and even lobbied for and promised the people democratic elections? Her father had used his great wealth to start his own political party. He called it the Party of God and Baseball and of course received the immediate blessing of the church, however valueless it might be, for what else could they do? And since baseball was the passion of Courteguay, who could vote against baseball?

"I will show you your grandfather," said Quita to the gentle swelling of her belly. She had told Julio in her last letter, "I am slowly filling with our son. He was conceived among the butterflies, he will be born the day you arrive home from the baseball wars, he will wait for you."

Julio was overjoyed, though he told no one but Esteban of his joy. As the father of a son he would truly be a man. Fathering a son was more important to Julio than all the shutouts pitched in the history of baseball.

ON A SUNNY MORNING, after a breakfast of guava juice, grits and pheasant breast with mango sauce, Quita set out for the capital. She wore white sandals, her new sun-yellow frock patterned with white daisies, and carried a reed basket-purse bright as a tropical bird. Quita crammed herself into the grumbling bus that spewed thick black fumes. There were boxes and crates of live goats and chickens tied to the roof. The bus was so crowded that people hung from the windows like decorations. A small, terrified dog nuzzled Quita's ankle. At the next stop a dozen more people forced their way inside, a few more were pulled in via the windows, the black fumes followed the passengers, making the air thick and stifling.

In the city Quita asked directions to the Hall of Baseball Immortals and after a short walk found herself in front of a half-moon-shaped building with a fountain in front and in the fountain a statue of a baseball player swinging a handful of bats. Water poured out of the business end of each bat, out of the eyes, ears, mouth and nose of the baseball player. There was a ten guilermo admission charge, which Quita was proud to be able to afford.

"I am the daughter of Milan Garza. I have come to see my father," she told the sleepily insolent clerk who ignored her and went back to dozing, after pushing a brightly colored ticket at her.

But as soon as Quita had entered the quiet, air-conditioned display area, the clerk picked up her telephone and pressed a single digit that had been circled in red on the face of the phone. When it was answered, she spoke the words, "Quita Garza," into the mouthpiece and hung up, her sleepy expression gone, her black eyes now bright with greed.

The inside of the Hall of Baseball Immortals was an open expanse, full of glass cases displaying memorabilia, the walls lined with photographs. In the cases were autographed baseballs, old uniforms, baseball cleats, stories from the world press on the exploits of Courteguayan players. There were also some unusual items. In a glass bottle was the poisonous insect that had bitten the middle finger of Cedeno Crispo's pitching hand, eventually causing the finger to be amputated at the first joint, the amputated finger allowing Crispo to put a peculiar spin on the ball, turning him from an average minor league player to a two-time twenty-game winner for the Philadelphia Phillies. Beside the insect in another jar was a small black thing resting on a piece of cream-colored velvet that purported to be the amputated piece of finger. Quita shuddered.

In a nearby alcove Quita found an enclosed statue of a baseball player, a batter in full swing, a man she recognized from childhood as her father's occasional teammate Javier Porto de Legre, a utility infielder for a few seasons with a number of teams, mainly at the Triple A level.

Sixty feet six inches away was, also enclosed in clear glass, Cedeno Crispo himself, who, having delivered the ball, was falling toward first base as he was famous for doing. Quita walked up to the case and stared at Crispo's pitching hand, the shortened middle finger rounded and nail-less as a bread stick.

At the center of the half-moon-shaped display area Quita saw a sign over an alcove that read Milan Garza, National Hero. There was a steady stream of people viewing the contents of the Hall of Baseball Immortals. As Quita headed toward the alcove, two dozen children—first or second graders, all boys—and their teacher passed her, the children two by two holding hands, chattering in excitement.

She understood that each time Dr. Noir had seized power in Courteguay, though he had disbanded the baseball leagues and named soccer Courteguay's national sport, he did not close, or worse yet, destroy the Hall of Baseball Immortals. It was said that even his strongest supporters, his lieutenants in the Secret Police, being Courteguayan through and through, refused to even consider closing the Hall. They could stand having the baseball leagues banned, for a ban meant very little to Courteguayans, used to political repression regardless of who was in power. The ban simply meant that Jesus, Joseph and Mary Celestial Baseball Palace would be dark for a few years until the reins of power changed hands again.

The baseball games would continue surreptitiously. The baseball stars in the United States, like the Pimental Brothers, would keep their noses out of politics in Courteguay and concentrate on playing baseball, perhaps doing a commercial on American television promoting Courteguayan mangos, guava and passion fruit, where Julio and Esteban would each be shown drinking a large glass of colorful liquid and smiling wickedly at the camera, while beautiful girls pulled at the sleeves of their baseball uniforms, giving the young men of America the impression that if they drank whatever Julio and Esteban were drinking they too would have beautiful girls tugging at their sleeves.

The walls of the alcove were lined with photographs of Milan Garza in his heyday. His white teeth glittered in the sun and his smile was like a bank of floodlights. Quita gasped as she recognized herself in one of the photographs; she sat on Milan Garza's knee, her brothers huddled like small dogs at her father's feet, and he had a sturdy bronzed arm around the shoulder of his smiling wife, Phyllicia. Only happy photographs adorned the walls. There were no photographs of the family in poverty after the state, the state being Dr. Noir, confiscated every asset of Milan Garza. There were no photographs of her father sick with drink and humiliation, forced to engage in, or at least condone the vilest of acts in order to feed his family.

Quita stood in front of the coffin for a long time. It was made of burled oak with Milan Garza's head and shoulders visible under a crystal dome. She stared at the square jaw, the deep-set eyes, the furrow between his brows, the sleek black hair combed upward in the glamorous pompadour that was his trademark. Even in death Milan Garza looked as if he were troubled, puzzled by his sudden and horrific fall from grace. Quita wondered how he had died. There were stories, rumors: a suicide, a firing squad, drink or drugs, shot in the back while trying to escape from Dr. Noir, or Dr. Noir's secret police.

The last of the group of hand-holding children moved along to another attraction. While they were gawking, their teacher delivering a soliloquy on the greatness of Milan Garza, Quita stood behind the coffin, head bowed, tears streaming down her cheeks while the small boys stood at attention and sang the National Anthem of Courteguay, their little caps in their hands, their shrill voices like birds chirping.

Now, Quita stared around, eyes darting, she felt sneaky, as if she was about to shoplift something. Her heart pounded. She felt around the edge of the coffin until she encountered some metal fittings. She checked the alcove again to be certain she was alone, then knelt down and looked at the valves, there were several, one read Pressure, another Air, another had only the number twelve on it. She decided on the one reading Pressure. She wondered if Milan Garza might disintegrate if the coffin was opened. The thought of her father turning to dust before her eyes was not unpleasant, it would be a release for both of them. Milan Garza could go back to being happy in his photographs, his troubled death mask erased.

Quita turned the valve. There was a noticeable whistling and hissing of air as the seal of the coffin relaxed. She stared anxiously at Milan Garza's face waiting for something to happen. The corpse remained intact, the only difference Quita noted was an acrid chemical odor. She pried at the crystal dome, it loosened and she turned it back. She intended to examine the body for clues as to how her father had died. Quita stared around nervously, there was a guard at the entrance of the Hall but this alcove was totally out of his view. There was a momentary dearth of museumgoers. She lifted the oak lid that covered the rest of the body and the seal slowly parted. She gasped in horror. Her father was dressed in his Baltimore Orioles home team uniform, his arms at his sides. Nothing extended beyond the cuffs of his uniform, above or below. He had no hands or feet.

His glove and a pair of cleats were placed carefully at the foot of the coffin. What had happened? Many strange and horrific things went on in Courteguay. Had her father's hands and feet been sold as medicine, fetishes, charms? Had they been stolen after death or had their loss been a cause of death?

What would she do now? Quita heard footsteps and quickly closed the lids of the coffin. She would wait out a few more visitors then unbutton her father's uniform searching for wounds.

The crisp sound of boots on the marble floor drew closer. She felt the alcove darken. There was a hissing sound and she thought it was coming from the coffin but instead it was the breathing of the person who followed his shadow toward Quita and the coffin. She instantly recognized Dr. Lucius Noir.

The corpulent Dr. Noir bedecked in a blazing white uniform with an ice-blue sash and a chestful of decorations including Knight Commander of the Blue Camellia, the Order of Bougainvillea which spread like a bloodstain over his heart, and the Golden Order of Courteguay, a medal Dr. Noir created exclusively for himself, which consisted of several ounces of pure gold inset with rubies and emeralds. Dr. Noir wore a smart vizored military hat with gold braid and epaulets on his shoulders the size of giant hairbrushes. His cheeks were like black, pockmarked grapefruit halves, so black they might have been polished. A round surgical mask, white as an angel, covered his nose, hiding the huge, slug-like lips Quita knew well from photographs.

"Miss Garza, it is a pleasure to have you visit the Hall of Baseball Immortals," said Dr. Noir, his voice filtered, deep and threatening, as if it were coming from a distorted echo chamber.

"Dr. Noir," Quita said in a whisper. She involuntarily bowed slightly in front of the imposing presence.

"You look surprised. I often drop by to welcome illustrious visitors to the Hall of Baseball Immortals. You father is the greatest baseball player ever to come out of Courteguay."

Quita considered lashing out at Dr. Noir, screaming into his asthmatic face all the invective stored in her heart, but she sensed, in spite of his soft words, the presence of danger like a shark in shallow water.

"I have always wanted to see my father's final resting place."

"And now you have. However, it is unfortunate that you chose to tamper with public property, which, in the strictest of terms is what your father's remains are." Dr. Noir pointed to a tiny object high in a corner of the alcove. "You were filmed vandalizing public property." Dr. Noir's pockmarked cheeks rose like eyebrows as he attempted a smile behind the convex mast, his breath rattling in his chest like dominoes.

"Where are my father's hands and feet?" Quita shouted, staring into the malevolent eyes of Dr. Noir.

Dr. Noir was unfazed by the bitterness in her voice. He smiled again.

"You were very young at the time, you may or may not recall that your father, national sports hero that he was, chose to espouse a very unpopular political position. Now in politics, which I doubt that you understand, particularly in a volatile political climate which is always the case in Courteguay, it is the policy to reward one's friends and punish one's enemies. Because of his status as national hero, I was very reluctant to punish your father. Unfortunately, he left me no other choice."

"I don't care about politics. What happened to my father's hands and feet?" Dr. Noir breathed deeply through his porcelain-white mask; he shuddered, coughed, gasped, raised an ebony hand to his throat.

"What have you done?" he rasped, his asthma activated by the gases escaped from the coffin.

"I only wanted to see my father."

"Guards! Guards!" cried Dr. Noir. "Vandalism!"

He seized Quita by a thin arm. Within seconds museum security arrived. Quita was whisked away to a behind the scenes office where she was interrogated, first by museum security, then by military police.

The museum closed. Quita missed the last bus back to San Cristobel. She and her new dress began to wilt. She was denied food, water, and the use of a bathroom.

The military police questioned her about things she had not only never heard of but never even suspected, subversive organizations, guerrilla alliances supposedly set on overthrowing Dr. Noir. They wanted to know about the activities of a few survivors from General Bravura's followers who might be recruiting in San Cristobel, might be receiving clandestine aid from foreign powers, from traitors like the baseball twins, Julio and Esteban Pimental.

Quita's head swam. When she began to doze she was awakened by a sharp slap to her right cheek.

"A terrorist," said one interrogator to another. She was slapped again. "If you confess and name your conspirators Dr. Noir may display mercy. You may be imprisoned for life but be allowed to live."

"I only came to San Barnabas to see the corpse of my father in the Hall of Baseball immortals."

The interrogator struck her again.

The door opened and Dr. Noir entered. He was in a fresh uniform, his breath wailing like a north wind. The clock on the office wall said 3:00 A.M.

"I will take charge of the prisoner," said Dr. Noir, placing a large, cold hand on Quita's shoulder.

"I want to go home," Quita whispered, her bravado extinguished.

Dr. Noir's breath rattled.

"We have done all that we can here. Perhaps a practical demonstration," he said, snapping his fingers. Two lieutenants appeared, gliding into the room behind Dr. Noir, boots glinting, guns drawn.

"No," cried Quita as Dr. Noir seized her. But Dr. Noir paid no attention.

"Please come with me, Miss Garza." Dr. Noir remained firm but calm, though his grip bruised Quita's arm.

Having no choice, Quita, feeling very small, followed along behind the labored breathing of Dr. Noir, while the guards, guns still drawn, walked behind her, pushing the cold snubs of their guns into her back every few steps.

At the curb was the longest limousine Quita had ever seen. It was a creamy white with painted bougainvillea blossoms flowing down both sides and across the roof. The Courteguayan coat of arms was on the door. One of the guards opened the door for Quita.

"After you, Miss Garza," said Dr. Noir.

Inside, the limo was like a small house. Dr. Noir had a desk and chair, there was a bar, a television, though it didn't appear to work, the screen covered in gray snow. One guard drove while the other occupied a small space at the rear of the limousine. He peered through a sliding window that when closed would be opaque glass, his gun still trained on Quita's chest. Dr. Noir took a Coca-Cola from the bar refrigerator. Quita's mouth watered.

Dr. Noir, his breathing less labored in the cool car interior, snapped the cap off the bottle with his fingers, slipped his surgical mask aside and drank deeply. He noted Quita's amazement at his feat of strength, though if he noticed her thirst he ignored it.

"A little something I learned while developing my medical skills in the United States," Dr. Noir said, nodding toward the Coca-Cola cap that lay on the carpeted floor of the limousine, displaying his large hands with their short, powerful fingers.

Dr. Noir glowered at Quita, eyes boiling above the mask.

"I have my own ways of dealing with terrorists," Dr. Noir rumbled during the brief ride. "I should have known that anyone associated with someone as power-mad as Milan Garza would be trouble."

When they arrived at the Presidential palace, he marched Quita in the side door near the bullet-gouged wall where General Bravura and many others had died, and down marble stairs, long hallways, and more stairs until he unlocked a wide wooden door and, pushing Quita ahead of him, entered a vast mostly open area.

The smell was unbearable. Quita gasped as her eyes became accustomed to the dim light. The large gymnasium-like room was full of cubicles and unfamiliar apparatus. There were barred cells along one wall, some occupied, some empty. There was an eerie whining in the air, which after a moment Quita recognized as keening, moaning, the sounds of men and women in great pain.

"This is where we deal with terrorists," said Dr. Noir. "You'll forgive the unpleasant odor, such inconveniences are sometimes unavoidable. Perhaps a brief tour of the wound factory." He paused, allowing Quita to assimilate what he had said. "It is really a medical facility where we study the effects of certain stresses and traumas on the human body so that we may better understand how such misfortunes may be treated for the greater good.

"The odor that assails our senses is of cooked flesh. Does that shock you, Miss Garza? Come here, don't be afraid, the oven is quite empty now, though there is still some residue to be cleared away. See, what we have here is a 4'×6' oven, quite large enough to hold a patient. What we do is observe the patient, studying his reactions to see how those reactions may advance medical science. For instance, a patient is placed in the oven and the temperature turned rather low, say 110 degrees. The patient is given two, three, sometimes as many as four small pieces of non-heat-conducting material, somewhat like coasters. It is very interesting to see how imaginatively the patient uses the tools given him in order to protect various parts of his body from the heat, and of course, what parts he chooses to protect, and how those perspectives change as the temperature rises.

"I wouldn't want you to get the wrong idea. We don't cook up our prisoners like so many pigs on a spit. The study will often go on for days, weeks even, if the subject is imaginative enough.

"Now, over here we have a test of endurance."

Quita saw a board like a teeter-totter, with the subject strapped tightly to the board which, when at its lowest, submerged the subject's head beneath water.

"The test is quite simple," said Dr. Noir. "The subject must learn to be submerged for one minute. Not difficult at all. He is then withdrawn from the water for one minute, then submerged again, and so on. The study becomes interesting sometime during the second day when the subject must, if he is to continue living, teach himself to sleep during the minute his head is not under water. We've had some very interesting results, one subject was very adept at catnaps and lasted nearly two weeks. Others opted for suicide in as little as a few hours."

Quita gasped.

"Suicide is always an option here, Miss Garza, an option which saves the government, and ultimately the taxpayers huge sums of money. In all the jails in Courteguay every prisoner has a suicide capsule available at all times. Here, while I think of it."

He reached inside his tunic and produced a small tin box, he slid the lid back and extracted a blue capsule. He held it out to Quita.

"Take it, Miss Garza. Put it in the pocket of your dress. I'm sure you'll be most co-operative with us, but if you should choose not to, that little pill may prove to be a blessing."

He pulled Quita to another part of the room.

"We have other studies. The gentleman over here was a spy. I'm sure you agree with me, Miss Garza, that a spy deserves no mercy. You don't have to look at him, Miss Garza, though he can't help looking at you, for you see his eyelids have been removed. Mercifully there is a towel over his midsection though I see a few splotches of blood have oozed through. Each day he is forced to watch while certain surgeries are performed on his body and his, to be delicate, private parts."

"Do you ever show mercy to anyone?" Quita asked. The room seemed to be tilted slightly, rotating.

"It depends on the crime, Miss Garza. Over here we are experimenting with new kinds of scalpels, notice how our subject is held to the wall entirely by a series of stilettos so slim and sharp that they hardly draw blood when passed through the subject's appendages. To answer your question we show great mercy to minor transgressors, thieves, grifters, prostitutes. I often treat them myself, giving them a thorough physical examination, often painful enough to change their outlook toward society, but not damaging them enough that they cannot become useful members of that same society.

"To the right is another of our studies."

Quita saw a naked man on his back on the polished hardwood floor, his right leg seemingly disappearing into the side of a gleaming deep freeze, which had a slot a few inches wide cut in its side. Insulation had been packed about the leg at the point where it was inserted into the freezer.

Quita's knees felt weak.

"I'm told the subject was very noisy for the first few hours. You see the inside of the freezer is –40 degrees, but the leg now appears to be well anesthetized."

The prisoner, his hands cuffed behind him, appeared to be unconscious, but as they approached one pain-glazed eye stared up at them.

Dr. Noir opened the lid of the freezer and a cloud of frosty air escaped.

"Ah," sighed Dr. Noir, staring at Quita's horror-stricken face. "It is nothing really. You'll notice that most prisoners in this study volunteer for their continuing treatment. While the first installation may have to be accompanied by a certain amount of force, after that first treatment, when the afflicted extremity begins to thaw, why the patient experiences so much discomfort that they wish to return to their therapy, often begging to do so. Usually we manage to accommodate them. However, if they have been particularly unappreciative of our hospitality they may be left in the general population.

"Come here and look at a foot that has been frozen at –40 degrees, for what?" He nodded toward the soldier guarding the freezer, "six hours?"

The soldier nodded.

Quita held back.

Dr. Noir forced her to peer into the freezer. He reached in and, seizing something, flicked his arm and wrist in a deft movement. Quita screamed. Dr. Noir held up a toe for her inspection. The insentient man on the ground did not react. Quita fainted. She awoke where she had fallen. It was difficult to guess how much time had passed. She felt weak. She had bruised her face when she fell; her left eye was badly swollen.

"Now that you've toured our medical facilities, Miss Garza," Dr. Noir began as soon as he saw she was conscious, "I assume you would prefer not to be involved in any of the situations you've encountered. Therefore, while you were indisposed I had some papers drawn up."

He helped Quita to her feet.

"The confession is straightforward. You admit to an act of terrorism at the Hall of Baseball Immortals, as well as membership in an organization with plans to overthrow my government. I will personally recommend leniency: life in prison rather than death, and your beautiful body left intact." He paused.

"Well, not entirely intact."

As Quita shrank away he placed his hand on her slightly distended belly.

"I will take care of that little problem myself. As soon as you've signed the papers."

"Never," said Quita, her voice stronger than either of them would have thought possible.

"You are very brave now," Dr. Noir said, stretching her cuffed hands above her head. "I'm afraid you have no choice but to co-operate."

He fastened her handcuffs over a peg in a round wooden pole. Her toes just touched the floor. At his signal a soldier approached carrying a stout black leather belt, which gleamed from recently being oiled.

"I would prefer not to do this, Miss Garza. However, in a few hours when I ask what you will do to have the whipping stop, you will reply, 'Anything.' I know this from experience. In such a confrontation as this, the whip always wins."

Dr. Noir's cheeks bulged on each side of his mask.

"Never," whispered Quita.

"Just a small reminder," said Dr. Noir, as he prepared to leave. He reached down and forcing Quita to balance on one foot, raised her other one waist high. He balanced her sepia foot on the pink palm of his ebony hand. With one deft movement he dislocated her little toe.

Quita screamed.

He dislocated the toe next to it. Quita screamed louder.

Pointing to the soldier with the whip he said, "I'm sorry not to be able to participate fully myself, but such exercise aggravates my asthma. I'm sure you'll understand, but I have speakers in my office, and in my bedroom. I find the sounds of suffering very soothing. I'll check in frequently to listen to your screams."

HOURS LATER, DR. NOIR'S HEAVY BOOTS clattered on the floor of the wound factory. Quita was still suspended naked. Her body bore evidence of mayhem. She stared at him with wide, horror-filled eyes.

"Now, Miss Garza, assuming that a few hours of education has changed your perspective, let me ask you the same question I asked last night. What will you do in order for me to stop your punishments?"

"Anything! Anything!" gasped Quita.

"Much better. We'll repair to my private operating room and take care of your little problem."

"No," cried Quita.

"Really?" said Dr. Noir. "I thought you had grasped the situation, Miss Garza. What I desire will eventually happen. But we never conduct a procedure without the patient's consent. One more chance. Your answer is still negative?"

"Never," said Quita.

Dr. Noir Motioned to one of his lieutenants, who then spoke into squawky two-way radio. Almost immediately a squad of palace guards marched into the Wound Factory, eight heavyset young men in blazing white uniforms and pith helmets.

Turning to the squad Dr. Noir said, "You gentlemen are on limited furlough, but will of course be on call. Please accompany Miss Garza to the guest suite. I'm sure you will find everything there quite comfortable. I've taken the liberty of having a keg of coconut wine set up for your enjoyment. You will of course take care of all Miss Garza's needs, and she yours." He turned to his lieutenant. "When these gentlemen are quite exhausted, you may send in the second squad of guards, and then the third. I will monitor their progress from my quarters."

THREE DAYS PASSED, then a week.

"I understand Miss Garza remains uncooperative even though she has not been allowed to sleep for several days, the small electrodes attached to sensitive areas see to that," Dr. Noir said to his lieutenant. "Now, you will allow Miss Garza to sleep for three hours. When she wakes refreshed, shower her and bring her to my quarters. And bring with her a set of scalpels, and an adequate selection of pliers."

FIFTY-THREE
THE GRINGO JOURNALIST

There are many rumors about how Julio met his wives, most of them created by the tabloids. To my knowledge Julio has never been married. Oh, he would have married Quita Garza, but in that instance there were many obstacles.

Once at a hotel in Atlanta, deciding that he wanted to be alone, Julio stepped into the bubbling water of the hot tub beside the swimming pool, which smelled of sulphur. As he eased himself down into it, each part of his body that passed beneath the surface of the water disappeared, not just submerged, but disappeared.

A girl, whom he had met in the coffee shop of the hotel, and invited to join him in the hot tub, watched awestruck, not believing her eyes.

"How do you do that?" she finally croaked, when only Julio's head remained above the water.

"It is something my tutor in Courteguay showed me." She, being from Idaho, wherever that was, probably was not ready for the word wizard. Julio smiled his heavy-lidded smile. "Perhaps I will see you tomorrow at the ballpark?"

He ducked his head beneath the surface. All that was left was the odor of his hair tonic and the dumbfounded girl from Idaho.

FIFTY-FOUR
THE GRINGO JOURNALIST

The first complaints came from Moosey Battaglia, a bulbous-nosed Phillies first baseman, struggling, as he would through his long, sixteen-year career, just to stay on the club.

"There are times," Moosey said to a reporter, after a particularly humiliating afternoon where he struck out four times, fouling only one pitch during the whole losing game, "when I don't think that motherfucker throws the ball at all. Lots of times I think he just goes through all the motions but the catcher really has a ball hid in his mitt. The catcher makes the popping sound of ball hitting mitt with his mouth. I mean nobody's that fast."

The reporter paraphrased Moosey in the paper's early edition, leaving out the word motherfucker and the twenty-eight other profanities Moosey had used during the short interview.

Other hitters were quick to jump on the bandwagon.

Charlie Bizarrovitch of the *Sporting News* did a feature story the following week. Moosey Battaglia, whose batting average had slipped to .219, took the story to the Phillies corporate offices.

"What if we was to set up movie cameras, secretly of course, and catch this guy with the goods, or without the goods would be even better."

Moosey guffawed heartily until he saw the sober-faced executives across the table from him.

"Yeah, well, you know what I mean," Moosey said with his usual gift for clarity.

The next time the only Major League Baseball Club in the True South visited Philadelphia, a portion of the press box was boarded up, supposedly under renovation. A second high-speed camera was hidden behind the center field wall, the lens dotting the i in the Strike of Lucky Strike. Both cameras filmed every move Julio and Esteban made all that muggy June afternoon.

Once, in the sixth inning, while Moosey was batting with the bases loaded and two outs, Esteban called time and trotted to the mound. He and Julio talked until the umpire came and reprimanded them. Then Julio threw a pitch, the force of which almost knocked his crouching catcher brother onto his back. Moosey Battaglia swung half-heartedly, then spitting curses as if he had a mouthful of porcupine quills, retreated to the dugout.

The film took forty-eight hours to process, but in the meantime Phillie executives met several times with a jubilant Moosey Battaglia to gloat over what they were certain would appear on the film.

"We got him cold in the sixth," said Moosey. "There was no ball. The catcher threw himself back as if he'd caught something, and made the popping sound with his mouth. There was no ball."

Phillie executives were inclined to agree. There had been four clutch situations in the game and three had ended with strikeouts of a suspicious nature.

The film finally arrived. The executives and Moosey Battaglia gathered in the Phillie projection room. The film was grainy black-and-white.

"Look at the sixth inning first," said Moosey and the other agreed.

They watched each pitch Julio delivered to Esteban, while Moosey was dug in at the plate. The ball, while not exactly visible, was discernible both in Julio's hand as he delivered it, and as a comet-like blur traveling toward the plate.

"Now!" said Moosey as the critical moment approached.

"Slow it down," said a Phillie executive.

The film showed Julio Pimental in full wind-up, his left leg kicking toward the center of the sky, his arm swished forward and....

They replayed the sequences, from both cameras, perhaps forty times, and what they saw each time was the same: Julio striding forward and firing the ball. But it was not a ball, but a pale, delicate flower, almost certainly a camellia. The flower bloomed from Julio's fingers, glided toward the taut batter, slowly and softly as its perfume. Moosey Battaglia swung so hard the men in the room all thought they could hear his vertebrae cracking, though there was no sound with the movie.

"A flower?" said Moosey.

"Somebody's screwed with the film," said the Phillie president.

They watched a replay of Moosey's bat swinging through the camellia, watched as the umpire raised his right hand to indicate the strikeout, replayed again and again the few petals that floated in the air like disturbed feathers, observed Esteban roll a ball back toward the mound.

Their conference lasted deep into the night.

FIFTY-FIVE
THE GRINGO JOURNALIST

By June 1st, many days after it happened, the news of the revolution in Courteguay reached the United States, Julio was 8-1, with 2.12 ERA, and leading the National League in strikeouts.

The UPI dispatch read in part:

> SAN BARNABAS, COURTEGUAY—In an apparently bloodless coup in the early morning hours Tuesday, Dr. Lucius Noir, head of the Courteguayan Secret Police, seized power, ousting the aged dictator of Courteguay, El Presidente. Dr. Noir installed himself in the Presidential Palace and immediately issued a proclamation concerning the retirement of El Presidente. It is rumored that Dr. Noir, a native Haitian who once lived in America as a student while attending a chiropractic college in Davenport, Iowa, will ban baseball and name soccer as Courteguay's national game.

Knowing of Dr. Noir's hatred of baseball and guessing that Quita would not be safe under the new regime, Julio caught the first available flight to the Dominican Republic, not even notifying Esteban of his plans, never mind team management. He sneaked across the border into Courteguay in the dead of night and dressed like everyone else, in a cotton shirt and black slacks, made his way surreptitiously to his mother's mansion, where he discovered his premonition had been correct, but worse than he feared. Quita had been in Dr. Noir's power for nearly two weeks, since a few days after Dr. Noir had seized power again.

Julio dreamed all that night of herons, long, white, sleek as spears, the sky dappled with them. The flapping of wings gentle, but true, like his mother shaking a tablecloth outside her home in San Cristobel.

In the dream he and Esteban were walking on a beach; the herons filled the sky like cloud, the optical illusion became complete when he discerned that he could see black herons flying against a white backdrop, the backdrop too, being heron-shaped. Then they were in the water too, reflected on the sun-dazzled water; herons blue as Wedgwood, gray as fog.

In the morning Julio set out for San Barnabas.

As he was leaving Fernandella clung to his sleeve. "Don't go," she pleaded. "You don't understand what Courteguay has become. A police state. You will be stopped at a check point. You will disappear."

"Courteguay has always been a police state. I am no more afraid of Dr. Noir and his thugs than I was of his predecessor."

"Courage has nothing to do with anything. Hundreds of courageous young men and women are dead. They are the baseball martyrs," she said.

"The what?"

"The baseball martyrs. Baseball is Courteguay. You, if anyone, should know that. After Dr. Noir's edict that banned baseball, young people all over the country defied his wishes. It was instinct, I tell you. The Wizard tells a story, supposedly true, though one never knows with the Wizard, of monkeys in some country who were taught to swim by humans. Soon monkeys hundreds of miles away took up swimming. Who knows why? But young people all over Courteguay defied Dr. Noir by playing baseball.

"A ball and a bat would mysteriously appear, smiles would crease a half dozen faces, someone would dig frantically in the back yard and a glove would appear, someone else would appear clutching a base to their chest like a baby. This whole group would make their way to a park, a baseball diamond, and the game would begin. Dr. Noir's terrorists drove about the cities and towns in camouflaged trucks supplied by the United States. If someone was seen playing baseball they simply opened fire. If the players, who always had at least one lookout, saw the soldiers first, the players scattered wildly in all directions. Sometimes they would chase down one individual. Usually death was swift, the bullet-shattered body left behind as a reminder to those who escaped. But, occasionally the captured player was carried off to San Barnabas to the Presidential Palace where Dr. Noir would subject the player to days in the wound factory. What happened there is only rumor, but rumor too terrible to repeat."

"And where is the Wizard when I need him?" said Julio. "How come he who claims to be in two places at the same time, is nowhere to be found. I'll need some magic to find Quita."

"Gone to the jungle," said Fernandella. "It will be a while before it is safe for him to be in San Barnabas, even San Cristobel. The Wizard always tries to be on the side of both the Government and the Insurgents."

"Don't go!" Fernandella said again. "Go back to America. Stay there! I'm afraid there is nothing you can do for Quita now. She is one of the disappeared."

But Julio could not wait to start his search for Quita. He shot out into the clear, blue morning as if he were stealing a base.

Instead of walking the oiled gravel that passed for a road he lurked through the jungle fern ever watchful for Dr. Noir's soldiers. He decided he needed a weapon and stopped at the house of a boyhood friend, Ruiz Tata, where he hoped to borrow a machete.

The mother of Ruiz Tata answered the door. She was a large, smiling woman the color of toffee, but today she was not smiling.

"Julio, you don't know?" she said, after he asked for Ruiz. "Dead," she said, and hugged Julio to her. "One of the baseball martyrs. One of the first. A dozen boys were playing on the field where you got your start. The soldiers sneaked up on them, parked the truck a mile away and crawled through the jungle. Are they traitors those boys, the soldiers I mean? They are sworn to do a job, but it must be hard for them, if they were not in the army they would be on the baseball fields defying the ban. But there are bonuses for each kill of a baseball player. Ruiz was shot dead in the outfield, it is said the outline of his body remains on the grass as a reminder of evil. Two others were killed while running away. But by that night a dozen more, including Ruiz's girlfriend Melita Diaz were there in the dust tossing the ball in memoriam to their friends and lovers.

"Ruiz died a hero. A martyr. But what of you? Because you are a baseball player Dr. Noir will have you killed."

"I am not afraid of Dr. Noir. I came to borrow Ruiz's machete. I am on my way to the capital to rescue Quita Garza."

"You are very brave, so I will do what I can to aid you." The woman disappeared into the tin-roofed hut and returned with a small, gleaming machete, which she handed to Julio.

Julio spent the day wandering the streets of San Barnabas. He circled the Presidential palace a few times, counting the number of guards, estimating how high he would have to jump to clear the whitewashed wall. He wondered if he could bribe his way inside. He had more money in his pocket than all the guards made in a year. But he remembered something Esteban had said, to the effect that money meant nothing to zealots, that they derived their self-esteem and sexual pleasure from having a single purpose in life. In this case their purpose in life was serving Dr. Noir and fighting his enemies. As darkness fell Julio caught the bus back to San Cristobel.

FIFTY-SIX
THE WIZARD

It was Alonzo Encarnacion, the right fielder, who exhibited the properties of ice. How Encarnacion came to Courteguay is not known. He appeared one day near the steps of the capitol in San Barnabas, bearded, wearing a slouch hat, carrying a rifle, with cartridge belts forming an X across his chest.

He rested on the lush lawn of the capitol, ate from a package of white cheese and dark bread which he pulled from inside his filthy tunic. After he ate he sprawled in the sun and slept for most of the afternoon, his hat on the grass beside him. When he woke it was early evening and the sounds that reached his ears were like familiar bird-calls outside a childhood window. He heard the sounds of baseball: a ball thwacking into a mitt, the bat and ball meeting, the thumping of feet on the friendly earth, the encouraging babble of the players, the occasional gasp from the fans. When he rose up from where he lay his image was burned into the grass of the capitol lawn.

When Alonzo Encarnacion relieved himself, he passed an arc of yellow ice that broke into two-foot lengths when it came in contact with the earth. The pencil-thin rods of ice lay like lightning on the

Courteguayan grasses, melted with a sigh in the humid summer heat, but left behind black scars on the grass where the cold had taken its toll.

"Encarnacion cannot stand too long on one spot or he leaves his footprints on the earth," the other players said, mystified. The first baseman, who was a carpenter, built a 3×3 square of fresh lumber and set it in right field for Encarnacion to stand on. Two ragged urchins with ill-fitting baseball caps covering their eyes were paid ten centavos a game to carry the square of lumber on and off the field.

In the shower a crust of ice formed around Encarnacion's knees, slivers of ice, like shards of glass gathered like an aura. Encarnacion showered alone.

Alonzo Encarnacion combed his black hair back in a sleek pompadour until he looked like the villain in a melodrama. Women, thrilled by the danger implied by his dashing presence, arrived in record numbers at the baseball grounds. The wealthy arrived in limousines, driven by chauffeur, the peasant girls arrived on foot, all gathered along the right field line, giggling, acting the fool, hoisting their skirts, sometimes with one hand, sometimes with two.

With his baseball salary Alonzo Encarnacion bought himself a scarlet velvet jacket, dark trousers, patent leather shoes, a ruffled shirt.

After he handled a bat the batboy would claim the instrument was frozen through and through, and take it out of service in case it would explode.

"He has the coldest lips I have ever tasted," one of the girls exclaimed. After that he became even more desirable.

"That is all?" asked the Gringo Journalist, noting that the Wizard was taking a drink of mango juice and that his eyelids were drooping, indicating that he finished his story.

"What do you want? The rest of his life story is not very interesting. I only want to tell you interesting stories. When his unexceptional baseball career was over, after he had fucked perhaps five thousand groupies, he opened an ice cream store, which seemed a logical choice for him. He continued to piss ice until the day he died. Now, weren't you happier not knowing that?"

"You are right, as always," said the Gringo Journalist. "Still I have a concern."

"And that would be?"

"You tell me stories, but the time frame seems more than just a movement forward or backward in time. Some events appear non-chronological, out of order as it were."

"So. This is Courteguay," replied the Wizard. "The word chronological is not in our language, neither is sequence. Things happen. That is all there is to it."

"I need more of an explanation."

"I thought such expansions and contractions of time would be obvious to you by now. You are a very slow learner, though I'm sure you've been told that often."

"I'm not stupid."

"Really? Where you come from and in many other places, maybe most other places, time is like a long highway with you standing in the middle of a straightaway while the highway dissolves in the distance in both directions, past and future. In Courteguay, if you picture the same scene, time occasionally runs crossways so that something that will happen in the future might already be behind you, slowly receding, while something from the past may not yet have happened."

The Wizard smiled. "Pass the mango juice, please."

FIFTY-SEVEN
THE WIZARD

The second time Esteban was murdered, Fernandella insisted that the body be cremated. A woman named Mme. Luzon had in recent months done many tarot readings for Fernandella. One of the cards had something to do with fire.

"If you cremate Esteban you will have to stuff me into the furnace with the corpse," said Julio, his cheeks sunken, his eyes wild with grief.

"He is not only my brother but my catcher," he went on. "He will be buried, and not even in a cemetery but on the lower lawn of our house, and in the manner I prescribe," and Julio banged his fist on the glass-topped coffee table in the rose garden, where Fernandella took her morning coffee, making the delicate china cups jump and chatter like ghostly teeth.

"If you feel so strongly," said Fernandella, "I will not stand in your way. All I want to know is does the Wizard have anything to do with your decision?"

Within hours of the announcement of Esteban's murder, the Wizard, who now had sixteen first names in his self-appointed capacity as Grand Defender of the long-defunct One True Church of God's

Redemption and Reaffirmation, appointed Esteban Pimental Bishop of Courteguay, posthumously of course.

"The pension of a deceased bishop is even larger than that of a retired baseball player," said the Wizard, smiling benevolently.

In the days after the murder, the Wizard was everywhere, lurking like a spy on the grounds of the Courteguayan White House, appearing from behind a wing-back chair or by parting a set of silken curtains.

Hector was devastated that nothing was required of him. Julio took over funeral arrangements. The wizard sent out invitations to world leaders and religious dignitaries. The Pope, while he declined to attend the service personally, issued a broadly worded statement condemning violence, and in favor of tolerance, understanding, tithing, and opposing family planning.

Julio, once he had frightened off Fernandella, took complete charge of the burial plans. Esteban was to be buried in a Plexiglas coffin, in his favorite baseball uniform, wearing his glove, and in his accustomed position, the catcher's crouch.

The coffin had to be custom-manufactured in Atlanta, and the funeral had to be delayed twice, once for two days, and once for three, because of its late arrival. Some dignitaries grew tired of waiting for the funeral and returned home, the Canadian prime minister among them.

Visiting newspaper reporters, tired of recounting the details of the murder, began to explore the political situation in Courteguay, some even dared to comment on human rights.

Those dispatches were seized by the Freedom Censors, but each reporter received a case of imported liquor. Male reporters were given vouchers good for the services of any prostitute in Courteguay.

The offending material was replaced by press releases from the Courteguayan National Tourist Service, headed Courteguay, Land of Enchantment, and sent out under each reporter's byline.

JULIO HIRED AN AMERICAN, a Feng shui expert who was an immigrant from China, a man who specialized in the design of baseball stadiums, to pick the exact spot for Esteban's burial. A home plate was installed four feet in front of Esteban's head, and pitching rubbers were sunk in the lush grass, eight of them, all exactly 60' 6" from the plate, but at such angles that none of the eight proposed hurlers would strike any of his compatriots when the ball was hurled over the single plate. The intricate geometrical patterns were such that there could be eight catchers crowded in an appropriate circle about the plate, each receiving pitched baseballs, without interfering with any of the other pitchers or catchers.

The reason the coffin, if it could be called that, had taken so long to prepare—actually it was done in a very reasonable amount of time considering its complexity—was that the Plexiglas container, which allowed the corpse to remain in its preferred position, was equipped with a refrigeration unit complete with a thirty-day supply of energy. There was a huge, forklift-like contraption beneath the container, capable of raising the top of the coffin from three feet below the earth's surface to four feet above, at the push of a button.

Another button would then release the front wall of the container, allowing it to fall forward. The buttons were on the front inside wall of the container, within easy reach of Esteban's throwing hand, should he suddenly regain the ability to use it. Instructions for the use of the buttons were in red lettering on the wall, in English, Courteguayan, Spanish, Latin and French.

When Julio took Fernandella to look at Esteban's coffin at the Armadillo of Navaronne Funeral Parlor in San Cristobel, Julio felt the tingle from wrist to elbow that he used to experience in the moments before a game as he warmed up lazily with Esteban, throwing softly, his arm aware, like a third person, anxious to begin laboring.

Julio shook his right arm vigorously.

"What are you doing?" demanded Fernandella, who was dressed in black, her hair pulled back until she was bug-eyed, looking as if she were a hundred years old.

"He looks just as he did when we played in America," Julio said. "In fact, he doesn't look much different than when he was inside your belly so many years ago. My arm wants to toss the ball to him."

"Mfffft," said Fernandella. She had never really believed her sons' stories that they had played catch in her womb.

"He looks exactly as he did on the packet of baseball cards you sent," Fernandella said. "But why have you done this to him? Can't you let him find peace in death?"

"His body arrived from America in this position," replied Julio. "A catcher is what he was before he came to this earth, and what he will be in the next life as well."

"Then why not let him get on to the next life?"

"I'm not sure his time has come. He was killed by mistake. I think that counts for something."

Julio put his arm around Fernandella's crepe-covered shoulder. She felt fragile as a spiderweb.

"Mama, I love him very much. I can't let him go without giving my best effort. There! Did you feel my arm? It flexed by itself. It wants to pitch. It could only want to pitch if Esteban were nearby—his spirit, I mean. His life force."

"The Lord works in mysterious ways," said Fernandella, "but Esteban is dead. He should be allowed to rest in peace."

The day of the funeral was clear and white. A few thumb-sized bees buzzed lazily over the emerald grass.

"Beautifully symbolic," was how the Wizard described the burial plot—the pitcher's rubbers in a circle about the bone-white home plate. The pit, rectangular and black, gaped deep.

The Wizard shielded his eyes from the sun and gazed into the pit. He was eventually able to discern the blue-and-silver workings of the contraption Julio had installed in the bowels of the lawn. The excess dirt had been hauled away, only enough to fill the space from the top of the coffin to the edge of the lawn was left, resting benignly on a carpet of artificial turf.

Julio, dressed in a dark business suit and sunglasses, kept scanning the sky, looking for a sign. For the first time in years he had dreamed of herons, endless rows of them needling the sky, and he ached for Quita Garza, and wondered if Esteban were not the lucky one. The dream made Julio question what he was planning.

"Esteban's death will unite our people in grief," said the Wizard, his own eyes slitted against the burning sky. "We will revere Esteban Pimental in death as he was never revered in life. In death he will become larger than life, if you will pardon the contradiction.

"There are only two real powers in our society, baseball and the church. Drawing from both worlds the way he did will make Esteban an idol. And a country without idols is nothing. Politicians make poor idols as Dr. Noir and his many predecessors discovered, always too late."

"I intend to bring him back to life," said Julio. "I don't wish to offend you. But even if the idea does offend you, I intend to do it anyway."

"How soon?" the Wizard asked. He was wearing a full-length, pure white, silk caftan with scarlet fingers of flames blooming on each sleeve. A few small, mysterious symbols decorated the back of the caftan.

The Wizard who usually favored stars and crescents had never worn these particular signs before. Julio recognized them as being several of the mysterious code signs baseball fans used on their scorecards to record outs, hits, and the advance of base runners.

"Don't worry," said Julio, "I will allow the nation time to mourn. A good tragedy will make everyone feel better."

He recognized the last statement as a direct quote from the Wizard.

"Feel free to predict the resurrection," he said to the Wizard.

"I only predict sure things," said the Wizard. "I will be as surprised as everyone else if you succeed. Then, I'll claim to have known about it all along, but that I did not want to raise false hopes. Let other people take the risks. Remember that if you ever decide to become a politician."

Julio searched the sky above the brown ridge, which rose like the spine of a dinosaur above the white house. The sky was like fresh-hung sheets. Julio's eyes watered behind his sunglasses.

Before the funeral service began the international press were allowed five minutes to photograph Esteban sitting upright in his Plexiglas coffin, dressed in his baseball regalia, wearing his catcher's mitt, his clerical collar visible above his baseball shirt.

The Wizard had arranged to have pews moved from the long-defunct San Barnabas Cathedral, the pews so newly varnished they stuck to the clothes of the mourners. The Wizard thought it would be a nice gesture to allow the old priest who had first instructed Esteban in religion to perform the service.

The Wizard visited the priest personally and assured him it was all right to come out from behind the chain-link fence for the occasion.

The priest refused.

"Well," said the Wizard, "if one cannot bring the priest to the cathedral, then one brings the priest and the chain-link fence to the cathedral."

The already makeshift communion rail was replaced by an eight-foot-high piece of frost fencing.

"It is about the same size as the wolf cage at the San Barnabas Zoo," observed Fernandella wryly.

Beyond the infield the newly named Esteban Pimental Memorial Stadium was jammed with mourners. Various services were conducted, some vaguely religious, other full of swirling colors and mysterious winds, beyond Paganism. When the last ritual was finished, Julio and his family led the procession to the funeral cars and the drive to the mansion at San Cristobel.

Though by necessity the crowd was much smaller, there were still more rituals at the burial ground, including a contingent of teenage girls twirling ribbons until the lawn looked like a pink ocean.

Julio himself pressed the button that lowered the coffin into the earth. As the sod closed over the top of it, Julio signaled the mourners to keep their seats. Starting on the far right Julio, after taking off his jacket and rolling up the sleeves of his white-on-white shirt, produced a box of virginal baseballs and indicated that he was planning to throw a baseball from each of the eight pitchers' rubbers. He did not use a catcher. Earlier, the geometric genius of the design had been demonstrated by eight pitchers pitching to a circle of eight catchers, the balls flying simultaneously but never colliding.

Julio wound up and fired the ball, the fans sighed collectively to see the greatest pitcher in the world throw. The ball hurtled toward the plate, but instead of passing on to the backstop, it vanished as it crossed the plate. Julio moved to the next pitching rubber. He repeated the exercise eight times in all. Each time the ball vanished as if into the glove of an invisible catcher. Again Julio signaled the mourners to stay in their seats. He waited, expectantly watching the spot where his dead brother had been lowered from sight.

There was a gasp from those assembled as the earth twitched, followed by a sigh as it subsided. A moment later there was another gasp as the earth moved even more, then slowly, the coffin emerged from the ground. It seemed to shudder, shaking off the last of the dirt, like a dog shaking off water. Then the Plexiglas front opened outward and Esteban Pimental stepped from the coffin, white baseballs clutched in the crook of his arm like so many mangos.

Fernandella fainted, though only briefly. She had too many questions to ask to remain unconscious for long. Julio and Esteban embraced.

"You always know the right thing to do," said Esteban.

"I, too, can read minds," said Julio.

Under her thick, black veil the Gypsy girl, Celestina, smiled redly.

FIFTY-EIGHT
THE WIZARD

As he walked up the hill toward his mother's home Julio was suddenly confronted by three soldiers, their uniforms gleaming like colored steam under the reflection of a white moon and a single streetlight. Their gun barrels glowed blue as they backed him up against a wall, issuing short, terse commands, their movements robot-like.

"Beisbol hombre!" one of them said.

"I am on my way home," Julio said reasonably. Then, as the tallest pointed his rifle at him in a menacing manner Julio reluctantly raised his hands.

"Beisbol," repeated the other two soldiers as they cocked their rifles.

"Dr. Noir is my friend," Julio lied. "You know he has issued a directive that none of the men who play baseball in America are to be harmed."

Julio knew of no such directive.

The soldiers stepped back a few paces, signaling Julio to remain with his back against the white adobe wall. Julio thought he recognized one of them as a childhood playmate.

"Miguel?" he said. "Miguel Figueroa?"

Too late, Julio realized that the encounter was not by chance. The one who had mouthed the words *Beisbol hombre* was indeed an acquaintance from childhood. He recalled Miguel Figueroa as an aggressive player who hated to lose.

"Attentiona!" cried Miguel.

Julio slowly brought himself to attention.

From the pocket of his tunic Miguel slowly withdrew a baseball. His smile was pure evil as he held it up for Julio to see. The ball glowed in the moonlight like a prize pearl.

Fog swirled about the legs of the soldiers.

"Those who are found in possession of the evil accoutrements of the game of baseball shall be executed on the spot," said Miguel, "even if they are one of Dr. Noir's pets."

Julio decided that if they were really going to execute him, he would feign a faint and crumple to the cobblestones next to the fence. They would then have to stand over him in order to kill him, and might lack the nerve to do it. Even aggressive types like these, Julio knew, had a sense of the kill; they liked their victims alive and kicking. He discarded the idea of running for he would have to negotiate fifty yards of road with the moon, the light, and the whitewashed wall providing assistance to the soldiers, and illuminating his death.

Miguel Figueroa rolled the ball forward, it coasted to a stop against the wall, settling itself into a tiny depression.

"America will be angry," said Julio. "They'll overthrow Dr. Noir if you kill me, and if they overthrow Dr. Noir, you'll find yourselves back in the hills, boiling beetles for soup, and eating roots and flower petals."

"Dr. Noir wants an excuse to kill one of you," said Miguel. "Why do you think he gave every Night Captain a baseball?"

Julio had no answer. He wondered if he could slide down the rough surface of the wall without lacerating himself.

"At the ready!" called Miguel Figueroa.

Julio took a deep breath as if he were getting ready to throw a crucial pitch, while as he did so, the air was awakened by the sound of bird wings.

A second later Miguel Figueroa let out a high, a surprised cry of pain as a heron, the sleek grey of fog, wings folded, pierced his back and chest like a stiletto. He pitched forward on his face on the cobblestones, the bird wavering like a spear in his back.

The other two soldiers turned their raised guns toward the source of the attack, one revolved in time to take his death in the chest rather than the back. The other caught his attacker by surprise and the heron pierced his left arm just above the elbow, fusing it to his body, causing his gun to discharge into night, toward the pale moon. A second shot ricocheted off the cobblestones, making a sound like a tight spring uncoiling, before another bird pierced his heart.

Julio breathed deeply of the sweet, bougainvillea-scented air. He stared up at the moon suspended in a puddle of fog. He could hear the flapping of gray wings in the night. He stood perfectly still until the flapping died away.

Real or imagined, he could see the lonely, longing face of Quita Garza, like a moon dog, wavering as if sketched by fireflies in the night sky.

Julio mouthed her name, saluted, his eyes wet with longing, his chest constricted with love.

He bent and retrieved the contraband baseball. Taking a deep breath he wound up and hurled the ball in a high arc, over the bougainvillea along the roadside, deep into the mango groves.

FIFTY-NINE

DR. LUCIUS NOIR

His secret police reported to Dr. Noir that Julio Pimental was back in Courteguay. Dr. Noir pondered for several days on whether or not to have Julio killed. He finally decided against it. In America Julio was a baseball superstar. There could well be political repercussions, lost foreign aid, withdrawn military advisors. Killing retired sports heroes was, if not considered acceptable, at least not likely to create an international incident. But, besides being a superstar in America, Julio Pimental was revered almost as a god in Courteguay. What was he to do? There was no undoing what he had done to that impudent little bitch Quita Garza. He should have disposed of her completely, disappeared had such an excellent ring to it. A grave somewhere in the mango orchards, a couple of peasants sworn to secrecy, bribed, or killed by one of his lieutenants. What was he to do if Julio kept snooping? He could let him find her in her rather delicate condition. It would be a warning not to attempt what Milan Garza had tried. Was Julio Pimental smart enough to take a warning?

SIXTY
THE GRINGO JOURNALIST

Excerpt from a tourist brochure advertising Courteguay, found among material left behind by a fly-by-night travel agency that went bankrupt in Shreveport, Louisiana, leaving travelers stranded at ports of call all around the world, including several in San Barnabas, Courteguay:

> IN THE HARBOR OF SAN BARNABAS, the glamorous and ultramodern capital of Courteguay stands a sixty-foot tall statue of Sandor Boatly, the American who is credited with introducing baseball to Courteguay.
>
> Boatly stands, a sling about his shoulder, his right arm extended, tossing toward downtown San Barnabas instead of apple seeds, baseballs. Cleverly connected by virtually invisible wires the arc of baseballs appears to be crossing the gentle turquoise waters of the harbor, with their final destination being the Palace of Baseball Immortals next to the Capitol buildings.
>
> If tourists are out early to the grounds of the Capitol, and are lucky, our renowned President, Juarez Blanco will appear on the steps of the Capitol to personally tell of a time during the revolution, when the insurgents, lead by then General Blanco, were fighting the forces of since-deposed dictator Dr. Lucius Noir, when a bullet

struck and shattered one of the baseballs being benevolently distributed by Sandor Boatly.

Both sides immediately displayed white flags. Each side sent forth their best stonemasons, and all fighting ceased while supplies of concrete and tools were secured.

During the break in the fighting troops on both sides renewed old friendships, in fact balls, bats and gloves miraculously appeared, two teams were picked and the players headed off the few blocks to the Jesus, Joseph and Mary Celestial Baseball Palace for an impromptu game.

The two stonemasons worked to reconstruct and replace the damaged baseball, they also repaired chips to Boatly's statue, many caused by ricocheting bullets, erased political graffiti, and repaired the work of a vandal who had used blue paint to cross Boatly's eyes.

The brochure went on to explain how, after the statue was restored to its former beauty, after the baseball game at Jesus, Joseph and Mary Celestial Baseball Palace had been won 3-2 in eleven innings by the Insurgents, led by now President Blanco, who tripled in two runs and pitched an inning of scoreless relief, the troops returned to their own sides, regrouped and continued the war until sundown.

SIXTY-ONE
THE GRINGO JOURNALIST

It was, of course, the Wizard who developed the idea of using genetic engineering to manufacture perfect baseball players.

"Every shortstop will hit .300 and cover more ground than the best who ever lived ever dreamed of. Every one of them will be able to do back flips."

The idea had come to the Wizard full-blown, served to him like a delicately cooked pheasant on a polished silver platter. "All our exportable first basemen will be left-handed power hitters," he went on. "The question is, if we supply the leagues with perfect specimens at each fielding position, do we then also supply pitchers?"

"Why not?" said Julio.

"Because our perfect infielders and outfielders will all be .300 hitters. A perfect pitcher cannot allow the opposition to bat .300 against him. We have a dilemma."

"I had a dilemma once," said Esteban, who had been sitting quietly, reading a theology book in Spanish. "It was in a hospital in Kansas City and was a somewhat painful and embarrassingly personal thing for medical personnel to do to a patient," said Esteban slyly.

"Go back to your reading," said the Wizard.

"It does not appear to be a dilemma to me," said Julio, "we will supply players for only the positions of shortstop and second baseman. Nothing else."

"An excellent idea," said the Wizard.

"Should I have suffered the indignity of having such a procedure done to me, or should I have allowed myself to suffer through without medical attention?"

SIXTY-TWO
THE GRINGO JOURNALIST

The newspapers played the Moosey Battaglia Affair way out of proportion. Moosey Battaglia's one claim to fame was that he once hit a home run to clinch yet another pennant for the Yankees. He was a journeyman first baseman who played in over 1,600 games in his sixteen-year career. He batted .282 lifetime, and on the year of his eligibility for the Hall of Fame garnered one single vote.

Moosey Battaglia's only crime was that he had an uncle of questionable reputation, who had many connections with what the newspapers euphemistically called "known underworld figures." The uncle, "Benny the Bat" Benvenuchi, got Moosey a job managing a dry cleaning plant in Bayonne, N.J. after Moosey retired from baseball. Moosey proved to be a capable manager; he also had a soft spot in his heart for down-and-out baseball players. He peopled his dry cleaning plant with ex-baseball players who had taken one too many curve balls without a batting helmet. He aided those who had problems with liquor or drugs; he found employment for some of the men who were cut out to do nothing but play baseball, and who found themselves in total limbo once their careers were finished.

When Atlantic City suddenly became a center for legalized gambling, casinos sprouted out of the rubble of the boardwalk like magical flowers. Moosey's uncle Benny the Bat was involved right up to his ten-dollar cigar. Moosey Battaglia was appointed personnel manager for a major casino. He brought with him all his hangers-on from the dry cleaning plant. Ex-major leaguers gave out change, were washroom attendants, bellhops, parking jockeys, cook's helpers, and doormen. It was Moosey's idea to install Esteban Pimental as Priest-in-Residence at the Golden Goose Casino and Show bar.

Moosey flew to Courteguay to talk with the Most Reverend Esteban Pimental, Bishop of Courteguay. Since the church was not recognized in Courteguay Esteban's appointment had been made official by the Wizard, aka President for Life.

"Listen, Bishop Pimental," said Moosey, "we'll call it the Velvet Chapel. It will be located right off the main casino. You keep your own hours, but if you was to ask me 9:00 P.M. to 3:00 A.M. would be most felicitous."

Most Reverend Esteban Pimental stared questioningly at Moosey Battaglia.

"I mean, I know it's a comedown for you Bishop. But wouldn't you rather be a big frog in a little pond than a little frog in a big pond, if you get my drift?"

"Go on," said Esteban.

"I mean, I'm in a position to hear rumors, if you know what I mean," said Moosey. "The scam is that the government's about to be overthrown again. The rumor is that in spite of your connections with this guy in the dunce cap and funny robe that they're not going to just enclose the priests behind chain-link fence; they'll be more likely to line you up against it, if you get my drift."

"I get your drift," said Esteban.

"I think a small sojourn in Atlantic City might be very beneficial to your health."

"I will do my work from the other side of the fence, so to speak," said Esteban.

In previous years such baseball immortals as Mickey Mantle and Willie Mays had been told to sever all present and future associations with baseball because they had taken executive positions with firms in some way involved in gambling.

Thus it created quite a stir when an enterprising investigative reporter for the *St. Louis Sporting News* wrote a story stating that not only was ex-major leaguer Moosey Battaglia employed by a casino, but he had brought along sixty-eight former big league players, who did everything from cut the lawns to plan the menus for the Golden Goose Casino and Show bar.

The baseball commissioner immediately issued an edict banning Moosey Battaglia and his sixty-eight compatriots from ever having any association with baseball other than watching games on television. On the list of suspended players was the Most Reverend Esteban Pimental, Bishop of Courteguay, Priest-in-Residence at the Velvet Chapel of the Golden Goose Casino and Show bar.

The Wizard, when he read the edict, banged his fist on the glass top of his 10×10 desk, more perturbed that Bishop Pimental's full title had been printed, than by Esteban being banned for life from baseball. For a while that afternoon, the Wizard's epaulets turned into small, flamingo-colored birds and fluttered wildly about his office.

SIXTY-THREE
JULIO PIMENTAL

Julio decided it was no longer safe to ride the bus, consequently it took a good part of the next day for him to walk, via back roads, to San Barnabas. He arrived at dusk, stood in the shadows staring across Bougainvillea Square at the presidential palace. He had no plan. He circled the palace a few more times, found a spot at the rear that was heavily treed and lightly guarded, where he inserted himself into a hedge of oleander and waited for total darkness.

He crept out of the oleander sometime after midnight and felt his way along the wall. He encountered a row of fifteen garages, each occupied by a luxury car, BMWs, Lincolns, Cadillacs, Maseratis. He entered one of the garages, crept to the back and found to his surprise that a door into the palace was unlocked. He remembered that in time of revolution the government was usually overthrown elsewhere, allowing time for whoever was in power to make a graceful exit to the jungle, there to become the insurgents until the next turnover of power.

Inside, the palace was lit by gentle night-lights. Julio was somewhere in the kitchen storage areas. He found a set of service stairs and made his way down a level. Peeking around a corner he saw a guard holding some kind of automatic weapon standing at the top of yet another set of stairs. Suddenly, there were heavy footsteps behind him.

JULIO WAS CAUGHT. He began to raise his hands, knowing in his heart that the guard would fire anyway, also knowing that he had to run toward one guard in order to escape from another, run right into the path of an endless stream of bullets.

As Julio was preparing himself to die, the door behind the forward guard slammed open sending the soldier sprawling down the steps, followed by a burst of gunfire loud as a cannon in the concrete hallway. A stocky figure strode through the door, bounding down the stairs in one leap and disarming the stunned guard, seconds later killing him with another burst of gunfire when the guard drew a machete and attempted to fight the intruder.

The armed stranger turned toward Julio. It was Esteban.

"How...?" said Julio.

"I am your brother. How else? When I found you gone I knew where you were going, as surely as I know what pitch you are going to throw, even though we've exchanged no signs."

"But you are a pacifist," said Julio pointing at the dead guard.

"You are my brother. Blood surpasses all ideologies."

Julio and Esteban disappeared into the night and were several blocks away before the alarms sounded at the Presidential palace. Apparently it was not unusual for the guards to fire an occasional burst from their submachine guns to alleviate the boredom.

"I have to go back," Julio said. "He has Quita."

"Are you certain?" Esteban replied.

"She went to the Hall of Baseball Immortals and never returned. What else could have happened to her?"

"A thousand things," said Esteban. "But if you are certain she is inside the palace, then we will go back, but with a plan of action, perhaps with friends, all of us well armed."

"The Wizard says Dr. Noir is a superstitious person, that though he hates the priests he is afraid to dispose of them all just in case there is something to what they stand for," said Julio. "Dress me in your priestly costume and I will make inquiries, if the Wizard is right he won't try to kill a fumbling priest, until it is too late."

"You want to take a chance that the Wizard is right?"

Julio smiled. "I will trust whoever I have to trust in order to find Quita."

"You will be a fumbling Cardinal, not the St. Louis variety," said Esteban, making another of his infrequent jokes. "You will appear at an entry point from the Dominican Republic, stating that you wish an audience with Dr. Noir, only you will use all his titles including Electrifier of Souls and you will carry an emerald the size of a grape to show the Vatican's goodwill toward Dr. Noir and his regime."

SIXTY-FOUR
THE WIZARD

In the jungle, quietness rises like mist in the final seconds of pre-dawn. There had been a baseball diamond carved with machetes from the unforgiving foliage, but the battles between the Government and the Insurgents moved on, and nature would soon reclaim its own. However, as the first pink tendrils of dawn appeared, the silence is broken by the myriad sounds of baseball. First, the murmur of the crowd, a couple of hoarse whispers as a ball is thrown about the infield, thwacking resolutely into gloves; the crack of the bat as a ground ball is hit to an infielder, the exhalation of breath as the ball is fielded and fired toward first.

An umpire authoritatively calls, "Play ball!" The infield chatter increases as a batter scrapes the earth, digging in at the plate. There is the whir of a pitch, the whap of it striking the catcher's mitt, the whiff of a bat striking nothing but air.

A mile away a sentry at the insurgent camp hears the sounds transported through the fragrant air. His ears perk up like an animal's. He wakes a compadre, they listen, they vanish into the greenery as if breathed in by nature. They creep toward the sounds as if their shoes were moss. They peek through flowering ginger plants into the clearing that is much lighter now, but stands stark and deserted.

"Who?" the first sentry mouths to his friend, question marks in his eyes.

"Ghosts," the second man mouths back. He readies his weapon.

Understanding each other perfectly the duo begin to strafe the clearing, the sudden cacophony of sound carrying for miles, causing birds like flashes of colored scarves to rise out of the jungle. From miles away a mortar is fired from the Government camp toward the Insurgent military quarters.

The two men wait at the edge of the clearing. Silence settles down like disturbed water quieting itself. There is the crack of the bat, the excited babble of the crowd. But now the sounds appear to come from inside the jungle not from the field itself. The two men stand, strafe the jungle behind third base where the sound seems to come from. Silence falls again, the sounds begin again, only this time from behind the soldiers. They turn and fire; the sounds move to beyond centerfield. A voice calls clearly, "Slide! Slide!" there is a scuffling, another voice, "Out!" The gibbering crowd turns angry.

The soldiers stare at each other in terror, scuttle back into the jungle, ferns slapping their faces.

In the humid greenery, the baseball bird snickers, makes the sound of a scoreboard emitting whooshing fireworks, hears the soldiers increase their speed, blood on their faces from colliding with knifelike branches. The baseball bird is only a rumor, a rumor that will be spread by the soldiers when they return to the Insurgent camp. The bird, his cool feathers striped like a Yankee uniform, cackles in glee. *Hey! Batta, batta* he says.

SIXTY-FIVE
THE WIZARD

The Anthurium Rapists were, said the Wizard, one of the most unusual phenomena in Courteguay's history. Near the center of the island was a small tribe, two hundred people at most; they fished the bayous with wooden spears, snared monkeys, roasted sloth over open fires, ate mangos and coconuts, venerated the Anthurium flowers that grew in sheets across the mossy floor of the jungle.

The males were warlike, but seldom had need to stray more than a mile from their village so were never able to find a war.

That is until the Old Dictator sent troops to train at jungle warfare. That small tribe heard the groaning of machinery, the twig-snapping pop of rifles, and went to investigate. They peered at the strangers through the thick foliage and rejoiced at the prospects of a war, something that their mythology had long predicted. Their mythology had also predicted victory.

They concealed their women and children under reed mats on the floors of their huts, sharpened their spears with slivers of rock, and set out to attack the invaders.

They killed one sentry and wounded two others. This was going to be easy, they thought. Then they advanced on a soldier armed with a rifle; they raised their spears in the attack position; they waited in an almost gentlemanly manner for the soldiers to raise their guns like spears.

Needless to say, there were no survivors. The soldiers scoured the jungle the next day, found the women and children huddled beneath the reed mats. The women were small and excruciatingly ugly; the adult women wore decaying fish scales in their hair as evidence of their desirability and sexual prowess. The soldiers made sour faces and retreated.

The women and children existed for several months, a few children died, the last pregnant woman gave birth, an old woman died, the tribe was headed for extinction. That is until deep in the night, the Anthurium came creeping out of the forest, each rubbery-red flower walking on birdlike legs, with its long yellow and white organ at the ready.

The Anthurium crept into the huts and applied themselves with some vigor to the sex organs of the sleeping women. The women were happy to accept whatever substitute nature had provided for they were used to frequent and passionate couplings with their virile men, and most were in such a state of frustration they had been eying each other with not entirely pure hearts.

The moonlit jungle was alive with the moans of passion. In the final moments before dawn the Anthurium padded away and as the sun rose, were to be found in their usual places in shady spots on the edge of dewy footpaths and along the edges of bayous, like drops of blood splattered among the abundant foliage. Months later many of the women gave birth to babies with red, leathery skin, who were otherwise perfect. Boys outnumbered girls ten to one.

SIXTY-SIX
THE WIZARD

The ruse worked. Julio, dressed as a Cardinal and with Esteban as his assistant, were not only allowed into Courteguay, but met by a limousine and police escort, and transported with honor to San Barnabas.

Once inside the palace, with a minimum of security present, Julio drew from beneath his robes a gun and a machete, and sliced off the head of Dr. Noir's press secretary. Esteban killed the three nodding security guards, and as they discarded their robes they made their way down long flights of stairs in the direction of the Wound Factory.

They found Quita, unconscious, more dead than alive. Julio took her in his arms and made his way to the nearest exit, while Esteban followed behind, blasting his weapon at anything that moved.

As they made their way across the grounds toward the street a soldier appeared on the steps of the capitol and raised his powerful rifle. He was immediately impaled by a sleek blue heron, and the first shot that had been aimed at Julio's head, discharged into the empty sky.

As they headed through mango and guava orchards, making their way in the direction of a hospital, Julio stopped for a moment to rest.

"Where is that confounded wizard when I need him most?"

Quita stirred in his arms. She opened her eyes.

"You'll never make love with anyone but me," she whispered, as Julio cradled her in his arms.

Julio thought at first it was a question. Then he decided it was not. But was it a request?

"Of course not," he said.

It took great effort for Quita to speak. Julio took a cool linen handkerchief and wiped Quita's brow. He bent low and kissed her cheek, the tip of her nose.

"You mustn't think..." said Quita. "I don't mean for you to..." she sighed and the warm arm she had clamped around Julio's neck dropped away. "You'll understand when you have to..." she whispered, her breath shallow and rapid.

"Never anyone but you," said Julio. "Never."

And Quita was dead, light as a bird in his arms, the smell about her not of death but of sweet spring earth, water-sopped, sun-warmed, swelling toward birth.

Julio screamed his rage into the sky. He shrieked of the revenge he would take on Dr. Noir. He carried Quita's body through the streets of San Barnabas, marching down the middle of the road, making eye contact with soldiers at checkpoints, daring them to interfere with his mourning. The soldiers, superstitious, shy of death, allowed him to pass.

He carried her to his mother's house in San Cristobel. There he collapsed in sorrow. Fernandella washed Quita's body with Julio's tears. In the morning Julio set out for the valley of the butterflies. He carried Quita wrapped in a simple white sheet. The valley was orange and black, the scattered trees at the foot of the mountain covered completely with the velvety horde, looked like butterfly cones. Julio laid Quita's body down on a cushion of orange and black, then he lay beside her and waited to be covered by the gentle blanket. "I will never rise up," Julio thought. "Here I will stay forever with my beloved. My own life will ebb until we are equal in death."

Julio slept for many hours. When he awakened the butterflies were stirring, beginning a slow tremble that turned to a vibration, then to definite movement. Millions of them began to raise Quita off the earth and into the air. The butterflies, so soft, so gentle, so compassionate, were barely up to the task, but as Julio watched in stunned fascination they carried her aloft, at first only a foot or two from the ground, then to waist height, then to eye level, then treetop height. As Quita ascended to the throb of butterfly wings, it appeared to Julio that she took the shape of a beautiful blue heron and, slowly rising above the cushion of butterflies as if suspended in mid-air, she suddenly took flight and disappeared into the darkening sky.

Julio snuggled back down into the comfort of the butterflies and slept until dawn. When he awoke his energy had returned and instead of wishing himself dead he thought of what lay ahead, of how he would somehow avenge Quita's death, how he would make Dr. Noir suffer as the monstrous doctor had made Quita suffer.

SIXTY-SEVEN
THE GRINGO JOURNALIST

Quita had barely departed for the sky when clouds swept in from both directions, from Haiti and from the Dominican Republic, and though it was not the rainy season, the rains began, constant and unrelenting. Weather forecasters around the world were puzzled by the thick layers of soot-like clouds that covered only Courteguay, ending at its borders, dropping not one raindrop on Haiti or the Dominican Republic. The clouds stayed. The rain, slanted and cruel, torrential in volume, continued for weeks as the skies mourned.

Without Quita, Julio thought only of baseball and revenge. All through the rest of the season he lived like a monk, scarcely speaking to anyone but Esteban, avoiding his fellows, sportswriters, and especially women. He wore a black arm band on his uniform, lived principally on cornbread which Fernandella baked and had the Wizard mail to him weekly, and was in bed alone by 9:00 P.M. each night.

Esteban was completely unused to being allowed in his own room night after night.

Once, an opposing catcher remarked on the armband when Julio came to bat, actually he only inquired, if profanely, on why Julio was wearing such a thing. Julio, misunderstanding the gesture, interpreted it as a slight against his lost love, whipped off the catcher's mask and beat him about the head with it, causing him twenty-seven stitches worth of discomfort, and earning himself a fourteen day suspension.

"Time heals all wounds," was the best even the Wizard could offer in the way of comfort.

"Something good will come out of it," offered Esteban. "Trust in the Lord, for he works in mysterious ways."

"Things will get better," said Fernandella.

"You are all fools," said Julio. "My life as a man is over. I am now only a baseball player. Baseball is my avocation, my philosophy, my wife, my God."

As if in response to his new dedication, the sidearm curve began to break about two inches more; it now not only broke in on the bat handle, it either rose or dipped as it did so. It was not unusual for a player to have more than one bat shattered in his hands, and many players bailed out, taking a called third strike in preference to having their hands shattered. A sportswriter nicknamed Julio "Robot-o" and broadcasters picked it up. By the All-Star break he was 13-1, and was named to start for the American League, and once again he failed to play as organized baseball never fully comprehended that Julio would pitch to no one but Esteban.

SIXTY-EIGHT
THE WIZARD

Once, in the distant past, said the Wizard, continuing with his oral history of Courteguay, a famous hotel chain decided to expand into San Barnabas. But they did far more than build a brick building, a mansion with many rooms, as it were. They brought with them foreign customs. Like entertainment. San Barnabas had never experienced a lounge singer. But I suppose it was all right, for only visiting foreigners could afford to stay at the famous hotel chain, whose son and heir had once been married to Elizabeth Taylor. I have seen *National Velvet* many times and have dripped tears each time even though I know that a happy ending is imminent.

The staff would stand about the mostly empty lounge, leaning against the velvet-curtained walls and snicker at the sleek singer with the slippery hair and shiny suit who crooned untranslatable songs. The singer resembled one of the thousands of bright little chameleons that blended with the walls and ceilings, there would be white chameleons on the linen tablecloths, and pink ones on the sleazy singer's pink piano. It was in Courteguay that the term lounge lizard was coined.

"Cultures do not mix well," the Wizard said to Julio, who was sitting at the Wizard's feet listening absently to this seemingly endless reminiscence. A sign on the marquee read: WELCOME MAGICIANS.

A further sign near the front desk, and another near the entrance to the lounge read:

APPEARING NIGHTLY
THE MAGICIANS OF ARKANSAS.

"No thank you, we won't need any keys for our rooms," the handsome leader of the magicians said. He was perhaps fifty, with hair the color of spun silver, long but immaculately styled.

"Do you always wear a hamster in your blazer pocket, miss? Ha Ha," a second handsome magician said to the young desk clerk, who stared uncomprehendingly at the small rat-like creature he had pulled from her pocket.

A trail of red dust, fine as an eye vein, followed the tallest of the magicians toward the elevator.

The actual entertainment was another matter. The Magicians of Arkansas danced on stage and each began doing tricks: one produced an endless supply of playing cards from thin air which he scattered about the stage, the second pulled yards and yards of light bulbs from his mouth, each one blooming like a tiny sun, the third had a way of seeming to extract doves from his nose. As he released each bird it fluttered over the walls of the set, where a young man whom they had seen loitering in front of the hotel had been hired to catch the birds and return them to their cages.

Unfortunately, the employee, a scrawny young man named Philippe, had not had a good meal for several days and the prospect of tame doves was too much for him. He stuffed the docile birds into a sack and disappeared out the stage door toward his mother's hillside hovel where the whole family feasted on roasted doves.

The sparse audience scarcely noticed the entertainment. As a tourist in Courteguay it was best to stay drunk. Though it was advertised as a bargain destination, with the exchange rate for the guilermo extremely attractive, locals wanted no part of any guilermos; they wanted American dollars. The hotels charged American prices in American dollars for second and third-rate accommodation and meals, while the man-made beaches on the man-made lagoons were infested with sand flies.

A member of the kitchen staff, Quintana Pollo Loca, leaned against a wall watching the performance. "They get paid in American dollars for such subtle subterfuge?" she asked a waiter. He nodded. "But I can truly do magic," said Quintana. The waiter shrugged. "What is magic in one place is not necessarily magic in another," he said, having probably heard such a statement from me.

Quintana, however had heard no such statement. "I will show you magic," she said. She marched into the audience to where a young couple who had been duped into holidaying in Courteguay with their new baby by a travel agency in Miami that was rumored to be owned by the Wizard (pardon me for referring to myself in the third person) sat miserably at their table. Quintana held out her hands for the baby and the surprised young mother handed the child over. No sooner had the baby been placed in Quintana's hands than it disappeared.

The mother screamed. The small crowd turned toward her. The Magicians of Arkansas stopped performing.

Later that night, after local police reluctantly intervened, the baby was found forty miles outside San Barnabas, in a guava orchard, sleeping comfortably on a pillow. Quintana Pollo Loca left the country with the Magicians of Arkansas who added a disappearing baby act to their repertoire.

SIXTY-NINE
THE WIZARD

Umberto, the translator of dreams was, next to the Chief of Police—who had been born ninety miles away and was therefore considered a foreigner—the richest man in his village. But in order to keep his position, he lived in apparent poverty, though he hoarded a trove of silver beneath the floorboards in his hovel and counted it in the deepest part of each night by the glimmer of a guttering candle, or simply by the blue of the moon.

Umberto's gift was to see into the hearts of his inarticulate neighbors. He had an unspectacular talent as an artist. Under ordinary circumstances, he might have been able to turn out sad portraits of big-eyed children and animals from which he would have earned a few centavos to buy bread.

But his secret was an eye into the heart. When Cortez the sandal maker said, "I dreamed of a woman," Umberto knew that Cortez, who was lumpy and had a walleye, was wildly in love with Principetta, the beautiful daughter of the Chief of Police. Umberto paints on the outside wall of Cortez' adobe shop a woman who is, yet is not Principetta, and the man who Cortez would be—the man who Cortez is in his heart—

a tall, handsome man in formal attire and a scarlet cape. On the wall the two dance. The girl's black eyes look up at the man, full of adoration.

Umberto knows.

Vasquez, a miserly and pathetic man, dreams that he has won the lottery, but he argues over the fee he will pay Umberto, and cries poverty when asked to remove the sweet pea vines from the south adobe wall of his home so that Umberto may work. Eventually Umberto pulls down the vines himself. He paints the wall white, then creates a mural which shows Vasquez in a fine frock coat over a lace-collared shirt standing on a small rise tossing golden coins to a group of people. Vasquez's daughter whom he disowned when she was a teenager because he disapproved of her boyfriend, stands beside him smiling, one arm about Vasquez's shoulders, the other clutching her apron that is full of gold coins. Vasquez's son, who ran off a few years previously because Vasquez expected him to work for nothing in the small mango orchard that provided their livelihood, and to postpone or abandon his plans to marry because his first duty was to Vasquez, is kneeling in front of his father, stuffing his pockets with money. When it comes time to pay Vasquez coughs up only half the promised fee along with a basket of hard and worm-riddled mangos. Umberto says nothing. But the colors in the mural run wildly into each other after the first rain.

"My dream is of herons, long and sleek as stilettos, patterning the sky, one dark, one light, one dark, until the whole sky is nothing but herons in flight," Julio told Umberto. He had trekked many miles to Umberto's village.

"There are no walls left for me to paint on," said Umberto. "I serve the local population only. Strangers seldom come here."

"I will have a wall built," said Julio. "Or I will provide a large canvas so I can carry the painting back to San Cristobel with me."

"I do not work on canvas," said Umberto. "Nothing I paint must ever be removed from the village."

Julio hired Sergio Montanez the village carpenter to construct a wall, on a vacant lot next to Umberto's home, six feet high and eight feet long. Unpainted, it was propped securely from the back.

"The virginal wood awaits your paints," said Julio.

The portrait was not of herons. It was of the side of a mountain with small evergreens covered with millions of monarch butterflies, on the earth were the outlines of Quita and Julio buried beneath an avalanche of butterflies.

When it came time to pay, Julio deposited twice the agreed fee in Umberto's hand.

"No," said Umberto, "the painting cannot leave the village."

But Julio had already hired three husky boys to share the burden.

"It is mine. I will do with it as I please," said Julio forcefully. It took them two days to transport the wall to San Cristobel.

When Julio unwrapped the canvas that protected it, the wall, which smelled of freshly sawed lumber, was blank and virginal. Though Julio imagined he could see Umberto's laughing face lurking in the shadows of the pale wood.

SEVENTY
THE WIZARD

After Quita's death, Julio drifted through two mediocre seasons. The political situation kept him from returning to Courteguay. His promise to Quita kept him from moving on with his life. He alternately pined for Quita, while cursing himself for being so weak as to desire other women. Without earthly love Julio became depressed, pitched lackadaisically, even so his record was 16-8. He made all sorts of fundamental errors, like forgetting when there were runners on base. Once with the bases loaded a sharp grounder was hit on one bounce into his waiting glove, but Julio was thinking about a girl in a red sweater sitting directly behind first. He began to make a play to first, then heard Esteban's anguished cry from where he stood one size twelve planted firmly on the plate waiting for the force out. For some reason he looked to second before throwing to Esteban just as the sliding runner touched the plate.

It was in Boston that Julio, sick with guilt, decided he could no longer stand being without a woman. His promise to Quita was always with him, as night after night he fought back his desire but with diminishing success. He remembered Quita's dying words, "You will never make love with anyone but me," and vowed that he would remain true to her, at least in spirit.

The physical is on one level, the spiritual another, he rationalized; it is merely lust which demands to be satisfied. I will not make love; I will satisfy only my physical passions.

The season was half over. After every game Julio waited in the clubhouse until the other players had left. He listened to their joking, their chattering, as they speculated on what adventures awaited outside the player's gate. He pretended interest in his clothes and equipment as they wondered aloud which of the bizarre, wild, sensually-violent women would be their lot.

Julio would sit in the damp, silent clubhouse, amid the odors of sweat, chlorine and urine, dreaming of Courteguay, of Quita, of the winter of the butterflies, until he felt safe from temptation, until the streets around the ballpark would be deserted. Dressed so casually he could be mistaken for one of the park-cleaners, who by then would be arriving for work, Julio would slip out of the park and walk, hands deep in pockets, the few blocks to his hotel, where he would sneak in a side entrance and up to his room.

He had awakened that morning in Boston full of an unquenchable desire, the kind he knew could be satisfied only by a woman. He relieved himself, while calling up his memories of Quita, breathing her name. But the relief was pale and useless; desire continued to smolder within him like ground-fire.

That night he pitched indifferently, thinking more about what he would do after the game than the game itself. He tried to blot out the batter from his mind, tried to concentrate only on making the ball reach Esteban's mitt. But his success was marginal. His team won 7-6, though Esteban reprimanded him for his carelessness on more than one occasion for throwing pitches to the wrong location, and twice for throwing the completely wrong pitch.

After the game he dressed carefully, splashing lime-scented aftershave lotion on his smooth cheeks. He wore tight, fawn-colored slacks, a black silk shirt with buttons in the shape of silver nuggets. He combed his hair and donned his team jacket. By now the first rush of players would be on the street, signing autographs, eying the more aggressive groupies, who would be flaunting themselves, making their availability plain.

I will choose one from the background, Julio decided, one who might not be attracted solely by my uniform, one who, as my third baseman might say, won't spread her legs until she reaches the hotel room.

He emerged from the player's gate smiling, tossing a baseball in the air. If I could only be like Esteban, he thought almost hourly. Esteban was mainly indifferent to sex and the pleasures of the flesh. But I cannot, Julio concluded. As he signed autographs he studied the women who waited; he dismissed the predatory ones, the grasping ones, the lewd-mouthed ones, who demanded that he sign their clothing or parts of their bodies. At the rear of the semicircle he spotted a dark-complexioned girl in a blouse the color of outfield grass; her hair reached below her shoulders. She might be of Latin origin, he decided. Staring above the crowd he caught her eye, and aiming carefully tossed the baseball to her. She caught it awkwardly, cupping both hands as she did so.

He deliberately made her wait until last; he finished signing autographs for all the little boys in baseball uniforms; he fended off the more aggressive women, especially a persistent one in a thousand-dollar dress and floppy black hat who he had heard the other players speak of with a mixture of admiration and contempt.

Finally, the dark-haired girl was alone in front of him. He seized the baseball.

"Should I write, From the greatest pitcher in all baseball?" Julio asked, smiling to show off his even white teeth.

"Whatever you wish," the girl replied. She was not beautiful, Julio noticed. Her face was too long, her chin pointed.

"Do you by chance speak any language other than English?" Julio asked.

"Espanol," the girl whispered.

"Would you go for a walk with me?" Julio asked in his best Spanish, which while not perfect was far better than his English, adding before she could reply, "it is sometimes very lonely being a traveling baseball player."

The girl nodded, and as they set out Julio took her hand; the very touch of warm flesh made him draw in his breath. He had intended to be brash and brazen with this woman, the way he promised himself he would be with all women for the rest of his life. He had planned to make it clear that she meant nothing to him but a means of sexual release, a toy to be used and then held in mild contempt. He planned on behaving like Navarro the third baseman, who would fling a heavy arm around a woman's shoulders, grin jovially, and say something like, "Hey, honey, you like to get sucked off before you get fucked?"

Instead, Julio and the girl walked in silence for a block.

"I am Carmen," the girl said.

"Do you know who I am?" Julio asked.

"Of course, you are the handsome half of the Pimental twins," she replied.

"Of course," said Julio.

He bought some roasted nuts from a street vendor and they ate them as they walked. The girl's hand was warm in his; when his cheek brushed against her hair he could smell rose-scented soap, and the hair tickling his nose the way Quita's had, excited him. He was tempted to ask the girl why she was doing this, inquire as to why she was attracted to him, find out if it was the uniform, the fact that he was famous, find out if it was the money, his own good looks. At length he decided he really didn't want to know. He supposed there wasn't a logical answer anyway.

At the hotel he was solicitous as a bridegroom, ordering drinks and ice from room service, inquiring as to the girl's comfort an endless number of times, until she finally stepped into his arms and raised her mouth to his, beginning the kiss in the same aggressive way that Quita always had. Julio found himself trembling as Carmen's delicious tongue touched his.

Forgive me, Quita, he thought. This will be for physical satisfaction only. But when he mounted the girl, Carmen; when she seized his penis and guided it into her the way his beloved Quita had done, Julio felt his senses dissolve in an all-encompassing passion. He felt as if he were being slowly immersed in sweet, heated water. Carmen's tongue rattled in his mouth; her odors were of sun-sweet earth, leather, Quita's odors. As he abandoned himself totally to sexual pleasure, the woman in his arms seemed to become Quita. As he changed positions, tasted her body, felt her convulse against his tongue, her red nails scraped his shoulders in loving passion in the exact way Quita's used to do. Julio called her name into the sweet sexual warmth of the room.

As he lay gasping, his head on the pillow next to her, she licked her own taste off his lips, exactly as Quita used to do. And when she slid down and took him in her mouth it was like the slim fire-colored skaters he had seen on TV racing through his veins.

"Quita! Quita, my love...."

And she answered him in voice, and breath, and passion.

Hours later as they cuddled softly in the large bed, their aura seemed suddenly to lift like a cotton candy cloud. When he looked down Quita was no more. The girl, Carmen was there, plain, unremarkable, breathing softly into his shoulder.

After Carmen left Julio felt guilty for experiencing such unrestrained pleasure. But, he thought, it is the first happiness I have known in two years. Can it be wrong?

He could hardly wait for the game to end the next day. He picked a woman who, while not unattractive, was of a type not desirable to him. She was a black girl with a wild tumbleweed of hair. She wore a red skirt slit to the waist, and a turquoise blouse that showed off her sloping breasts. She was brazen, not very intelligent, and almost impossible to understand when she spoke. He hustled her back to the hotel and into bed. In the throes of sexual activity Julio, to his delight, experienced all the exotic passions he had enjoyed every time he made love with Quita.

Every night that week he took a different woman back to his hotel. In his bed, for a few blissful hours each one turned into the essence of Quita Garza. Slowly, that magical week, Julio came to understand the true meaning of Quita's dying words.

SEVENTY-ONE
THE GRINGO JOURNALIST

The player who rusted in the rain. Did this actually happen? The Wizard says it did. I am always noncommittal for I hate to spoil a good story.

His name was Pasqual Ruiz, says the Wizard. An average outfielder, an average hitter, destined never to rise above Triple A baseball, his one uniqueness was his abiding fear of rain. At the first sign of rolling black clouds he would become uneasy. He would spend more time watching the sky than watching the hitter. At the first spit of rain he would walk off the field and conceal himself in the dugout. The manager tolerated this eccentricity. If he was called upon to come to bat while it was raining, no matter how lightly, he refused to leave the dugout. The times this happened were few and the manager replaced him in the lineup when it was necessary.

"However, in the middle of his second season in America, management changed. The new field manager was a man with a reputation of never quitting, and of expecting his players to follow instructions with no questions asked. When he was told of the peculiarities of Pasqual Ruiz, he spit contemptuously on the field and said, "My players play when and where I tell them to. There are no exceptions."

A few days later a fine drizzle began while the team was batting. When Pasqual's turn came to bat he remained seated. The manager strode to a spot in front of him and demanded to know why he wasn't batting. Pasqual Ruiz instantly forgot whatever English he had learned. He signaled frantically for a fellow Courteguayan to come and explain the situation. The manager listened, then said, "Tell Pasquali here if he wants to continue playing baseball in America he'll go to bat, otherwise he'll be on the first plane back to whatever heathen hinterland he came from, a place where he'll have to spend a whole year burning off rain forest in order to earn half as much as he gets for one day's meal money."

Pasqual Ruiz listened. He picked up a bat and walked out into the drizzle, where he swung at the first three pitches, none of which were near the strike zone, and trotted back to the dugout.

When the inning ended he was the last player to leave the dugout, in fact he waited until the manager had stared at him for several seconds and was about to make his way down the bench to confront him again, when he reluctantly ventured into the outfield. He stood the whole half inning in the ever increasing drizzle, and when the inning ended he walked stiffly back to the bench. The next inning it was raining harder, so hard that about twenty minutes into a four-run inning the umpires called the game. The players ran toward the dugout, all but Pasqual Ruiz.

"What's the matter with Pasqual? I thought he hated the rain?" said the manager.

"He is rusted," said a utility infielder.

"People don't rust," said the manager.

"Unless they are from Courteguay," said the infielder who, it was rumored, had been conceived from a union between a glove and a bat, and had been discovered when he was a few hours old, in an equipment bag.

Ruiz never played again. He remained in right field for two seasons while the fielders played around him. Gradually it became known that there was a statue in the right field of the baseball park. Pigeons sat on Ruiz's head. Young thugs painted graffiti on his body.

"What became of him?"

"The team, somewhere in the Midwest, lost its Major League affiliation, the ballpark was closed, eventually torn down. Ruiz stands now in a cornfield, I am told, no longer visible from any road, longing to again someday hear the crack of the bat."

"Is that how it happened?" I ask the Wizard.

"If it isn't, it's the way it should have happened," replied the Wizard.

SEVENTY-TWO
THE GRINGO JOURNALIST

Dr. Noir, his instinct for survival more delicate than most, became suspicious of herons. Though Courteguay was land-locked and there was no lake close to the presidential palace, Dr. Noir noticed that there were an inordinate number of herons on the palace grounds. The tall, blue birds stood like statues on the manicured lawns, walked slowly and softly in the gardens, stared with squinted eyes at anyone who approached them, displayed a certain arrogance as they let guards or visitors get almost close enough to touch before slicing the air with their dark wings.

"Where have they come from?" Dr. Noir demanded of his chief of security.

"They are only harmless birds," came the reply. "A change in migration patterns, who knows? They are non-destructive, virtually silent, nothing to worry about."

"But I do worry," said Dr. Noir.

"I assure you, sir...."

"Kill them!" said Dr. Noir. "Not now..." he grabbed the sleeve of the security chief to keep him from drawing his weapon. "Instruct the guards. I want an attack. I want them all killed at once."

As if they had heard, the herons suddenly took flight, their giant shadows darkening the sun for a few seconds. The security chief barked into his radio. A gunshot shattered the quiet of the palace grounds, a heron landed with a thud near the Japanese garden thirty yards from the palace.

Like feathered spears the herons attacked. There was a crackling of rifle fire, more herons dropped on the lawns. Two hurtled toward the presidential balcony. The security chief bellowed into a radio held in his left hand, in his right he waved his handgun. But before he could get off a shot a heron arrived from above and to his right; he screamed as his right arm was pinned to his body, the gun fired wildly. Dr. Noir held a wooden deck chair in front of him, and just in time, for a heron impaled the seat of the chair, its beak driving all the way through. Dr. Noir, holding the chair as a shield hurried into his apartment, quickly closing the door and drawing the curtains.

SEVENTY-THREE
THE GRINGO JOURNALIST

During their twentieth season in the Major leagues, when everyone but the Wizard and their parents thought they were thirty-six years old, Esteban decided he had had enough. He had been studying for the priesthood for several years and was nearly ready for ordination in the outside world, but not the world of Courteguay where he was already a bishop, with a good opportunity of becoming a cardinal.

Julio, while moderate in most of his habits, was gregarious and outgoing, even more so after he learned to speak English, if not well, still well enough to understand the offers that were being made to him by the Baseball Sadies. He was delighted by media attention and the attention of women, many of whom were not Baseball Sadies at all, but professional models, and actresses. Julio's reputation was that he never turned a Baseball Sadie away unsatisfied. His reputation of course was inflated by the tabloid press; colorful people in sports are at a minimum, and their color can and will be enhanced by the tabloids. On the other hand Esteban became accustomed to being ignored. When they were younger Esteban wished that he and Julio might have been identical twins so he could have impersonated

Julio on occasion. Esteban found himself uncomfortable with even the most aggressive groupies, and after his experience with the mysterious Gypsy girl, had been very selective when it came to female company for nearly five years.

Julio won over 300 games during his career, and would certainly have won more if he had not played for a perennially second division team. Julio and Esteban never got to play in a World Series.

Even in the most humid days of July, the President of the United States attended many games when Julio started. A secret service man would emerge from the shadows of the locker room, his shoulders bulging with hidden weaponry, and state that the President would appreciate it if Julio would stop by his box and say hello.

"We would like to help Courteguay achieve freedom for itself and its people," the President of the United States said to Julio.

Julio noticed that when the President smiled the left corner of his mouth turned up, and a dimple like a small pentastar appeared at the left corner of his mouth.

"I would be grateful for any help you could offer," said Julio carefully.

This was the third time in a month he had been invited to dinner with the President. He did not know what to make of it.

The President smiled again, picking up one of the linen napkins that Julio noticed were heavier than most of the drapes on the windows.

"Our problem is, as international politics goes, we do not have a solid reason to invade Courteguay, even temporarily."

"I still think we can use repression of human rights," said the Attorney General.

"Courteguay is no worse than, in fact in many ways it is much freer than, many nations in Central and South America. Dr. Noir persecutes only baseball players and some priests, so far as we can gather." The President looked to Julio for confirmation.

"The economy has certainly improved under his dictatorship," said Julio. "But he has murdered children for playing baseball. He uses his skill as a chiropractor to personally mutilate his enemies, to break their backs and limbs and rearrange their bodies in grotesque shapes. Is that not reason enough to intervene?"

"Not according to international protocol. During the off-season when you are in Courteguay, are you or your brother's lives at risk? You're somewhat of a national treasure. The death of one of you two might be excuse enough."

"But which one?" asked Esteban, proving that he had been listening after all. "I would suggest Julio, since I have already been murdered twice."

"Dr. Noir is intelligent," said Julio. "He knows what will create an international incident and what will not. After our retirement it is another matter. Once we are not in the public eye of the United States Dr. Noir will kill us like dogs. We will not be able to retire in safety to our homeland."

"If he would just consummate diplomatic ties with Cuba or some other of our enemies. But he rejects all their offers. Bulgaria sent its national soccer team to tour Courteguay. They even offered Dr. Noir box seats for the World Cup final in Brazil," said the secretary of state. "Just to be safe he's deported every American from Courteguay, even the three who had become Courteguayan citizens. He takes no chances."

"I would like to help with his overthrow," said Julio. "I have personal reasons for hating Dr. Noir."

"And your brother?"

"Esteban lives life on a more ethereal plane. He is opposed to violence. He turns the proverbial other cheek."

"Being referred to in the third person is always a pleasure," said Esteban.

"Would you consider becoming President of Courteguay?" The President asked Julio. Then glancing at Esteban, he added, "Perhaps co-presidents?"

"Neither of us have political aspirations, other than removing Dr. Noir from power. But we have a friend, the man who discovered us so to speak. We will refer to him as Jorge Blanco, and I assure you he will continue in the tradition of all Courteguayan El Presidentes. Looting the treasury and pocketing foreign aid for his personal gain will be his most endearing qualities."

"I believe I have met your Mr. Blanco," said the President. "He dresses in a rather flashy manner, if I remember correctly. Yes, I think he has leadership qualities."

Later it would be determined that it was because of Julio that the Wizard became President of the Republic of Courteguay.

SEVENTY-FOUR
THE GRINGO JOURNALIST

When Julio and Esteban returned to Courteguay in retirement, they decided for their own safety to take whatever American aid was available and start the process of overthrowing Dr. Noir.

As he discussed the overthrow of Dr. Noir with the Wizard, Julio noticed that the Wizard was dressed in a new silk robe with red embellishments brighter than scarlet, purer than vermilion.

"I want to visit the Hall of Baseball Immortals," said Julio.

The Wizard's eyes shifted rapidly for a split second. He produced a baseball from thin air, tossed it to Julio.

"Of course you should familiarize yourself with the baseball greats of the past. I should like to see the Hall of Baseball Immortals myself. If you could see fit to pay my way I could accompany you. It is in a place called Cooperstown in the great state of New York. Just before the season starts would be a good time...."

"I mean the Courteguayan Hall of Baseball Immortals."

The Wizard's eyes reflected pastoral sunsets. He picked up a silver table lighter from his desk, flicked it and a rainbow-hued parakeet appeared.

"There is no Courteguayan Baseball Hall of Fame. Where did you get such an idea?"

"You must remember that I loved Milan Garza's daughter," said Julio. "Everyone knows he was murdered and his body is on display there in a crystal coffin."

"Are you losing your mind?" asked the Wizard. "Milan Garza had no daughter. He was the most wasted talent in Courteguayan baseball history. He died of alcohol poisoning, on a cot in a flophouse when he was only twenty-nine."

SEVENTY-FIVE
THE GRINGO JOURNALIST

There are certain protocols even to a revolution. El Presidente, even when it was Dr. Noir holding the office, was given sufficient notice of his overthrow that he had time to make an unhurried escape to the jungle, taking with him a sufficient amount of treasure and cash to eventually finance his return to power.

There were other protocols to follow concerning the insurgents, whose forces were in a particularly pitiful condition, consisting of only a few dozen physically and mentally ravaged soldiers, short of courage, weapons, and leadership. Dr. Noir had done something unprecedented. When he overthrew El Presidente, he had also killed the insurgent leader General Bravura and his highest ranking Lieutenants. One of the escaped Baseball Martyrs, Jose Rincon Valenzuela, had taken command of the insurgents almost by default. He had not even promoted himself; he was still Sergeant Valenzuela, and his piteous group has no plans to attack Dr. Noir and friends.

Julio called the President of the United States who promised five hundred military advisors, who united with Julio, Esteban and their friends, along with Sergeant Valenzeula's bearded and moldy two dozen should be able to turn out Dr. Noir.

But the Doctor did something else unprecedented; he gathered his army and his secret police and determined that they would defend the capitol to the death. This had never happened before. No matter how often the government and insurgents changed places, all warfare was conducted in the jungle. San Barnabas never suffered any damage. Both El Presidente, whoever he might be, and the leader of the insurgents were gentlemen and an outmanned El Presidente retreated safely to the jungle and awaited his turn at power to come.

The Wizard remained in the background, letting Sergeant Valenzuela lead the insurgents; the Wizard wanted no part of responsibility for a failed coup, if it indeed failed, and the prospects of success diminished one hundred percent when the American advisors failed to arrive as scheduled. Someone in the CIA forgot that Courteguay was landlocked. The advisors were turned away at the border of first Haiti and later the Dominican Republic. They had to retreat to a hastily summoned aircraft carrier, where forty-eight hours after their estimated time of arrival, they took off in a fleet of helicopters for San Barnabas.

Dr. Noir in one of his most resplendent uniforms stood on the balcony of the Presidential Palace and appeared to unleash spirals of smoke from his short, black fingers. The helicopters froze in position where they circled the palace. The aircraft idled absently, as they became fixtures in the sky.

The squads of secret police and soldiers sworn to loyalty to Dr. Noir prepared to attack Julio and Esteban and their ragged collection of baseball martyrs.

SEVENTY-SIX

THE GRINGO JOURNALIST

"They say there are no atheists in battle," said Esteban. "Have you had a change of heart?"

"I see no reason to change my beliefs simply because my life is about to end," said Julio. "I will take as many of Dr. Noir's secret police with me as possible. Where is that damned Wizard?"

"This will be my third time to die," said Esteban, "and I think I may be turning more to your point of view, particularly the premise that there is no need for God in a warm climate."

As Dr. Noir's soldiers moved forward, Julio and Esteban raised their weapons, and their compatriots, already sensing the best option was to live to fight another day, had already begun retreating when a mammoth spiral of butterflies darkened first the sun, then the windows of the presidential palace.

The Secret Police understood firepower, but not the silent river of butterflies. The hired help fled like thieves as the butterflies piled in drifts against the doors and windows of the Presidential Palace until a latch gave way and a spiral of spun gold the size of a muscled arm bore into the palace. Hour after hour the unending horde filled the palace to overflowing. Window after window groaned, cracked, glass toppled inward and a flat tunnel of butterflies the circumference of the missing pane plunged into the palace.

Dr. Noir in his scarlet and white general's uniform with the crossed bandoleers full of bullets, stayed on the balcony as long as possible, urging his forces to annihilate the scrubby army led by the Pimental brothers.

But for the first time in years there was a tinge of fear in Dr. Noir's heart as he paced the empty palace, batting aside the onslaught of butterflies. They must be harmless, he thought. Not poisonous. What could butterflies do to Dr. Lucius Noir? Still, their sheer numbers frightened him. Could they take up all the air? Her remembered stories of cats curling on the faces of babies, sucking the air out of them. Suddenly a butterfly entered a nostril. Dr. Noir swatted his large nose. The fluttering stopped. He blew the dead butterfly onto the marble floor of the palace.

SEVENTY-SEVEN
THE GRINGO JOURNALIST

Dr. Noir died, not at all as he deserved to die, not at all in keeping with his life, but smothered by millions of curiously soft and beautiful butterflies. With his death Courteguay was in momentary chaos. Until someone remembered the Wizard's dictum that "It matters not what your qualifications are, it is only important that you look like a leader," and it was looking like a leader that led to the Wizard becoming President of the Republic of Courteguay.

The Wizard loved to tell the story of the Chinese warlord who was so huge and scary in his full military regalia that armies often bolted when he came into view. The warlord was stricken, perhaps with cholera, and died a few days later, just as his army was preparing to face yet another battle and feared defeat without the old warlord to lead them. Desperate, his officers dressed the corpse in its finest regalia, strapped him to his horse and set him at the head of their army. The opposing army stared across a small valley at the imposing figure of the warlord, turned and quietly slunk away.

With Dr. Noir dead, the army and civil service was in chaos. General Bravura was gone, in fact all of the military who showed any signs of leadership were gone, so tight had Dr. Noir's grip been on Courteguay. The Wizard sent a message for Julio and Esteban and Hector to meet him at his home. There, the Wizard had all three help him dress in his finest and brightest uniform.

"Once, in America, I saw the world covered in snow," said Julio, "and it was not as white as the linen of your uniform."

The Wizard beamed.

"These crossed ammunition belts are heavy," grumbled the Wizard, "but it is what is expected of me. Politicians have to sacrifice so much for their country." His tunic had a scarlet sash that put fresh blood to shame. His epaulets were of flamingo feathers, his cap the ice blue and white of an airline pilot. The Wizard preened in front of his mirror, which no longer showed the reflection of Dr. Noir.

SEVENTY-EIGHT
THE WIZARD

The tabloid story, so far as I know strictly a rumor, which I may have had some small something to do with, stated that when Julio returned to Courteguay he was accompanied by four women, all beautiful, all former models, all natural blondes, none of whom could speak a word of Courteguayan, all of whom were pregnant.

Fernandella was happy at the prospect of a houseful of grandchildren. Fernandella's youngest, Jorge, was nearly two years of age, and she often lost track of the number of her children all together, as Hector had never stopped hoping for and trying to produce another set of magical offspring.

The Wizard, even though he was now President of the Republic, still booked bets on baseball games, and still cheated Hector out of his allowance, even though he now had the ability to steal from the public purse, which he was not hesitant to do. The Wizard calculated that his winnings from Hector Pimental paid for the precious metals on his uniforms.

"IS THERE LIFE AFTER BASEBALL?" a reporter asked Julio.

"It leaves a great void," said Julio, making a circle of his arms, to show how his insides were missing. "But we must go on. My brother is still tuned to the mysteries of religion for solace, although not so much as before. While I have taken on a far greater challenge; I have turned to the mysteries of women."

"There are many rumors about your women," said the reporter.

"Most of them created by the Wizard," replied Julio.

"Rumors are so much more wonderful than truth. I've heard that you have five wives, all pregnant, that you bring your women to the office of the President of the Republic so he can examine their bellies. And that his fee for the examination was enough for him to add another balloon to his fleet."

"I notice," said Julio, "that you speak of the Wizard and El Presidente in the same breath as if they are one and the same."

"I am a slow learner," replied the reporter.

WHAT THE TABLOIDS reported is this.

"An infield," said the Wizard, smiling broadly, after he had poked and prodded the quartet of taut-skinned beauties.

"First base, second base, third base, shortstop," he proclaimed. "The greatest infield in the history of baseball. And they will be born on the day their father is inducted into the American Baseball Hall of Fame." The Wizard's epaulets fluttered about the room, beat enthusiastically against the window for a few seconds before returning to their place on the shoulders of his uniform.

"But I am not eligible for induction for nearly five years, if I'm elected on the first ballot," said an alarmed Julio.

"The Infield will be worth waiting for," said the Wizard, ending his audience.

The tabloids also reported that Julio called his women, not by name but by their place of origin: I-owa, I-DA-ho, Tenn-Essee, and the Blessed Virginia. The women grew to full term, and waited, and waited, and waited. They went for a walk each afternoon in the rose garden of the Pimental mansion, and blurry photos of what might have been four pregnant women in a row in a garden appeared on the covers of more than one magazine. The tabloids reported that they walked in single file, led by Julio, the women pale and beautiful, looking like magazine models displaying maternity clothes.

The Wizard who claimed the Presidency upon the death of Dr. Noir knew the secret of adequate government. In addition to his spectacular appearance there was the delegation of authority; he also knew that there was no such thing as good government. He knew that eventually he would be overthrown, and deciding that he was too old to head for the jungles and become the guerrilla leader, his policy would be to make hay while the sun shone, so to speak. The Wizard loved foreign bank accounts. He felt that anything Ferdinand Marcos, Idi Amin, or Baby Doc Duvalier could do, he could do better.

"TELL ME THE TRUTH about your women," The Gringo Journalist said. "Better yet introduce me. Can it be true that they are all pregnant? Can it be that the births have been postponed until you are elected to the American Baseball Hall of Fame?"

"That all could be," said Julio, smiling enigmatically. "Of course the Wizard and I might have also dreamed the whole thing up, with the help of a few tabloid journalists. As someone once said, my mother's mansion has many rooms."

The gringo journalist was allowed to stay in a wing of Fernandella's mansion that faced on acres of vegetable gardens. His meals were sent to him and Julio came for an hour each afternoon to continue their interview.

Though he asked many times, he did not see Julio's women, until one midnight a sound awakened him and he walked to the window to see an acre of cabbages waltzing in the moonlight, pair by pair, rock solid, so green they appeared blue in the moonglow. As the cabbages swirled to the unheard music, the Gringo Journalist heard a giggle and noticed four women standing at the edge of the dancers, they were young and lithe, dressed in trailing dresses that appeared to be made of gossamer. All were extravagantly pregnant. The women murmured, giggled. Julio appeared, smiling, and one after another waltzed his women about the garden, swirling to the ethereal music, as if dancing in a marble-floored ballroom to a Strauss waltz.

The next day when Julio arrived for his interview the Gringo Journalist brought up the subject of what he had seen the previous night.

"Are you going to believe your eyes or what I tell you?" asked Julio. "I have only one woman, Celestina, whom I have known for many years, though she is able to take on many forms. She is a Gypsy girl with a green scarf in her hair, she is a revolutionary in fatigues, dirt smeared on her beautiful face, a bazooka pressed against her shoulder, she is pregnant with a quartet of my handsome sons. When I make love with her she is Quita Garza and no one else, although she does not know that. The rest is rumor. Or so they say."

AS THE TIME FOR JULIO'S ELECTION and induction into the Hall of Fame approached, there was a frenzy of activity around both San Barnabas and San Cristobel. The Wizard hissed from one edge of the country to the other making plans for the celebrations. He granted amnesty to hundreds of political prisoners. He announced that the surviving priests were free to come out from behind their chain-link fences, though the priests hastily declined, having found life much easier when not having to deal with parishioners except through protective fencing. Since their incarceration the incidence of sex crimes in Courteguay dropped to practically zero, although the Wizard did his best to suppress that information. Though when it was seized upon by the scurrilous tabloids, he did not deny it.

It was also reported that Julio was seen in San Barnabas' finest department stores buying large quantities of stuffed toys and miniature baseball uniforms.

Hector Pimental, the father of the twins, had secretly been in touch with Jerry Springer and several of the most outrageous trash television shows offering to sell rights to the approaching births.

Then, the events had to be postponed for at least a year when Julio fell three votes short of election for the American Baseball Hall of Fame on the first ballot. His non-election generated little interest in America, for although a complete baseball player Julio was after all a foreigner, and a foreigner who had returned to his native country after retirement.

"Ah," sighed the Wizard, who had proclaimed himself President for Life of Courteguay, and who, although he had sixteen first names, called himself Pedro Angel Guilermo Cayetano Umberto Salvador Alfredo Jorge Blanco for short.

"If Julio could only have died like Roberto Clemente," the Wizard lamented. "Clemente was so lucky to die while on a mission of mercy at the height of his career. About the only mistake I have ever made was not allowing his kidnappers to execute Julio Pimental."

A tabloid headline read:

JULIO'S WOMEN GROAN IN DISAPPOINTMENT

Politicians, both friends and foes, lobbied the Wizard to invade Florida. A one barge invasion they suggested. A quick surrender, the only stipulation of their surrender being Julio's election to the Baseball Hall of Fame.

"What if I am never elected?" wailed Julio.

"Trust me, I know what I'm doing," answered the Wizard who, several times during the following months burned condor dung and incense in the Presidential Palace, at odd hours of the day and night.

On his first year of eligibility Julio was passed over even though his statistics were far better than a dozen Hall of Fame pitchers, passed over because he was Courteguayan, but more because he never showed the proper respect for the game that the American Press required. He was bitterly resented because he never pitched in an All-Star Game since he refused to throw the ball to anyone but his brother, he was also resented because he spoke, or at least pretended he only spoke, passable English and then as infrequently as possible, resented because women threw themselves at his feet like he was a movie star, while the sportswriters in their Hawaiian shirts and beer bellies drooled over his success, and cursed him because they couldn't even pick up the overflow.

On Julio's second year of eligibility, the sportswriters, feeling he had been punished sufficiently, elected him by a sizable number of votes.

The morning of the day Julio Pimental was to be inducted into the American Baseball Hall of Fame dawned clear and sparkling as the new ruby and crystal epaulets on the shoulders of the President for Life of Courteguay.

Julio, partly for genuine personal reasons and partly in pique that he had never been accorded the respect he felt he deserved, wired the Hall of Fame that pressing business obligations required him to remain in Courteguay. That, of course, did not sit well with the American media.

The tabloid press reported he was at the bedsides of his four brides, (some still said five; the fifth would be a utility player) waiting for the birth of his infield. They reported that the nursery in Fernandella's mansion was in the shape of a baseball field with a crib waiting at each infield position.

At precisely 10:00 A.M. a fleet of hot air balloons rose like tropical birds from the steamy jungle outside San Barnabas. The hiss of the balloons was gentle as a baby's breath. The balloons were all perfectly round, shaped and colored to be exact replicas of baseballs. Some of the gondolas were filled with tropical flowers, the eleven national flowers of Courteguay plus long red lilies, violet and lemon-colored orchids with petals soft as velvet. Other gondolas were filled with waving greenery, tough spindly grasses, carnivorous plants testing the air for food.

President for life Pedro Angel Guilermo Cayetano Umberto Salvador Alfredo Jorge Blanco and his chiefs of staff rode in the lead balloon, each bedecked in uniforms so stupefyingly gaudy that only science fiction could do them justice.

The one unhappy note on this occasion of jubilance was that the American newspapers all but ignored the eight-page press release, issued on the thick, cream-colored stationery of the President for Life, its edges bordered by the eleven national flowers of Courteguay.

USA Today condensed the eight pages to five short lines:

> SAN BARNABAS, COURTEGUAY—President Pedro Blanco bestowed the Order of the Great Knight Commander on former baseball star Julio Pimental in honor of his induction into the Baseball Hall of Fame at Cooperstown.

"Americans have no sense of tradition or spectacle," grumbled the Wizard, discarding the newspaper. Besides ignoring the Wizard's titles and names the papers reported only one of the titles bestowed on Julio. Following Great Knight Commander there was Head of the Civil Service Defense Corps, Honorable Air Commodore, Defender of the Avocado, Commander-in-Chief of the Garment Worker's Union, plus seven more.

In the rose garden the Wizard led the singing of the Courteguayan National Anthem; the Wizard sang while above the mansion nine baseball-shaped balloons sketched an ethereal diamond in the pure blue sky.

Earlier in the day he had taken Esteban aside.

"I have decided to retire from politics and spend the rest of my life concentrating on magical happenings. I think you would make the perfect successor. I think you can govern Courteguay wisely and never be overthrown. You can be El Presidente for life without proclaiming yourself such."

"What makes you think I would want to be El Presidente?"

"You have all the qualifications. You are overqualified. You speak too many languages. You read books no one else in Courteguay has ever read or even heard of. You support a church that is obsolete in the extreme. Dr. Noir was right about one thing. There is no need for God in a warm climate. However, you are a thoughtful patient man who longs for justice. You have the stamina for endless cabinet meetings, listening to reports from toadying politicos, and to hours and hours of whining zealots pleading for their often insane causes—something that is necessary if people are to think they have some say in government."

"I'm sorry," said Esteban, "I wasn't listening," making a joke, possibly for one of the first times in his life.

The Wizard stared at him in surprise.

"But I looked sincere while I wasn't listening, didn't I?"

"I take it your answer is yes?"

FROM INSIDE THE MANSION the Wizard's ears discerned the sounds of babies crying, a grandmother fussing, a father's chest expanding, a grandfather's brain plotting.

The Wizard breathed the fragrance of the orchids, observed the blue fish darting in the frothing stream, watched the two dozen lemon-and-white cockatoos perched in a row on the rose garden fence, and smiling benevolently at all present decided that when the time was right he himself would negotiate contracts for The Infield.

AT COOPERSTOWN, Julio, his beautiful wife Celestina by his side, a dark haired girl baby named Quita in her arms, received his honors with grace and humbleness. He gave a moving speech in slightly accented English, praising his brother for impeccably calling his every game; he praised his family, his loving mother, his inventive father, and his old friend, Jorge Blanco, President for Life of Courteguay.